Praise for *The Case of the Man Who Died Laughing*

A *Seattle Times* Best Crime Novel of the Year
A *Pittsburgh Tribune-Review* Notable Book for Summer

"As tasty as Puri's favorite aloo parantha."

—*Kirkus Reviews*

"The perfect dog day novel for readers who like their murder mysteries spiced with unforgettable characters and a good dose of humor. Embrace the heat this summer in this vibrant (and flavorful) new murder mystery series set in New Delhi, India."

—Lauren Nemroff, Amazon Best Books of the Month, June 2010

"Highly amusing . . . Hall has an unerring ear for the vagaries of Indian English, the Indian penchant for punning acronyms, peculiarly Indian problems."

—*Publishers Weekly* (starred review)

"Fictional detectives come in all shapes, sizes and ethnic backgrounds these days, and Tarquin Hall has created one of the most memorable. Entertaining and enlightening."

—Yvonne Crittenden, *The Toronto Sun*

"Unlike those of Alexander McCall Smith, the books in this series are genuine detective stories, but they are every bit as warm and entertaining and should appeal to much the same readership."

—Tom and Enid Schantz, *The Denver Post*

"Delightful . . . This second in the series is a terrific book with a wonderful puzzle plot and a great setting."

—*The Globe and Mail*

Praise for *The Case of the Missing Servant*

"Speaking of sweet stuff, consider *The Case of the Missing Servant* by Tarquin Hall. This first novel is set in Delhi, where Vish Puri, founder and director of Most Private Investigators, Ltd., performs discreet investigations into the backgrounds of prospective grooms, with surprising and often comic results."

—Marilyn Stasio, *New York Times Book Review*

"India, captured in all its pungent, vivid glory, fascinates almost as much as the crime itself. [A–]"

—*Entertainment Weekly*

"Hall turns to fiction with the debut of what promises to be an outstanding series. . . . An excellent, delightfully humorous mystery with an unforgettable cast of characters, *The Case of the Missing Servant* immediately joins the *No. 1 Ladies' Detective Agency* as representing the best in international cozies."

—*Booklist* (starred review)

"An amusing, timely whodunit . . . Hall has woven his impressive knowledge of India into a tautly constructed novel."

—*The Guardian* (UK)

"This novel could easily have been just a playful pastiche of the traditional British mystery, but through its comic tone and ironic point of view, the novel becomes a take on justice in post-colonial India."

—Carole E. Barrowman, *Minneapolis Star-Tribune*

"Tubby, ingenious and hilarious, Delhi's most trusted PI, Vish Puri, is not easily forgotten. Properly disdainful of unoriginal crime-busters like Sherlock Holmes and James

Bond, his unique methods of detection deserve to be widely known and feted."

—David Davidar, author of *The Solitude of Emperors*

"Vish Puri is the most original detective in years. Tarquin Hall has captured India in a way few Western writers have managed since Kipling. The country's humor, commotion, and vibrancy bursts from every page, exposing its vast, labyrinthine underbelly. Scintillating!"

—Tahir Shah, author of *The Caliph's House*

Also by Tarquin Hall

The Case of the Missing Servant: From the Files of Vish Puri, India's Most Private Investigator

Mercenaries, Missionaries and Misfits: Adventures of an Under-age Journalist

To the Elephant Graveyard: A True Story of the Hunt for a Man-killing Indian Elephant

Salaam Brick Lane: A Year in the New East End

The Case of the Man Who Died Laughing

From the Files of
Vish Puri, India's Most Private Investigator

TARQUIN HALL

SIMON & SCHUSTER PAPERBACKS
New York London Toronto Sydney

Simon & Schuster Paperbacks
A Division of Simon & Schuster, Inc.
1230 Avenue of the Americas
New York, NY 10020

First Simon & Schuster trade paperback edition June 2011

Manufactured in the United States of America

10 9 8 7 6 5 4 3 2 1

The Library of Congress has cataloged the hardcover edition as follows:
Hall, Tarquin.
The case of the man who died laughing : From the files of Vish Puri, India's most private investigator / Tarquin Hall.
p. cm.
Sequel to: The case of the missing servant.
1. Private investigators—India—Fiction. 2. India—Fiction. I. Title.
PR6108.A495C36 2010
823'.92—dc22 2009048308

ISBN 978-1-4165-8369-1
ISBN 978-1-4391-7238-4 (pbk)
ISBN 978-1-4165-8403-2 (ebook)

For the midwives of Homerton Hospital, East London

One

Ensconced on the backseat of his Ambassador with the windows rolled up and the air-conditioning working full blast, Vish Puri kept a wary eye on the crack in the car's windscreen. It had started off as a chink—the work of a loose stone shot from the wheels of a speeding truck on Mathura Road that afternoon. But despite the sticky tape fixed to the glass like a bandage, the fissure was beginning to spread.

Delhi's infernal heat pressed down on the windscreen, trying to exploit its weakness, determined to conquer the defiant pocket of cool air within. The detective imagined what it must feel like to be a deep-sea explorer, listening to your tiny craft creaking under thousands of tons of pressure.

That Monday in early June, the top temperature in the capital had been 44 Celsius, or 111 Fahrenheit—so hot, the tarmac on the roads had grown pliable and sticky like licorice. So hot that even now, an hour after darkness had fallen, the air felt like fire in the lungs.

Nothing dampened the frenetic spirit of Delhi's rush hour, however. Everywhere Puri looked, thousands upon thousands of people were making their way through the heat, the roar of the traffic, and the belching fumes illuminated in the headlights. Laborers, servants, and students crowded into non-air-conditioned buses; bicyclists in sweat-soaked shirts strained against their pedals; families of three, four, even five rode on scooters, mothers sitting sidesaddle, infants in their laps and older children sandwiched in between.

And everywhere commerce flourished. Chunks of ice-cooled coconut and bootleg copies of Booker Prize novels were being sold by children meandering through the crawling traffic. Watermelons were heaped on the pavements. Handbills advertising the powers of a hakim,* who promised to exorcise malignant spirits and counteract curses, were being slipped under windshield wipers.

As Puri watched countless faces slick and shiny with sweat, eyes blinking in the pollution, lips parched with thirst, he was struck by how stoically "Dilli wallahs," as Delhiites were known, went about their lives, seemingly resigned to the capital's harsh and, for most, worsening conditions. Part of him admired their resilience, their surprising good humor in the face of such grinding adversity; but he also mourned humanity's capacity to adjust to any conditions and perceive them as normal.

"The survival instinct is both blessing and curse, also," was how he put it.

For his part, the detective had grown accustomed to air-conditioning. Without it, dressed in his trademark safari suits and Sandown caps, he fared badly. At the height of summer, he stayed inside as much as possible. When venturing out was unavoidable, Handbrake, his driver, had to walk next to him with an umbrella to ensure that his employer remained in the shade. Puri had also invested in a small battery-powered hand fan. But in temperatures like these

* For a glossary of unfamiliar terms, see page 297.

it had the opposite effect for which it was intended—like putting your face in front of an exhaust vent.

He could only pray that the windscreen would hold. Tomorrow was the earliest he could afford to send Handbrake to get it replaced.

It was going to be a long night.

Puri glanced at his watch. Ten minutes to eight—ten minutes until the drop was due to be made at Fun 'N' Food Village.

"Subject is approaching IGI overbridge, over," he said into his walkie-talkie.

The silver Safari he was tailing left the gated colonies and posh villas of South Delhi and headed onto the new, elevated three-lane expressway that snaked past Indira Gandhi International Airport.

"In position, Boss," came back a voice. It belonged to one of Most Private Investigators's top undercover operatives. Puri, who was in the habit of giving nicknames to people, called him Tubelight because he was usually "slow to flicker on" in the morning.

"Tip-top," replied the detective. "Should be we're with you shortly. If only this bloody fellow will get a move on. By God, such a slow coach!"

From the moment they'd started to tail the Safari, the detective had watched its slow progress with incredulity. Unlike all the other cars, which treated the road like a Formula One racetrack, slaloming through the lumbering heavy-goods vehicles and diesel-belching buses, it had kept precisely to the speed limit. It was the only vehicle on the road that didn't straddle two lanes at once and have its headlights on full beam. And its horn remained silent despite the instructions painted on the backs of the trucks, HORN OK PLEASE!

"Arrrrey!" exclaimed Puri in frustration as the Safari gave way to a lowly auto rickshaw. "I'm all for sensible driving—speed thrills but kills, after all. But this man is some sort of joker, no?"

Handbrake was equally bewildered: "Where did he learn to drive, sir?" he asked in Hindi. "Ladies' college?"

"No, United States," the detective answered with a laugh.

In fact, Shanmuga Sundaram Rathinasabapathy, Most Private Investigators Ltd.'s latest client, had got his license in Raleigh, North Carolina.

According to Rathinasabapathy's dossier—Puri had managed to get hold of a copy from one of his military academy batchmates who was now working in Indian intelligence—"Sam" Rathinasabapathy was the son of a Tamil heart surgeon who had been born and brought up in the Tar Heel State. A nuclear physicist and MIT graduate, he had "returned" to India a month ago, bringing with him his fellow "non-resident Indian" (NRI) wife and two young children. He was meant to be working for a joint American-Indian partnership building a new generation of nuclear reactors but had so far spent all his time dealing with problems and corrupt practices as he had tried to rent an apartment, enroll his children in school and find his way around the city.

Three days ago, facing a crisis, Sam Rathinasabapathy had come to see Puri in his Khan Market office and outlined his predicament.

"This is my children we're talking about! What am I going to do? I'm absolutely desperate!"

The detective had agreed to help him, advising the earnest, clean-cut Rathinasabapathy to play along with the demands of the middleman who had contacted him.

"Pay this bloody goonda the two lakhs and leave the rest to me," was how he'd put it.

After that first meeting, Puri had marveled to his private secretary, Elizabeth Rani, about the naïveté of "these NRI types." More and more of them were being posted to India by top financial institutions and multinationals. Like the Britishers before them, the majority lived in pampered luxury, spent a good deal of their time complaining about their servants and Delhi belly, and didn't have the first clue about how things were done in India.

"A topper this Sam fellow might be, but here in India he is quite at sea," the detective had said. "What is required in this situation is experience and aptitude. Fortunately, Vish Puri can easily and willingly supply both."

Having bestowed on his new client the sobriquet Coconut—"The fellow might be brown on the outside but he is one hundred ten percent gora inside"—the detective had put his plan into action.

That afternoon, Sam Rathinasabapathy had withdrawn the two hundred thousand rupees demanded—a hundred K for each of his children—from the bank. He had brought the cash to Most Private Investigators Ltd., where Puri had made a note of the serial numbers and packed the wads of notes in a brown duffel bag.

The call from the middleman explaining where to make the drop had come at six o'clock. This had given Tubelight enough time to get to Fun 'N' Food Village first and move into position.

Now all Rathinasabapathy had to do was hand over the money.

"Estimated time of arrival ten . . . by God, better make that fifteen minutes, over," Puri said with a sigh as Rathinasabapathy's Safari turned off the expressway and onto a dusty single-lane road.

Here, confronted with potholes and unmarked speed

bumps, as well as the usual honking cacophony of traffic, the vehicle slowed to a crawl, narrowly missing a bicyclist transporting a tall stack of full egg trays. Handbrake, struggling to keep a safe distance and incurring the wrath of a Bedford truck, was forced to brake suddenly. At the same time, he instinctively leaned on his horn.

"Sorry, Boss!" the driver quickly said apologetically. "But he drives like an old woman!"

"All Americans drive in this style," affirmed the detective.

"They must be having a lot of accidents in Am-ree-ka," muttered Handbrake.

It was a quarter past eight by the time Rathinasabapathy reached his destination and parked outside Fun 'N' Food Village. He hurried to the ticket office, duffel bag in hand, and got in line.

Bracing himself, Puri opened his door and the heat and humidity hit him full on. He felt winded and had to steady himself. It was only a matter of seconds before the first trickle of sweat ran down his neck. Perspiration began to form on his upper lip beneath his wide handlebar moustache.

Fanning himself with a newspaper, the detective bought himself an entry token and followed his client through the turnstile.

Fun 'N' Food Village, a distinctly Indian amusement park with popular water features, was packed with giddy children. Squeals filled the air as they careered down Aqua Shutes and doggy-paddled along the Lazy River: "Phir, phir! Again, again!" Mothers in bright Punjabi cotton suits, with their baggy trousers rolled up just beneath their knees, stood half-soaked in the shallow end of the Tiny Tots Pond playing with their toddlers. In the Wave Pool, a group of Sikh boys in swimming trunks and patkas played volleyball. On benches arranged along the sidelines, aunties dipped their toes into the cool water and ate spicy dhokla garnished with fresh coriander and green chilies. Occasionally, cheeky grandsons and nephews splashed them with water.

Puri followed Rathinasabapathy as he squeezed through the crowd toward one of the many plaster-of-paris characters dotted about the park: a fearsome ten-foot-tall effigy of the ferocious, ten-headed demon king Ravana. With savage eyes and sneering lip, he brandished a great scimitar with which he was preparing to smite a hideous serpent.

It was in front of Ravana that the middleman had instructed Puri's client to wait.

Rathinasabapathy stopped in the shadow of the towering divinity. His apprehensive eyes scanned the crowd of revelers passing back and forth. Meanwhile, the detective, keeping his client in his sights, joined the unruly queue in front of a nearby dhaba. When it came to his turn, he ordered a plate of aloo tikki masala. It might be hours before he got to eat again, he reasoned, and the Gymkhana Club's lunchtime special of "veg cutlet" had left him craving something spicy—no matter that he had drenched the food in a quarter-bottle of Maggi Chili Sauce.

The food was delicious and when he had scraped every last bit of chutney off the bottom of the tobacco-leaf plate, he ordered another. This was followed by a chuski, a jeera cola one with extra syrup, which he had to eat quickly before it melted, avoiding incriminating stains on his clothes that would be noticed by his eagle-eyed wife.

By eight thirty, there was still no sign of the middleman. Puri was beginning to wonder if the plan had been blown. He cursed under his breath for not having anticipated his client's poor driving skills. But then what sort of fellow didn't employ a driver?

An announcement sounded over the PA system, first in Hindi and then in English. "Namashkar," said a pleasant singsong voice. "Guests are kindly requested not to do urination in water. WC facilities are provided in rear. Your kind cooperation is appreciated."

Another five minutes passed. Puri diligently avoided eye contact with his client in case the middleman was close by. A balloon wallah, who had been doing brisk business in front of the Wave Pool, came and stood a few feet to the left of Rathinasabapathy.

Then a short, chunky man with a thick neck and dyed black hair approached the nuclear physicist. His back was turned to the dhaba so that the detective was unable to see his face. But beyond the obvious—that the man was in his early to mid-fifties, married, owned a dog and had reached the rendezvous within the past few minutes—Puri was able to deduce that he was having an affair (there was a clear impression of an unwrapped condom in his back pocket) and had grown up in a rural area where the drinking water was contaminated by arsenic (his hands were covered in black blotches).

Puri pressed the mini receiver he was wearing deeper into his ear. It was tuned to the listening device housed in a flag of India pinned to his client's shirt pocket.

"Mr. Rathinasabapathy, is it?" the detective heard the middleman ask over the din of the children. His voice suggested a confident smugness.

"Yeah, that's right," answered the nuclear physicist, sounding apprehensive. "Who are you?"

"We spoke earlier on phone."

"You said to be here at eight o'clock. I've been waiting nearly half an hour."

"Eight o'clock *Indian* time, scientist sahib. You know

what is Indian time? Always later than you would expect." The middleman let out a little chuckle. "By that account I'm extremely punctual. But enough of that, haa? What is that you're carrying? Something for me I hope?"

"Look, I'm not handing over any money until I know exactly whom I'm dealing with," insisted Rathinasabapathy, repeating the words Puri had coached him to say.

The middleman gave a petulant shake of the head and turned his back on the balloon wallah.

"Don't be so concerned with my identity. Important thing is, I'm a man who gets things done," he said.

"You must have a name. What am I supposed to call you?"

"Some people know me as Mr. Ten Percent."

"That's very amusing," said Rathinasabapathy drily.

"So glad you think so, scientist sahib. But I'm not a joker to do rib tickling. So let's do business, haa? You've got the full amount exactly and precisely?"

"Yes, I've brought your two lakh rupees," said Rathinasabapathy, returning to the dialogue Puri had scripted for him. "But how do I know you'll keep up your end of the bargain? How do I know you won't just take the cash and my kids still won't—"

"Listen, Textbook!" interjected Mr. Ten Percent. "In India deal is deal. This is not America with your Enron. Everything's arranged. Now, you're going to give over the cash or what?"

Rathinasabapathy hesitated for a moment and then handed over the duffel bag. "It's all in there. Two—hundred—thousand—rupees," he said, raising his voice and enunciating each word clearly.

The middleman took hold of the bag and held it by the straps in his right hand, gauging its weight.

"Very good," he said, apparently satisfied.

"You're not going to count it?"

"Here? In such a public place?" He chuckled. "Someone seeing so much of cash might get a wrong idea. Who knows? They might rob me. I tell you there's dacoity all about these days. One more piece advice to you, scientist sahib: keep hold of your wallet, ha? The other day, only, a thief grabbed my portable straight out my hand. Can you believe? Right there on the street in daylight hours. Luckily for me I got it back one hour later. The thief himself returned it. That is after discovering to whom it belonged. He was most apologetic."

Mr. Ten Percent extended his hand. "Good doing business with you," he said. "Welcome to India, haa, and best of luck."

"That's it? When will I hear from you again?"

"You'll not be hearing from me. Next communication will come from the principal."

With that, the middleman walked off in the direction of the exit, soon vanishing amidst the crowd.

The balloon wallah was close behind him.

His bunch of silver helium balloons bobbed along above the heads of all the happy children and parents, indicating his position and that of his mark as accurately as a homing device.

Puri watched their progress for a few seconds. Then the detective signaled to his client to stay put for at least ten minutes as per the plan and went in pursuit of Tubelight and his balloons—and Mr. Ten Percent.

Two

At five forty-five the following morning, Dr. Suresh Jha reached India Gate, the centerpiece of Lutyens's colonial New Delhi. He looked calm, in spite of having been told this was the day he was going to die.

Leaving his old Premier Padmini Fiat in the usual spot in the car park, he set off along Rajpath, the grand imperial boulevard that led past Parliament House and the Secretariat to the gates of Rashtrapati Bhavan—once the home of the British viceroy, but now the official residence of the president of India.

There had not been a hint of a breeze for days and the collective emissions of sixteen million souls hung heavily in the morning air. The dense haze created halos around the Victorian streetlamps and made keen edges of the headlights of passing vehicles. The rising sun was but a feeble glow in the sky. With visibility down to less than a hundred feet, the sandstone domes and chuttris of the Indian seats of power lay far off in the distance, shrouded from view.

On either side of the tarmac boulevard lay sandy paths and, on either side of these, wide lawns edged with trees. Dr. Jha made his way down the path on the left-hand side, having first smeared a dab of eucalyptus balm on his upper lip to disguise the nauseating pong emanating from the Yamuna River a mile and a half away.

Despite the hour, he was far from alone. Many of the other regulars who came to Rajpath every morning to exercise before the heat of the day made such activity unthinkable passed him along the way: the flabby, middle-aged couple in matching sun visors who did rigorous "brisk walking" but never seemed to lose any weight; the tall, muscular Muslim army officer who always jogged the full length of Rajpath and back in a sweat-soaked T-shirt; the decrepit gentleman with the pained expression whose servant had to push him along in his wheelchair.

Dr. Jha, too, cut an instantly recognizable figure. He had a long, white beard and wore open-toed sandals and a dhoti. Anyone seeing him for the first time might have been forgiven for assuming that he was an ascetic. But the retired mathematician was the very antithesis of the ecclesiastic. The founder of the Delhi Institute for Rationalism and Education, or DIRE, he was known to millions of viewers who had watched him debunking and unmasking India's Godmen on national TV. They knew him as the "Guru Buster."

This newfound celebrity was something Dr. Jha had neither sought nor welcomed. It had crept up on him over the past few years since the twenty-four-hour news channels had started reporting on so-called miracles as if they were newsworthy events, leaving him with no choice but to take to the airwaves and preach the gospel of reason and logic.

In doing so, he had lost his anonymity. Starstruck admirers were forever approaching him in public to shake his hand. And he was often hassled by ignorant people who, having seen him on TV demonstrating how simple "miracles" were performed—like walking on red-hot coals or making holy ash pour from the hands—believed he had acquired the very powers he was trying to discredit. Only last week, for example, he had been asked to exorcise an evil spirit from a boy of five who was unable to speak. Subsequently, Dr. Jha had made some inquiries and learned that the boy had suffered from jaundice during infancy, was partially deaf and therefore unable to mimic sounds like normal children.

But here on Rajpath, where the early birds were drawn from the educated middle classes, Dr. Jha's privacy was rarely invaded. It helped that his body language was reserved. He walked with arms held studiously behind his back and head stooped in contemplation.

On this particular morning, as his mind mulled over the death threat he had received the day before, his thoughts turned to his childhood and the first time he had set foot on Rajpath.

Suresh Jha had been seven at the time, still small enough to sit on his father's shoulders. From that dizzying height, the view in all directions had been unforgettable: a vast ocean of people, their heads adorned with every kind of gear—pagris, Maharashtrian turbans, Gandhian topis—surging around the walls of the Secretariat and Parliament House.

The date: August 15, 1947, the day India gained its independence and, at the stroke of midnight, Jawaharlal Nehru, the country's first prime minister, made his famous "tryst with destiny" speech.

"A moment comes which comes but rarely in history, when we step out from the old to the new . . . when the soul of a nation, long suppressed, finds utterance," Pandit-ji had said. "We end today a period of ill fortune and India discovers herself again."

Nehru's enthusiasm, his belief that as a secular, socialist democracy India would modernize, build factories and power stations, schools and universities, clinics and hospitals—that it would retake its rightful place as a leader of the civilized world—had been infectious. The young Suresh Jha, brimming with optimism for the future, had been one of the first students to enter the newly formed Indian Institute of Technology in Delhi. Later he'd helped design India's first indigenous telecommunications network.

But during the 1970s and '80s, while China, South Korea and Taiwan pumped billions of dollars into research and development, Indian technology lagged far behind. Economically, the country fared no better. The so-called License Raj ensured that a small number of industrial families monopolized manufacturing. Corruption ate at the heart of the political system.

Now in his sixties, Dr. Jha felt bitterly disappointed by his country's failures.

"While the middle-class elite grow richer and maintain an exceptionally high degree of tolerance for the inhuman levels of deprivation around them, India still languishes among some of the poorest countries in the world—on the Human Development Index just behind Equatorial Guinea and Solomon Islands," he had written in the latest edition of *Proof,* the DIRE quarterly of which he was editor in chief. "India will remain a feudal society as long as people continue to believe their destinies are governed by some nonexistent higher power, whether it be God, Allah or Vishnu, and don't take control of their lives for themselves."

His campaign had made him countless enemies. Many a village fakir and traveling sadhu had sworn vengeance after the Guru Buster had unmasked them as frauds. Dr. Jha had been denounced as a "devil" and a "monkey" by the church and the mullahs. He had also provoked the ire of India's Hindu right. But his most famous—and arguably most powerful—adversary was His Holiness Maharaj Swami.

"Swami-ji," as everyone referred to him, had risen to prominence in the past three years. Revered as a living saint by more than thirty million followers and watched by millions more around the world on Channel OM, the saffron-robed Godman claimed miraculous powers. He often levitated, produced precious stones and valuable objects out of thin air and communed with an ancient rishi whose ghostly face thousands claimed to have seen materialize before their very eyes.

Dr. Jha had described him in the past as a "fraud," a "crook," "David Blaine in saffron robes." On numerous occasions he had also challenged Swami-ji's claim to be able to cure the sick of cancer, diabetes and HIV/AIDS.

And then a month ago, the two men had finally come face-to-face when, unbeknownst to one another, they had been invited onto the same live TV talk show for what the host had billed as a "showdown."

Seizing the opportunity to rail against Maharaj Swami before an audience of millions, Dr. Jha had angrily denounced him as a "charlatan" who was swindling the public.

"You should be prosecuted as a common criminal," he'd said, adding: "If you can levitate, show us now!"

With his equable, beatific smile, Swami-ji had calmly explained that he only performed miracles when "there is a purpose and a need" and that such feats were designed to "inspire humanity to understand its true potential." He'd also added that he was not "a circus performer."

"Scientists seek to undermine our belief in the divine," the guru had continued, fingering his Rudraksha rosary. "The power of the intellect and modern technology is insignificant compared to the power of love that each and every one of us carries in our hearts. At times, people must be reminded of this—they must be shown something truly miraculous. This helps to renew their faith. Thus within the month, I will perform a spectacular miracle that will leave no one—not even atheists like my friend Dr. Jha here—in any doubt about my powers."

The talk show host had pressed the Godman to explain the nature of the "supernatural occurrence" he had predicted, but Maharaj Swami had refused to elaborate. He had promised, however, that Dr. Jha would "be left speechless."

Then yesterday the death threat had been delivered.

> WHENEVER THERE IS A WITHERING OF THE LAW
> AND AN UPRISING OF LAWLESSNESS ON ALL SIDES
> THEN I MANIFEST MYSELF.
> FOR THE SALVATION OF THE RIGHTEOUS
> AND THE DESTRUCTION OF SUCH AS DO EVIL,
> FOR THE FIRM ESTABLISHING OF THE LAW,
> I COME TO BIRTH, AGE AFTER AGE.
> UNBELIEVER! TOMORROW YOU DIE!

The Hindi words had been made up of letters cut from a newspaper and pasted onto a piece of paper.

Terrified, Dr. Jha's wife had called the police. They in turn had advised her husband to stay indoors. But the Guru Buster had been determined to keep his regular early morning appointment.

Dr. Jha passed several other groups on the wide lawn that lay to the left of Rajpath: the first was a ladies' yoga session, the supple participants arching their backs so that they looked like giant snails. Next, five bare-chested south Indian men were practicing the ancient Keralan martial art of Kalaripayat, the sound of their long wooden staves clattering against one another sounded like drumbeats. And finally, members of the local chapter of the Rashtriya Swayamsevak Sangh (RSS) were conducting their morning drill in Hitler Youth–style khaki uniforms.

In the past, Dr. Jha had challenged the RSS's right to gather on Rajpath; in his view, the group presented a clear threat to public law and order no matter how much social work it carried out. The swayamsevaks had not taken kindly to his protests, and on a number of occasions there had been heated exchanges between them. But this morning the Guru Buster passed the "hate-mongering fascists," as he had often referred to them, without incident.

A quarter of a mile farther on, in the shadow of a jamun tree, four men dressed for exercise were standing in a circle.

As Dr. Jha approached them, they raised their arms and stretched toward the sky. An instructor's voice called out a command and they lowered their hands to their hips. Then all but one of the men tilted their heads back and began to laugh. Not a titter, chortle or snigger: they ejaculated hee-haws like drunken men.

For ten seconds, they shook with infectious mirth, going abruptly silent as if the joke that had caused their collective amusement had suddenly lost its appeal. The instructor's voice boomed out again and, with varying degrees of success and groans of discomfort, the men bent forward to touch their toes. Then they flung their arms wide and burst into another bout of joyful hysterics.

"Welcome, Dr. Sahib!" said the beaming instructor, Professor Pandey, who was in his late fifties. He had a big face surmounted by a shock of white hair partially stained yellow from smoking a pipe. "Welcome, welcome, welcome! We're doing our warm-up! Join us!"

Dr. Jha, who had been a member of the Rajpath Laughing Club for two years, greeted the other men before taking his place in the circle.

"Unfortunately, there are only a few of us present today because so many people are away on holiday," continued Professor Pandey.

The Laughing Club was usually attended by at least a dozen regulars. Their morning sessions were always noisy and rambunctious and there had been complaints from some of the other exercise groups, which was why they gathered so far down Rajpath.

"Now that we're all assembled presently and correctly, good morning to you all!" said Professor Pandey.

"Good morning!" chorused the group.

"I'm delighted to see you, gentlemen!" The instructor carried on, grinning as he spoke. "First order of the day, we have a newcomer. Allow me to introduce Mr. Shivraj Sharma. Please make him welcome."

"Good morning!" chorused the others with a round of applause.

"Mr. Sharma, what is your profession, please?" asked Professor Pandey, addressing the distinguished, middle-aged gentleman in the purple tracksuit.

"I'm a senior archaeologist with the Survey of India," he answered haughtily.

"Very good, Mr. Sharma," Professor Pandey said, smiling, as if he were talking to a child who had correctly recited his twelve-times table. "Now, you must know that here at the Laughing Club, we do laughter therapy. It's a really wonderful approach that involves exercise and breathing as well as laughter, which is good for the heart and the soul. And what are we without heart and soul?"

There was a collective "Nothing!" from everyone except Mr. Sharma.

"Exactly! The ultimate goal of laughter therapy is to bring about world peace. People anywhere belonging to any culture can laugh. Laughter is the common language we all share. So how can we bring world peace through laughter? Very simple! When you laugh . . ."

Here the other men joined in again, chorusing: "You change. And when you change, the whole world changes with you!"

"Very good, very good, very good!" exclaimed Professor Pandey, addressing each part of the circle in turn. "So, Mr. Sharma, do you know what a jester is?"

Before the archaeologist could answer, the instructor continued: "He is a comedian and therefore laughs loudest of all. So let us now do jester laughter. On the count of three. One, two . . ."

On three, Professor Pandey pointed at the man opposite him in the circle, as if he had just told the funniest joke the world had ever heard, and started giggling feverishly.

The other men mimicked him, staggering about like intoxicated teenagers while holding their hands over their mouths.

Sharma tried his best to join in but looked awkward and self-conscious.

"Ho ho, ha-ha-ha! Ho ho, ha-ha-ha!" sang the group at the end of the Jester Exercise, doing a little jig and clapping their hands together.

"Very good, very good, very good!" cried Professor Pandey. "Next, Gibberish Exercise! What is gibberish, Mr. Sharma?"

The newcomer's scowl suggested he was thinking: "Everything that comes out of your mouth!" But again Professor Pandey answered for him. "Gibberish is nonsense," he said. "What infants speak." He grinned again. "So let us now pretend we are two years old again."

Professor Pandey spent the next minute uttering embarrassing baby noises while swinging his arms around him like a windmill.

More exercises followed: Silent Laughter (which involved puffing out their cheeks, holding their fingers over their lips, wheezing like old bellows and pumping their shoulders up and down) and finally the Chicken.

"Ho ho, ha-ha-ha! Very good, very good, very good!"

At the conclusion of the session, which lasted thirty minutes, Professor Pandey invited anyone with a funny joke to share it with the rest of the group.

"Strictly no non-veg jokes, thank you very much!" he said. "Nothing you wouldn't tell your nani-ji!"

"But, Pandey Sahib, my nani-ji is telling the dirtiest jokes of all!" cried out Mr. Karat, one of the other regulars, who could do an alarmingly realistic chicken impersonation.

This comment provoked more laughter—genuine, natural and wholly spontaneous laughter, that is. And then another regular, Mr. Gupta, announced that he had heard a cracker the night before.

"Manager asked a Sardar-ji at an interview: 'Can you spell a word that has more than five letters in it?' Sardar replies: 'P-O-S-T-B-O-X.'"

Professor Pandey followed this up with a knock-knock joke.

"Knock, knock," he said.

"Who's there?"

"Bunty."

"Bunty who?"

"Bunty," repeated Pandey with a giggle.

"Bunty who?" the others said, prompting him again.

But the professor could not answer. Like Uncle Albert in *Mary Poppins,* laughter had got the better of him.

"Really, Professor Pandey, you must finish your joke. Otherwise what is the point?" said Mr. Karat, smiling. But then he, too, erupted into a fit of giggles.

Dr. Jha and Mr. Gupta followed suit, chortling like little girls.

This time, however, it was different; this time they were unable to stop.

"I . . . I . . . can't control my . . . myself!" Professor Pandey declared through his laughter. "And I . . . I can't move my feet!"

Dr. Jha said he felt rooted to the spot as well. To their alarm, Karat and Gupta felt the same. They all looked down at the ground, trying to ascertain what was holding them in place. As they did so, a mist started to form around their ankles. Soon, it blanketed the earth, lapping up around their shins.

Only Sharma was not affected by what was happening. But he dared not shift from his position. The stray dogs that had been lazing in the shade of the trees along Rajpath had started to surround the group of men, howling and barking. Dozens of crows were also circling overhead, cawing menacingly.

The sky seemed to darken. Thunder rumbled. There was a blinding flash. And then, in the middle of the group, a terrifying figure appeared.

Hideously ugly, with four writhing arms, a jet-black face and a large tongue slithering from her bloody mouth, she wore a garland of human skulls around her neck.

The men, still laughing but struck by sheer horror, recognized her instantly as the goddess Kali.

"Unbeliever!" boomed a screeching witch's voice as the mist rose up around her.

The goddess pointed one of her long, wizened index fingers at Dr. Jha and rose up into the air, hovering several feet off the ground. In one hand, she wielded a bloodstained sword, in another a man's severed head.

"I am Kali, consort of Shiva! I am the Redeemer! I am Death!"

A jet of fire shot from her mouth.

"You! Who have dared to insult me! You who have dared to mock my power! You will taste blood!"

The goddess glided through the air toward Dr. Jha, spewing more flames. The cawing of the crows and the howling of the dogs grew louder.

"Mere mortal! *Now* you are speechless!" she cackled.

Dr. Jha was now face-to-face with the goddess, still unable to move his feet thanks to some invisible force. He looked terrified and yet he was still laughing.

"Now die!" screeched Kali in a chorus of voices.

She raised her sword and drove it down into his chest. Blood flowed from the wound and spewed from his mouth. Clutching his chest, the Guru Buster uttered a last guffaw and then fell backward onto the grass, dead.

Three

Puri's day began without any indication that he would soon be investigating a "supernatural occurrence" destined to capture the imagination of the entire nation—a case that he would later describe as "a first in the annals of crime."

His Ambassador pulled into the car park behind Khan Market at ten o'clock. Handbrake was dispatched to replace the windscreen while the detective walked his usual route to his office.

Now the most expensive commercial real estate in all of India, Khan Market was home to new boutiques selling exorbitantly priced cushion covers and "size zero" Indian couture. Trendy bars and restaurants had sprung up, the nocturnal playground for Delhi's nouveaux riches. Where a greengrocer had once traded, trays of American-style macadamia chocolate chunk cookies were on offer at 80 rupees each, more than a day's wage for most of the country's working population.

But a number of the old family-owned businesses still thrived and the place remained scruffy and unkempt, retaining—in Puri's eyes at least—a reassuring character lacking in the new sanitized shopping malls. Paint blistered and peeled from concrete walls, and spaghetti tangles of wires and cables hung overhead. Many of the shop signs leaned at angles. And the Punjabi princesses who flocked here with their proprietorial airs, high heels and oversize designer sunglasses had to negotiate cracked, uneven pavements cluttered with sleeping pye-dogs and hawkers.

"Kaise ho?" Puri called out to Mr. Saluja, who stood outside his tailor's shop, overseeing one of his employees sprinkling water on the pavement to keep down the dust. The key wallah was also getting ready for the morning trade, laying out his medieval tools on a potato sack on a small patch of pavement: hammer, chisels, long metal files and a giant rusty key ring holding the uncut blanks he would use to make duplicates for his customers.

Mounting the steep, narrow steps that led up to the Most Private Investigators offices above Bahri Sons bookshop, Puri was greeted with a warm smile and a "Good morning, sir" by Elizabeth Rani, whose desk took up a quarter of the small reception.

The first thing he did upon entering his office—that is, after turning on the air-conditioning—was to light an incense stick in the little puja shrine below the two frames hanging on the wall to the right of his desk. One contained a photograph of his father, Om Chander Puri, the other a likeness of Chanakya, the detective's guide and guru who had lived around 300 BC and founded the arts of espionage and investigation. The detective said a short prayer, asking for guidance from them both, and then buzzed in his secretary.

Elizabeth Rani brought his post and messages and ran through a list of mundane matters that required his attention: "Kanwal Sibal's wife birthed a son. You'll visit them or I should send nuts and fruit?"

Door Stop, the tea boy, then brought Puri his morning

cup of kahwa, Kashmiri tea steamed with saffron, cardamom, cinnamon, sugar and slivered almonds.

The detective savored the sweet liquid while bringing himself up to date with the cases on his books. Most Private Investigators was as busy as ever. So far this month, the agency had dealt with seven matrimonial investigations, which required background and character checks to be done on prospective brides and grooms having arranged marriages. An insurance company had hired the firm to ascertain whether a certain Mrs. Aastha Jain, seventy-four, had died of natural causes during the annual pilgrimage to Gangotri (the detective had found her alive and well, living it up in Goa under an assumed name). And Puri had brought to a speedy conclusion the unusual kidnapping of Mr. Satish Sinha's father. Sinha Senior had been reincarnated as a monkey, and the detective had located him by following the local banana wallah's best customer home.

Still, it had been a while since he had dealt with a truly challenging, sensational case. The Case of the Blue Turban League had been a good six months ago.

As for nuclear scientist Rathinasabapathy's crisis, well, that was standard fare, albeit satisfying and decently remunerated work. Puri was looking forward to his client's visit at twelve o'clock, when he would dazzle him with his results. In preparation, he spent ten minutes putting all the photographic evidence in order.

It was then that he noticed something outside his window—a loaf of white bread dangling like bait on a string.

It dropped out of sight. But soon a carton of cornflakes appeared. A minute later, a carton of Mango Frooti.

Zahir, who was blind and owned the tiny general store next to Bahri Sons, was restocking from the storage space he rented upstairs.

Puri was not altogether happy about this practice. Only recently he had been in the middle of a meeting with a distressed client whose husband had been murdered when pots of instant masala noodles had started knocking against his window. But beyond cutting the string with a pair of scissors, there was little to be done.

Besides, Puri was particularly partial to some of the products stocked by kindly Zahir—like those nice coconut biscuits, for example. And sometimes, when they appeared in his window, he hauled them in and settled his bill later.

It was almost uncanny the way packets of coconut biscuits often appeared around the same time every afternoon.

Soon after eleven o'clock, Elizabeth Rani entered Puri's office, her voice trembling as she placed a copy of the *Delhi Midday Standard* in front of him.

"I thought you would want to see this, sir. It's terrible news, I'm afraid. Such a kindly old gentleman he was. Really, I don't know what the world is coming to."

FLOATING GODDESS STABS TO DEATH

LAUGHING GURU BUSTER. COPS CLUELESS.

"By God!" exclaimed the detective, sitting up straight in his executive leather chair. He studied the coverage of Dr. Suresh Jha's murder intently, letting out several sighs and, on three occasions, a pained "Hai!"

The newspaper quoted the members of the Laughing Club, who described how, after killing Dr. Suresh Jha, the "apparition" had "vanished in a big flash."

"She was at least twenty feet high, a terrifying sight, like something from a nightmare," said eyewitness Professor R. K. Pandey. "I thought we would all be killed."

Senior advocate N. K. Gupta added: "There is no doubt in my mind it was the goddess Kali. Today we have witnessed a supernatural occurrence. No one should be in any doubt."

The article continued: "Many Delhiites have started flocking to temples across the city to seek protection, while hundreds of Kali worshippers have converged on Rajpath to celebrate the goddess's appearance, which they believe is a divine event."

SKEPTICS SKEPTICAL read the headline of another article on page two, which quoted a Mumbai-based rationalist as saying that he was certain Dr. Jha had been murdered not by the goddess—"How could she have done it when she does not exist?"—but by someone masquerading as her.

"The rationalist was unable to explain, however, how a murderer could have carried out the crime in broad daylight in front of so many witnesses," the article continued. "He noted that last month, during a live altercation between Dr. Jha and Maharaj Swami, the Godman had promised a miracle to prove his powers. When asked for comment this morning, one of Swami-ji's aides said off the record that His Holiness was certainly capable of summoning Kali. But so far the Godman himself has been mute on this point."

Puri pushed the paper aside with a look of anger and disgust.

"Madam Rani, you remember this deceased fellow?"

"Of course, sir, he's—"

"Dr. Suresh Jha, the Guru Buster," said the detective, finishing her sentence for her. "I did one investigation for him a few years back. You remember?"

She did indeed and indicated as much with a nod. But Elizabeth Rani had worked for Puri long enough to know that he was going to recount the details of the Case of the Astrologer Who Predicted His Own Death regardless.

"It started when one astrologer by name of Baba Bhola Ram predicted the time and date of his very own death," he began. "Twenty-four-hour news channels, forever chasing eyeballs, got hold the story and turned it into a national spectacle."

Elizabeth Rani remembered watching the live coverage on the *Action News!* station.

"Vedika, is there any indication yet of how he's supposed to die?" the anchor had asked a young lady reporter standing outside the astrologer's front door before the appointed hour.

"There's been a good deal of speculation on that point," the reporter had answered without the slightest hint of irony. "One local tarot card reader is claiming she's foreseen that something will fall out of the sky and hit him on the head. Baba Bhola Ram himself says he knows only when he'll die, not how. Will his prediction come true? Certainly he has a lot riding on the outcome, not least his reputation. Back to you in the studio."

"Millions tuned in to find out whether this fellow Baba Bhola Ram would live or die," continued Puri. "Minutes after the predicted hour, only, the astrologer's wife came out and, in floods of tears, announced that her husband 'by grace of God almighty went to great abode in sky.' "

Dr. Suresh Jha visited Most Private Investigators Ltd. the following morning. His charity-cum-foundation, DIRE, labored to "explain the unexplained" and the rationalist wanted to hire Puri to disprove the so-called miracle performed by Baba Bhola Ram.

"The wool is being pulled over our eyes," he'd told the detective at the time. "If people carry on believing in this kind of thing, they will remain blind."

"Through deductive reasoning and the most thorough examination of evidence at hand, I came to know Dr. Jha's suspicions were quite correct," recounted Puri. "The astrologer had indeed been murdered. The evildoers were Baba Bhola Ram's most trusted and dedicated disciples themselves. Fearful of their guru's reputation getting ruined, they took it upon themselves to make certain his prediction came true. Knowing of his weak heart, they put some ground castor beans into their master's chai and thus he expired."

Puri lapsed into a contemplative silence. By now, he was leaning forward with his elbows planted on his desk.

"Naturally I saw to it justice was done," he added. "But one thing about the case has always been there—one thing that frankly and honestly to this very day troubles me."

"What is it, sir?" asked Elizabeth Rani, although she could anticipate what he was going to say.

"Would Baba Bhola Ram have died at that hour had he not predicted his own death?"

"I believe that is something we will never know in this lifetime, sir," said Puri's secretary.

"Undoubtedly, Madam Rani!" said the detective, shaking off his mournfulness. "As usual you are quite correct. Only the God can know, isn't it?"

Puri's mobile phone rang and he looked at the name on the screen: JAGAT. He answered it.

"Inspector! Kidd-an?"

The call lasted no more than two minutes. It ended with the detective saying: "I will be reaching in one hour."

He glanced at the clock on his desk, a gift from the Federation of Automobile Dealers Associations (India).

"Mr. Sam Rathinasabapathy would be here any moment," he told Elizabeth Rani. "Thirty minutes maximum is required. After, my presence is requested on Rajpath. Not for the first time, Inspector Jagat Prakash Singh would be needing my expert guidance."

"You're going to investigate Dr. Jha's murder, sir?" asked his secretary, sounding hopeful.

"Nothing is confirmed, Madam Rani. But I can hardly be expected to stand by and watch this crime go unpunished, no? Myself and Dr. Jha were not in agreement on all matters, that much is certain, but he was a most upstanding fellow all round."

Elizabeth returned to her desk, fully confident that her employer would be taking on the case, even though it would mean working without pay.

The idea that Vish Puri could resist getting involved in such a tantalizing murder was preposterous. There was as much chance of him going without his lunch.

Sam Rathinasabapathy was fifteen minutes late. A traffic jawan had issued him a challan on Panchsheel Marg.

"The cop said I failed to signal when I turned right! Can you believe that? I mean, Mr. Puri, have you ever seen *anyone* in this country use their signals—ever? Personally, I think he was after a bribe. He kept mentioning the word 'lifafa.' That means 'envelope,' right?"

"Correct, sir," said Puri patiently, the faintest hint of a smile on his lips.

"I can't *believe* how corrupt this place is. Everyone's got their hand out the whole time. I can't even get a cooking gas canister without paying baksheesh. No wonder the country's such a mess!"

"Sir, no need to do tension," said Puri, motioning Rathinasabapathy into one of the comfortable chairs in front of his desk. "Allow me to give you some advice. Most definitely you will thank me for it later."

"Sure, Mr. Puri," said the nuclear physicist with a sigh as he took a seat.

"An educated, well-to-do gentleman such as yourself should not go round hither and thither without a good driver. Frankly speaking, sir, it does not look right. Just you should sit in the backseat, only. That way you won't be facing this type of harassment. Police wallahs will know you're someone of importance and not a part of the riffraff." Puri rolled his Rs with gusto.

"But I'm used to driving myself," protested Rathinasabapathy.

"Believe me, sir, I understand. You value your independence. But allow me to find a suitable driver. He should be of good character and naturally not a drunkard. Those from hill states are best. Such types have to learn to control their vehicles on all those tight bends. Otherwise they'd go right off the edge."

"Yes, well, I suppose that would be an advantage," said Rathinasabapathy.

"Very good! Later, I'll get my man to revert with some candidates. You need pay five, six thousand per month maxi-mum."

"OK, Mr. Puri, whatever you say. Now are you going to tell me what happened last night at the Food Village place? Where's my money?"

Puri reached down behind his desk and picked up a sports bag, setting it down on his desk.

"It's in here, sir. Two lakhs exactly."

"You got it back! But how?"

"Actually, sir, it never left this room."

"I don't follow."

"Just I'll explain. It was necessary for you to make the withdrawal in case they were keeping an eye on you. But the cash you gifted was not the money you withdrew from the bank."

"I don't get it. What was in the bag I gave to what's-his-name? The fat guy in the silk shirt. Mr. Ten Percent."

Puri smiled. "His real name is Rupinder Khullar. He's a professional lizer."

"A what?"

"Lizer," repeated the detective. "Means a man who gets things fixed up. Delhi is full of such types. I tell you, throw a stone in any direction and most definitely you will hit one. Such individuals will arrange anything for the right fee. Get your son a job in a government ministry, lobby the right MLA to get emissions certificates passed on your factory. Mr. Rupinder Khullar is particularly well connected politically. You might say he's got a finger in every samosa." Here Puri uttered a light chuckle.

"So what did I give him?" asked Rathinasabapathy, who didn't seem to find the metaphor humorous.

"Counterfeit money," answered the detective.

"I gave him *what*?" cried the nuclear physicist, rising half out of his chair.

"Please, sir, remain calm. Rest assured everything is two hundred percent all right. Pukka! I borrowed it from an old batchmate in the Anti-Counterfeit Section. Naturally on condition every last note be returned. It is evidence from another case. These days so much of funny money is being sent across our borders by Pakistan, I tell you."

"Is that legal?"

"Sir, in India the line between what is legal and what is not is often somewhat of a fuzz."

Puri opened the Rathinasabapathy file and pulled out the photographs that Tubelight had taken of Mr. Ten Percent. They served to illustrate the narrative about the middleman's movements after the meeting.

His first stop had been a hotel bar, where he had "taken

a few pegs imported whisky" with a local politician. Two hours later, Mr. Ten Percent visited an apartment in Sector Nine, DLF City, where he spent a couple of fun-filled hours with his mistress, a twenty-six-year-old VJ with a job he had fixed for her on a prominent music channel.

"The place is registered in his name. She is a PG, so to speak."

"PG?"

"Means 'paying guest.'"

Mr. Ten Percent then returned to Raja Garden, his home, wife, two children, three servants and a Pekinese.

"This morning first thing, he drove to Ultra Modern School," continued Puri. "There, he handed over the two hundred thousand to Mr. S. C. Bhatnagar."

Bhatnagar was the school principal. Last week he had offered Rathinasabapathy two places for his children in return for a hefty bribe.

"Their entire conversation was captured on hidden video cameras secreted inside Mr. Bhatnagar's office," continued Puri. "On tape, these two can be clearly seen and heard, also, discussing your case and Rupinder Khullar's fee."

"Let me guess. Ten percent?"

"Correct."

"But how did you get the money back—the counterfeit money?"

"I called this principal fellow and made the situation perfectly clear—that we are having all evidence to take to authorities and he is in possession of so much funny money. Forthwith, I gave him instructions where to return it—that is, two lakhs total. He was most accommodating." Puri paused. "Sir, I am pleased to say he has also kindly assured me your two darling children have confirmed places in Ultra Modern School."

"You mean they're in?" exclaimed Rathinasabapathy. He was half out of his chair again.

"They may start Monday, only."

Relief swept over Puri's client. "That's fantastic news, Mr. Puri!" he said. "I don't know how to thank you. I was *so* worried. I had tried so many schools and they all wanted kickbacks. The thought of the kids not getting into a good institution . . . well, I don't know what I would have done."

Rathinasabapathy sighed, relaxing his shoulders, and leaned back in his chair. But then a thought occurred to him and he frowned. "Hang on a minute . . . what about Mr. Ten Percent? He's going to be pretty upset!" he said.

"That one will keep quiet. He would not wish to be on tonight's news."

"But won't he come after me?"

Puri shook his head.

"Won't he come after you?"

"Not to worry about me," said the detective with a chuckle. "I have my connections, also. Besides, my identity remains top secret. Vish Puri is a voice on the phone, only."

Rathinasabapathy's forehead was still creased with anxiety.

"I don't know, Mr. Puri," he said at length, shifting in his chair. "I'm not sure how I feel about all this. It all seems . . . well, risky as hell."

The detective held up both his hands and shook them, a gesture that communicated "Why worry?"

"Trust me, sir," he said smugly. "I have taken care of everything."

Rathinasabapathy stared at the floor for a while, weighing it all up in his mind, and then said, "Well, if you say so. But I still can't believe how much people in this city go through to get their kids into schools."

"I told you when we met few days back, no, schools in India are a huge racket. Any business is about supply and demand. In this case there is excess of demand and nowhere near the supply. Thus schools can charge a premium for admittance. I tell you parents in Delhi go to hell getting their children into good schools.

"What all my niece Chiki went through you wouldn't believe," continued the detective. "She made applications to six schools total. All demanded a registration fee of four hundred to seven hundred rupees. Naturally there were countless forms to complete. Each and every time, the boy had to sit a test and do the interview. And each and every time, his parents were interviewed, also."

"The parents?" exclaimed Rathinasabapathy.

"Most certainly. They were interviewed separately in order to cross-reference their answers. What all were their aspirations? Their views on discipline? Chiki joked she and her husband had to cram for the test themselves. Made University look like ABC."

"So what happened?"

"Thank the God, Ragev got a place at Sunny Dale. But only after his father made a donation toward the new school bus."

"Unbelievable."

"Sir, I tell you, that is nothing. I know one family—they run a dry-cleaning business. In return for admittance to Vallabhbhai Jhaverbhai School, they agreed to do the head teacher's family's laundry! Six years now they've been washing their shirts and undergarments."

"Why don't people send their kids to state schools?"

Puri clicked his tongue dismissively.

"Sir, my maid's son goes to our local school. As it is, I had to intervene to get him in, such is the demand. Standards are quite frankly shocking. Teachers don't turn up. Food is substandard. Her boy often complains of bugs in his daal. For females, there are not even toilet facilities. Nowadays standards are only getting worse. What with the liberalization of the economy, government is withdrawing from its responsibilities more day by day."

Rathinasabapathy shook his head in disbelief. "Can't something be done?" he asked. "What about this evidence you have against the principal of Ultra Modern School? We should go public with it!"

"Most certainly we can," said Puri. "TV channels love such footage. But then your children won't get admittance. And you will be back at square number one dealing with Mr. Ten Percent—or one of his many competitors."

The nuclear physicist paused for thought and then said: "Yeah, well, I guess maybe we should let sleeping dogs lie, right? I mean the main thing is we didn't have to pay a bribe and the kids are going to go to a good school."

"Sir, I can see you're getting a hang of how things work here in India," said Puri with a smile, rising from his chair and handing Rathinasabapathy his money. "And now if there's nothing else, I'll take my leaves. I have a most puzzling murder to look into."

Four

As soon as Rathinasabapathy had left, Elizabeth Rani called Puri over the intercom and suggested he turn on his TV.

"Apparently there's some amazing video of the murder," she said.

Action News! was indeed running exclusive footage taken by a French tourist that morning.

At exactly 6:37 AM, Edouard Lecomte had been riding in a tour bus toward the Presidential Palace. While filming out the window, his attention had been drawn to what looked like some kind of "exotic Hindu ritual" being enacted by a small group of people on one of the lawns. Only later did he realize what he had captured: Dr. Jha's murder.

The footage was unsteady and hazy thanks to the smog and the distance at which it had been shot. But it showed the goddess Kali, complete with four writhing arms and a hideous red tongue, floating three feet above the ground. She could be seen driving her sword through Dr. Jha and cackling wildly. Then came a bright flash. Evidently, this had startled the Frenchman, who had lowered his camera and could be heard muttering, "*Putain de merde!*"

The channel was playing the thirty or so seconds over

and over again, slowing it down, enlarging key frames and drawing little circles around certain details. It proved beyond doubt that whoever or whatever had killed the Guru Buster had not hung from wires suspended from overhanging branches. The graceful manner in which "the apparition" glided through the air suggested it was standing on neither stilts nor a box.

"Could it be someone wearing a jet pack?" postulated one of the *Action News!* TV anchors.

"You'd see evidence of that," a science commentator answered. "There'd be an exhaust and the movement would be jerky. Those things are hard to control. I can't explain what we're seeing here."

Puri, who watched the footage numerous times on the small set he kept in his office, agreed with this last assessment.

"Absolutely mind-blowing," he kept muttering to himself.

A part of him wanted to believe that it was a genuine supernatural occurrence—that the goddess Kali really had materialized on earth. Believing in something fantastic, something inexplicable, was always easier than accepting the mundane truth. But Puri was certain that his eyes were being deceived, that a mere mortal had killed Dr. Jha, and he felt roused to the challenge of hunting down the murderer.

The video convinced him of one other thing: the general public would believe there had been a miracle.

The authorities had evidently come to the same conclusion.

Riot police armed with lathis, tear gas and water cannons had sealed off all the approach roads to Rajpath. And as Puri soon discovered, setting off in his Ambassador complete with new windscreen, this had brought gridlock to the British bungalow-lined streets of New Delhi. The many roundabouts, congested and chaotic at the best of times, were a logjam of cars and auto rickshaws playing a discordant symphony for horns.

After ninety minutes, the detective had only reached Safdarjung Road, and it was here that he decided to abandon his car. Having made arrangements with the incharge at the front desk of the Gymkhana Club to leave the Ambassador unattended in the car park (and passed up the opportunity to have some lunch—the special was kadi chaaval followed by moong daal halwa), he and Handbrake continued on foot.

Puri found the going hard. By now it was blisteringly hot and muggy and it was not long before he felt as if he were swimming in his safari suit. The unusually high curbs built by the Angrezi along their fastidiously laid-out avenues—presumably to deter bicyclists and motorcyclists from using the pavements—presented Puri with a formidable challenge thanks to the shortness of his left leg. Every time he had to cross the road or the entrance to one of the many bungalows, he needed a hand up.

For Handbrake the going was hardly easy either. While exposed to the full force of the midday sun, he had to walk alongside Boss, shielding him with a black umbrella. But of the two men, the driver reached the corner of Janpath and Maulana Azad Road (where police barriers prevented them from going any farther) in better shape and without complaint. Puri, on the other hand, looked close to fainting and had to rest in the shade of a tree for ten minutes in order to recover. Glugging down a bottle of chilled water purchased from a passing ice cream wallah, he bemoaned the fact that he could go no farther and thanked the heavens when Inspector Jagat Prakash Singh came to the rescue in his air-conditioned jeep.

"What took you so much of time?" asked the detective as he climbed inside the vehicle, leaving Handbrake outside, and sat panting in the cool air like an overheated dog. "It is hotter than hell out there."

"Press conference, sir," answered the inspector in his deep baritone.

Inspector Singh was a stern bear of a man, six foot two inches tall with enormous hands and size 14 feet. He was sitting on the backseat of his jeep (his driver was behind the wheel) with the top of his head touching the roof, his neck and spine bent like a bow and his knees pressed into the back of the seat in front of him. Although a Sikh, he kept his black beard trimmed. His hair, too, was short and he didn't wear a turban.

But while Singh's religious identity was liberal, his investigative style was conventional. A graduate of the Sardar Vallabhbhai Patel National Police Academy and the son and grandson of former officers, he had a good track record when it came to solving bank robberies, rapes, kidnappings, burglaries and crimes of passion where the clues were staring him in the face and the choice of suspects was few. But when dealing with more sophisticated crimes, like cunningly orchestrated, premeditated murders for example, the inspector often found himself stumped.

In such circumstances, he turned to Puri.

The detective had solved a number of Singh's cases, and pointed him in the right direction on various others, but never taken credit for his work. This rankled him; Puri relished the glare of the cameras and the opportunity to impress everyone with his acumen and skills. And yet the currency he received in return for his anonymous assistance was invaluable. He could count on information and cooperation with his own cases. And it often helped having an ally in the department to keep the chief, who reviled him as a "filthy jasoos," off his back.

There was not another man on the Delhi force with whom Puri would have entered into such an arrangement. Singh was incorruptible. It didn't hurt that, being only thirty-four, he was suitably deferential as well. Nor that he was Punjabi and enjoyed a couple of stiff pegs at the end of a hard day's work.

"So, Inspector, what progress you've made till date?" asked the detective, wiping his face with his handkerchief and drinking more water.

The Sikh splayed his enormous fingers across his knees, studying his hairy knuckles and wedding ring.

"Honestly? I can't make head or tail of it," he admitted. "I'm starting to believe something supernatural *did* occur. I mean that. People don't just vanish into thin air, sir. Furthermore, no one saw anyone coming or going. Plus I've got four witnesses who *swear* they saw the goddess murder Dr. Jha. And then there's that video. You've seen it?"

Puri nodded.

"It looks so . . . well, so *real,* sir. That face, the arms—the fact that she's levitating. The murder occurred close to a tree and some of the branches overhang the spot. But I examined those branches myself and there's no sign of any rope marks. The only thing I found was some holes drilled into the side of the tree trunk."

"Inspector, believe me, I am one man who believes in miracles. Unlike Dr. Jha, I know such things can and do occur. But because gold exists, it does not mean there is not fool's gold, also."

Singh made a face. "Sorry, sir?"

"Not every strange occurrence is automatically a miracle," the detective clarified. "Take that incident few years back when Ganesh statues started drinking milk. Millions believed something miraculous occurred. A kind of pandemonium there was nationwide. But it was all a total nonsense. Just some unscrupulous individuals took advantage of people's beliefs and superstitions. Got them believing something had happened which had not. Word spread like wildfires. Same is true now. I guarantee you no miracle has taken place."

"I'm sure you're right, sir, but I've never come across anything like this."

"What all does Delhi's 'top cop' have to say on the matter?" As ever when Puri referred to the chief, his voice was loaded with sarcasm.

"You know him, sir. If it can't be solved, don't bother solving it. Concentrate on cases where we can get quick, easy results. That's his credo. Had the victim been the twelve-year-old daughter of a doctor or engineer it would be different. But none of his superiors are pressuring him on this one."

Puri drained his bottle of water; he was beginning to cool off.

"Swami-ji's whereabouts early this morning are known, is it?" he asked.

"He was in Delhi, a guest of the health minister, Vikram Bhatt. The minister himself called the chief first thing this morning to let him know."

"By God," muttered Puri.

"Do you think Swami-ji could be behind all this?" asked Singh.

"Too early to tell, no? But certainly he claims miraculous powers, levitation being one only. It is said he can be in two places at once. He had motive, also, after making one promise on national TV of some kind of miracle in Delhi to prove his power."

Singh looked worried.

"Something is wrong?" asked Puri, although he could guess what it was.

"The chief wants Maharaj Swami left alone. Hands off. He's not to be investigated."

The detective sighed.

"No surprise there, Inspector," he said. "But if you are asking for my help—and seems you are—I can hardly be expected to do a proper and thorough investigation while ignoring the main suspect?"

"Sir, all I'm saying is that we have to tread carefully."

"That much goes without saying, Inspector. Now let us not waste more of time sitting idle. Take me to the spot."

The crime scene had been cordoned off with metal barricades. But from even the most cursory examination, Puri could tell they had been put in place far too late to serve any useful purpose. Dozens of discarded bidi and cigarette butts, gobs of paan spit and fresh piss stains on the nearby jamun tree, which stood approximately eight feet to the north of the spot where Dr. Jha had been slain, indicated the size of the crowd that had gathered at the scene before the police had taken charge.

Plenty of traces also pointed to the earlier presence of opportunistic vendors as well. They had set up pitches selling cold drinks (bottle tops littered the entire area), peanuts (there were shells as well) and Hindi newspapers (flyers for a 50 percent mid-season sale at Jessy's Shoe Palace in Pahar Ganj lay everywhere). Someone had also been doing a roaring trade in incense sticks: dozens had been stuck into the ground and lit on the spot where the goddess was believed to have appeared.

"Quite a carnival scene it must have been, isn't it?" said

Puri as he stood inside the cordon wearing his tinted aviator sunglasses with Handbrake by his side, umbrella aloft.

Singh was the only other person in the immediate vicinity. He had sent away his subordinates on some pretext (in case one of them reported Puri's visit to the chief) and the media had been penned into a position in front of India Gate. Between there and the crime scene, Rajpath dissolved into a rippling, liquid mirage. Cars along the road melted as if made of chocolate. Figures took on alien dimensions.

"Constables patrolling the area reached first, is it?" asked Puri.

"Yes, sir. Constable R. V. Dubey arrived ten minutes after the murder occurred."

Puri made a note of his name as Singh continued: "By then there was already a crowd of one hundred plus—passing auto rickshaw drivers, schoolkids, some women who'd been doing yoga. Their numbers quickly grew."

The inspector himself had not reached Rajpath until eight thirty. By that time, hundreds of people, including the entire Delhi media pack, had trampled the crime scene.

"Could be the murderer left his business card, but we'll never know," commented the detective drily.

Singh did not respond to this gibe. He knew all too well that the response time of the Delhi police force was abysmal. There was no point trying to defend it.

"You know where the members of this Laughing Club were standing?" asked Puri.

Singh took out his notebook and read out the names one by one, indicating where each man had been at the time of the murder. Puri plotted their positions on a page in his own notebook. He marked the spot where Dr. Jha had stood with an X; in the middle of the circle he drew a question mark.

"These other fellows: they were all present when you arrived?"

"No, sir, they'd been taken to the station to give statements. But I interviewed each of them personally. I'll have the transcripts brought to your office. One of them, Shivraj Sharma, an archaeologist, says he didn't see what happened because he dropped his glasses. But the others are all convinced they witnessed a paranormal event—although of course their descriptions vary. Mr. Ved Karat, a political speechwriter, described the goddess as being twenty feet high. Mr. Gupta, a High Court advocate, says her eyes 'burned like coals.'"

"Witness accounts always differ, Inspector," said Puri. "Eyes all work the same, but the mind . . . that is something altogether different, isn't it?"

"Yes, sir," intoned Singh, who had learned to put up with Puri's little lectures.

"I would be needing to do interrogation of all these gentlemen myself, also," said the detective.

The inspector had already anticipated this and written their names and addresses down on a piece of paper. Without a word, he handed it to Puri.

"You know me better than I know myself, isn't it?" He smiled before beginning a more thorough examination of the scene.

Singh stood nearby watching the detective's actions closely as if he was trying to decipher some hidden method.

"Inspector, your boys' boot prints are everywhere," scolded Puri after a minute or so. "A three-legged dog was present, also. But there is nothing else here apart from one bloodstain." He paused. "Anything is missing?"

His question anticipated key evidence having been removed from the scene by petty criminals. In the past, Puri had known pickpockets posing as doctors to rob corpses of wallets, wedding rings, even shoes. It was not unknown for constables to do the same.

"Sir, regretfully, the murder weapon itself is nowhere to be found," answered Singh.

"Could be anyone stole it."

"It's possible, sir, but . . ." The inspector looked suddenly unsure of himself.

"Tell me," prompted Puri.

"It's ridiculous, I know, but Professor Pandey says he saw the sword disintegrate before his very eyes while still in the victim's chest."

"Disintegrate?"

"Into ash, sir."

"You found any of this ash?"

"I found some gray dust next to the spot where Dr. Jha fell. I've sent it to the lab. The results won't be back for a few days."

Puri referred to his notebook again.

"This fellow Pandey was closest to the body. Could be why he saw the blade disintegrate and others didn't."

"But, sir, you told me you didn't believe anything paranormal occurred!" objected Singh.

"Correct, Inspector. But it may be the blade *did* in fact disintegrate. A good detective keeps an open mind."

By now, Puri was stooped over the bloodstain, the only indication of where Dr. Jha had fallen.

"Seems there was a good deal of blood," he said. "How long the body lay here?"

"Five minutes at the most. Professor Pandey drove the victim to AIIMS, where he was declared 'arrived dead.'"

Puri inquired about the wound.

"I saw it myself, sir, an inch to the left of the heart. The medical officer says he died quickly."

"You released the body?"

"Yes, sir. The cremation will be later today." Puri nodded. There was nothing unusual about this; funerals in India were usually held within hours of death.

"Do one thing, Inspector," said the detective. "Go and stand behind the tree."

Singh did as he was asked while Puri went and stood in each of the spots where the Laughing Club members had been.

"It is as I suspected," he announced. "Anyone hiding behind the tree would have gone unseen. The trunk is too wide."

"But surely they would have seen the murderer approaching," said Singh as he reappeared.

"Not if they came directly from the south. From there the tree is providing more than adequate cover."

"They?" asked Singh.

"There were at least two persons, no? One to do the actual deed, another to release the fog and make those flashes so as to distract the witnesses."

"That makes sense, sir," said Singh, sounding encouraged. "I suppose the second man hiding behind the tree could also have released some laughing gas—that would explain why the members all started laughing uncontrollably."

"That is one possibility, Inspector. Why not check into how readily laughter gas is available? Who all is having access to it? No doubt there are small canisters available that are readily portable." The two went quiet for a moment, both deep in thought. Then Singh asked: "Sir, do you have any theories about how the murderer levitated?"

"As of now, I am certain of one thing only," replied Puri.

"And that is?"

"This is one of the most extraordinary crimes I have encountered during my long and distinguished career. Those behind it are master criminals. No doubt about it at all." He paused. "But tell me, Inspector. These holes you mentioned earlier. They're where exactly?"

Singh led the detective to the east side of the tree and pointed out four small holes bored into the bark at a height of about ten feet.

"Looks like they held some type of bracket," suggested Puri on tiptoe.

"For holding up a winch perhaps?"

"A small one, possibly. But only time will tell."

They made their way back across the lawn to the jeep.

"So you're willing to take on the case, sir?" asked Singh, sounding hopeful.

"More than willing. But usual rules apply. I will update you on any and all major developments. Meantime I work alone."

"But if there's an arrest to be made . . ."

"Not to worry, Inspector, that is your department. When the time comes, I will be calling you, only."

Singh was frowning again.

"Sir, one thing still worries me: Maharaj Swami. Some of the richest men in India bow down to touch his feet. Even the prime minister visited his ashram not long back. You should be careful."

Puri smiled. "No need to worry about me, Inspector. Danger is my ally after all."

Having called the Jha household and been given the time and place of the funeral, the detective traveled north along Ring Road, past the sheer, red sandstone walls of the Old

City, the Mughal emperor Shah Jahan's once magnificent capital. He passed the milky white audience hall, which once housed the Peacock Throne, and the octagonal tower of the Shahi Burj, the king of the world's library.

Ten minutes later, the Ambassador pulled up at the entrance to Delhi's principal cremation ground on the west bank of the Yamuna River.

To Puri, no other place served as such a powerful reminder of man's mortality, the fact that for all of us there is but a single breath between this life and the next. Facing that reality was no bad thing. But the place held sad memories for him all the same. The first time he had come here had been as a five-year-old for the funeral of his great-grandmother; more recently, he had brought his beloved papa to be cremated.

Om Chander Puri had suffered a massive heart attack while out on his early morning walk. Less than twelve hours later, in accordance with Hindu custom, Puri and his brothers had carried their father's body into the cremation ground on a stretcher and placed him in one of the forty or so shallow cremation pits that lay just a few feet apart under a blackened metal roof. A crowd of "near or dear" had gathered round as a pandit had performed antim-samskara, the last rites, helping to bring the union of the soul, atma, with the Holy Spirit. Sprinkling Ganga water on the body, the priest had pulled back the cotton shroud to reveal Papa's face, and a little honey and a small dollop of ghee had been poured into the mouth.

Slowly—carefully—Puri and his three brothers had piled pieces of wood on top of the body. Two bags of fragrant-smelling mulch had been scattered over the pyre to disguise the smell of burning flesh. And then Puri's elder brother had applied a flame to the kindling.

Now the detective watched another family enacting the

same timeless rituals in more or less the same spot where his father, and thousands of others since, had been cremated. The heat of a blaze burning nearby felt hot against his right cheek. Six other pits contained charred, smoldering hunks of wood and blackened bones. They would there remain undisturbed until the following morning, when the male relatives of the respective families would return to sift through the ashes by hand and retrieve the remains of their loved ones.

This was not where Dr. Jha was to be cremated, however. The Guru Buster, who had spent his adult life railing against religious ceremony (not to mention the precious wood that the traditional Hindu funeral demands), had left strict instructions for his body to be cremated, without fuss, in a gas incinerator.

Puri therefore turned away from the fire pits and walked the short distance to the nearby CNG (compressed natural gas) crematorium.

A more soulless structure could hardly have been imagined. Like something out of a Nazi death camp, it was built of cinder blocks and corrugated iron and there was a big, ugly chimney sticking out of the roof.

It was here that the city's unclaimed and unidentified bodies were brought, along with the poorest of the poor. A no-frills funeral cost just 500 rupees and was devoid of aesthetics. A cavernous concourse housed six giant ovens replete with gauges, knobs and levers.

Puri arrived in time to see Dr. Jha's body, which had been sewn into a shroud, carried onto the heavy metal trolley that fed oven number five. His widow, Ashima, who was some twelve years younger than her late husband, stood in front of it dressed in white. Her daughter had one arm around her. Both women were sobbing quietly. About seventy family members and friends were gathered around them.

The detective stood toward the back of the gathering, hands held respectfully in front of him, as one of Dr. Jha's former colleagues from the Wireless Planning and Communications Wing, where the two had worked for some thirty years, read a touching tribute. It included a quote from Marx and an anecdote about how the deceased had once asked the Godman Sai Baba why he gave the gold chains he claimed to materialize out of thin air to the wealthy and not the poor.

This brought fond smiles to many faces.

And then Puri noticed a man standing in the shadow cast by oven number four. He was holding a video camera. Judging by the red light on the front of the device, he was recording Dr. Jha's funeral.

It occurred to the detective that this individual might be working for a news channel, which would explain why he was standing at a distance, apparently trying to remain inconspicuous. But the camera he was holding was much smaller than the ones used by professional cameramen.

Curious, Puri began to inch to his right, hoping to get a look at the man's face. But as he did so, everyone was asked to step back from the oven and the detective found himself hemmed in by his fellow mourners.

Two crematorium employees pushed the trolley inside the gaping mouth of the oven and the detective's attention was drawn back to the proceedings.

A heavy metal door came down with a clang. Unceremoniously, the crematorium foreman turned a couple of knobs on the control panel, waited a couple of seconds and then pressed a red button. The oven trembled as the gas inside ignited.

The temperature gauge rose abruptly and settled on red.

A moment later, when Puri looked for the man with the video camera, he was gone.

Five

Puri hurried home to greet his second daughter, Jaiya, who was driving from Agra with her husband.

Jaiya's baby, Puri's third grandchild, was due in eight weeks. As tradition demanded, she was returning to her parents' house, where she would remain until the infant was at least a month old.

Over the past few weeks, frenetic preparations had been under way for Jaiya's arrival, and every evening Puri had arrived home to learn that his bank balance had taken another hit. Rumpi, who could usually be relied upon to be frugal, had called in the decorators to paint the largest of the three guest rooms. The adjacent bathroom had also been retiled in matching pink. An imported coil-spring Slumber mattress (14,000 rupees!) had been procured, along with an unusually large cot, numerous sets of sheets and pillowcases printed with motifs of elephants and penguins, and countless baby outfits. A strange, boomerang-shaped pillow had also been bought at one of the exorbitant shops in the Great Mall of India—"A Mall for All."

The detective, who kept a close watch on everything that

transpired inside his house, sometimes even bugging the servants, had also discovered a large stash of imported disposable nappies hidden away in the servants' quarters.

This had prompted him to object to the exorbitant sums being spent.

"Why you're buying so much of everything? How many outfits this child will need? You think paisa can be plucked from trees in the jungle, my dear?"

Rumpi had said nothing to this. Emboldened, Puri had continued with his protest: "No need for all these imported products. Made in India is just as good, if not better. We were all fitted with cloth nappies and our bottoms never suffered."

At that, his wife scowled, telling him that he was the one who needed nappies.

"Why exactly, my dear?" an incensed, bemused Puri had asked.

"Because of so much of verbal diarrhea!" she'd snapped.

The next day, the detective had opened his lunch tiffin to find it packed with celery sticks. The day after that plain bean sprouts. And so on . . .

To make amends, he had bought Rumpi a new mixie, something he had been putting off for months (the old one was only nine years old, after all). The model he had purchased was one of the best on the market, made in China, as almost everything was these days. According to that bloody bastard of a salesman who had refused to give a discount, "It slices and dices in a thrice."

There had been a marked improvement in the quality of Puri's lunches after that. But the frivolous spending had not abated.

The latest purchase, which Puri found propped against

the wall in the corridor when he reached home at seven o'clock, was a plastic tub shaped like a whale. The attached price tag was for 3,500 rupees.

"By God," muttered Puri, "it is practically a swimming pool!"

"What was that you said, husband?" asked Rumpi as she emerged from the kitchen to greet him.

"Nothing at all, my dear," he said with a smile, refraining from pointing out that he and his brothers had all been bathed in a steel bucket and it had done them no harm. "Just I was admiring this beautiful tub. The child is going to learn swimming, is it?"

"Nothing of the sort, Chubby," Rumpi said brusquely. "And I don't want to hear about how you were washed in some balti of yours."

"Yes, my dear. Nikhee must be getting close, is it?" Nikhee, Little One, was Jaiya's nickname.

"She called twenty minutes back. A truck turned turtle on the road. She won't reach here for another hour at least."

Rumpi brought Puri up to date with the rest of the affairs of the house: all the food apart from the kadi, which Malika had burnt, was ready; the geyser in the downstairs washroom wasn't working again; the diyas needed filling with oil.

"Now don't just stand around, Chubby. Make yourself useful. Our son-in-law will be arriving soon!"

Rumpi returned to the kitchen.

"Yes, my dear," murmured Puri as he took off his shoes and slipped on his monogrammed VP slippers.

He mounted the stairs. Halfway up, he stopped and suddenly bawled at the top of his lungs, "Sweetu!"

The houseboy came running out of the kitchen.

"Sir?" he asked, standing to attention in the hallway with an alertness that pleased his employer.

"Sweetu, what is five times six—tell me?" Puri asked him in Hindi.

"Five times six, sahib?" He murmured to himself nervously and then declared: "Thirty . . . sahib?"

"Very good. You've done your homework?"

Puri had enrolled Sweetu, who had been working in the house for over a year now, in afternoon maths classes. Next year, the orphan boy would begin an apprenticeship as a mechanic; when he was old enough, the detective would also find him a wife. This was the sort of help all well-off Indians should have been providing to those less fortunate than themselves, in the detective's opinion. It was their dharma, their duty, if only they knew it.

"All done, sahib," replied Sweetu.

"Very good. Go help madam."

Puri went upstairs, had a cold bucket wash, changed into a freshly pressed kurta pyjama, splashed on some Sexy Men aftershave, and donned a cloth flat cap.

A few minutes later, he was standing up on the roof, a generous tumbler of Royal Challenge whisky in hand. He watered his prized chili plants and then stood for a few minutes looking out over the lights dotted across the landscape twinkling in the polluted night air.

When Puri had moved to Gurgaon some sixteen years ago, it had still been a flyspeck of a village. He had built his house, a mock Spanish villa with an orange tiled roof and matching awnings, on land surrounded for miles by mustard and sugarcane fields. But there had been no escaping the city. In the past decade, it had expanded at a dizzying rate. Gurgaon, a part of the NCR, the National Capital Region—

now the largest human agglomeration on the planet with a population fast approaching 17 million people—had been quickly transformed into a land of housing estates, monster shopping complexes and shiny glass office blocks that seemed to grow overnight as if they came from magic beans. Were the cranes that loomed over the concrete superstructures giant watering cans?

In the cracks and shadows of this newfangled, corporate world, on plots of yet-to-be-developed land, tens of thousands of migrant workers were living in makeshift shelters without toilets or running water. Rickety stands selling chai, tarra and one-rupee shampoo sachets had rooted along the sides of the roads, as tenacious as Japanese bindweed. Barbers and earwax cleaners were to be found plying their trade between yet-to-be-laid concrete sewage pipes.

As he gazed out, Puri's thoughts turned to his guru. In his great work of 300 BC, *The Arthashastra,* literally *The Science of Material Gain,* Chanakya had emphasized the importance of wealth creation. Perhaps the world's first economist, not to mention a political genius, he was also an ardent capitalist.

Chanakya would have ridiculed the Nehru dynasty's protectionist policies and applauded India's recent economic rebirth, Puri reflected. But the slums and poverty, the inequality and rampant abuse of natural resources—all this would have appalled him. More than two millennia ago, he had stressed the necessity of honest and just governance. And yet today, a handful of politicians aside, India was ruled by a bunch of bloody goondas.

Sometimes, Puri wondered if the best thing might not be a revolution. But he doubted that would ever happen. The majority of Indians were farmers, not fighters. War had always been the preserve of the Kshatriya caste, and nowadays most of them were traders, businessmen and software engineers. Some even worked as private investigators.

A honk at the gate brought Puri to the front door with an expectant grin on his face.

His face fell when a red Indica with a crumpled bumper, a bashed-in fender and a Punjab number plate entered. It belonged to his sister's husband, Bagga-ji, who lived in Ludhiana.

"Don't tell me," the detective moaned to Rumpi, who was standing next to him on the porch. By now she had changed into a light chiffon sari, which had been part of her wedding trousseau, and rubbed sindoor into the parting of her hair.

"Chubby, stop it. Be nice. They've got some good news."

"They're getting divorced, is it?"

"Now that's enough. Be a good host and don't get into any more arguments with him."

Bagga-ji pulled up and stepped out of the car. Everything about him screamed cheapness, from his polyester shirt to the big gaps in his blackened teeth.

"Namaste-ji!" he cried, sounding as if he had cotton wool in his mouth. "How are you, Mr. Sherluck?"

Puri groaned inwardly. He hated people comparing him to Sherlock Holmes. Bagga-ji's thick Punjabi pronunciation made it all the more irritating.

"Hello, sir-ji!" said the detective, pronouncing "sir" "saar." "Good journey?"

"Fine, fine, fine, fine, fine," replied his brother-in-law.

The detective's older sister, Preeti, alighted from the other side of the Indica. Of all the minor but nonetheless enfeebling ailments from which this large, quiet woman suffered, the most serious was acute Bagga-itis.

"Chubby, you've lost some weight, is it?" she asked as they greeted one another with a loose, sideways hug.

This was said with concern rather than admiration.

"Not that I'm aware," said Puri, observing his belly, which spilled over his belt.

Bagga-ji had already gone inside the house.

Five minutes later, when Puri, Preeti and Rumpi reached the sitting room, he was sprawled on the floor. On the carpet in front of him lay a large glass of Royal Challenge and a collage of irregularly shaped pieces of paper with names and phone numbers in spidery writing. The backs of cigarette packets, old cinema tickets, strips torn from old envelopes—these served as Bagga-ji's phone directory and lived, for the most part, as a big lump stuffed into the pocket of his half-sleeve shirts.

"Sorry, ji. Long-distance. Five minutes only. Don't mind, huh?" he said, holding the receiver of the home phone to his ear.

"Please, sir-ji," replied Puri. "Make yourself at home. You'd like a cushion? A foot rub?"

The detective's sarcasm was lost on his brother-in-law.

"Fine, fine, fine, fine, fine, fine!"

The detective still found it hard to believe that his sister had married such a prize Charlie. But Preeti had never attracted many suitors thanks to her weight and bad skin. She'd been twenty-seven by the time Jaideep Bagga had come along in his secondhand three-piece suit.

"Good for nothing much, na," had been Mummy's appraisal after meeting him for the first time.

But Papa and Bagga-ji's father had got along and Mummy had been overruled.

The family astrologer had sealed Preeti's fate. Jaideep Bagga was a perfect match. Never mind that the young man had only displayed an aptitude for playing carrom board and eating large quantities of ladoos.

During the thirty-three years that had passed since then, Bagga-ji—whom Puri privately referred to as "Baggage"—had proven a constant embarrassment to the family. The detective dreaded inviting him to any family function, especially since his performance at Jaiya's wedding. Tipsy on whisky, he had tried to ingratiate himself with the minister of chemicals and fertilizers and asked him for a job for his eldest son. Despite receiving a sharp rebuke, Bagga-ji had spent the rest of the evening trying to worm his way into all the photographs taken of the MP from Chandigarh.

Anecdotes about Bagga-ji's business dealings abounded. His deceased father's transport business was long gone. And acre by acre, he had sold off most of the land he had inherited, sinking the proceedings into harebrained schemes. At one point he'd even invested in a Nepali yak-burger joint. But like all his enterprises, the Big Yak had gone under.

Now, it seemed, he had something else brewing. No doubt it was "foolproof" and was going to make him the richest man in all Punjab.

"Lakshmi has finally smiled on me!" he said in Punjabi with a grandiose sweep of his hands once he was off the phone.

The detective cast him a weary look. "What's the plan this time?" he asked, switching to Punjabi as well. "Camel-milk ice cream again, is it?"

"Actually that was not such a bad idea," interjected Preeti. It was rare for her to come to her husband's defense; usually she suffered in silence. "The ice cream itself was quite delicious."

"Problem was milking those bloody camels!" Puri chuckled.

"Laugh all you like," said Bagga-ji. "But you'll soon be congratulating me. A construction company wants to build a shopping mall on my land. They're offering me one crore."

"Which company?" asked the detective, sounding dubious.

"A big, respected one. I visited their offices. Very modern. They're offering Western-style contract."

Preeti added: "It all seems pukka, Chubby."

Another horn sounded at the gate. Puri looked outside in time to see Jaiya being helped out of the car by her husband.

Her belly had grown large and round.

"Hi, Papa!" she said, waddling over to him with a big smile.

"Nikhee, beta, so wonderful to see you. Just look at you! How many you've got in there?" he joked.

"Well, actually, we've been waiting to surprise you, Papa," she said with a grin, rubbing her bump.

His eyes widened. "Don't tell me."

"Yes, Papa, we're having twins."

"By God! My dear, you heard the news?" he called to Rumpi. "Nikhee has got two in the tandoor!"

"What wonderful news!" she replied, trying to sound surprised, although it was obvious she already knew. "All I can say is it's a good thing we're well prepared. Isn't it, Chubby?" She gave Jaiya a mischievous wink.

"Yes, my dear," intoned Puri.

Six

No one spotting the auto rickshaw driver who parked his three-wheeler down Basant Lane behind Connaught Circus would have guessed that he was a sattri—in ancient Chanakyan terminology, a spy. Nor that he knew every brothel, illegal cricket-gambling den and cockerel-fighting venue in the city—not to mention most of its best forgers, fencers, smugglers, safecrackers and purveyors of everything from used Johnnie Walker bottles to wedding-night porn. Blind in one eye, with henna-dyed hair and tatty, oil-stained clothes, he blended into the cityscape as seamlessly as Delhi's omnipresent crows.

Not even his family knew about his secret life.

Perhaps one day, when his three children were old enough, Baldev Pawar would tell them. But for now it was too risky. If word of his true identity ever leaked out, his life would be in jeopardy and his ability to operate seriously compromised.

Worse, he would be disgraced in the eyes of his father.

Papa Pawar had, in the best family tradition, spent his life working as a professional thief. And like his father and his father's father, he had worked diligently to ensure that his sons became proficient, capable crooks themselves.

From the age of seven, Baldev had been trained to pick pockets and relieve aunties of their handbags. As a teenager, he had graduated to locks, ignitions and safes. And in his mid-twenties he had started robbing banks. But after he was caught emptying the safe of the Faridabad branch of the Punjab National Bank and subsequently confined to a rat-infested cell for five years, he had decided to do the unthinkable and go straight. Papa Pawar had been devastated. It was his son's destiny to rob and cheat; dacoity was in their blood, he'd argued. But India was changing. Just because you were born into a certain caste, tribe or clan didn't mean that you had to stick to the job description of your forebears, Baldev had argued.

How Baldev, aka Tubelight, had become one of Vish Puri's operatives was a story in itself. Suffice it to say, it was not one he would ever share with his father or his brothers, all of whom were still in the family business and living nearby. Better that they believe him to be a lowly auto rickshaw driver than find out the truth, that he worked for one of their natural enemies: a jasoos.

Besides, a rickshaw wallah was the perfect cover for the type of work Tubelight was now engaged in—tailing grooms, spying on errant husbands, befriending servants and milking them for their employers' secrets. He didn't have to account for his whereabouts to anyone; he could hang around on any street corner or in front of any chai stand without raising suspicion; and—requisite bribes demanded by the police aside—the three-wheeler was an economical and agile means of transport.

Refusing fares was not a problem, either. Dilli wallahs were well accustomed to gruff, unaccommodating auto rickshaw drivers forgoing their custom whenever a requested destination did not suit them.

Still, as Tubelight crisscrossed the city, he sometimes took on board paying punters. Besides making a few extra rupees, it was an excellent way of keeping his finger on the pulse of the city.

This morning, en route to his rendezvous with Puri, all the talk from the backseat had been about yesterday's sensational murder. An elderly couple had described Kali as if they'd seen her themselves. Towering a hundred feet tall, she had slain dozens of people, hence the police cordon around the area, they said.

"Let us hope she rids us of our politicians!" the old woman had declared.

A fertilizer salesman from Indore believed Kali was going to cleanse the world of sinners. Judging by his terrified expression, it seemed the man had sinned a good deal.

Dainik Jagran, the bestselling Hindi newspaper (readership 56 million), was also preoccupied by the same news.

As Tubelight waited for Puri on the backseat of his auto rickshaw, he read a description of how, last night, "in the interests of national security," the police had cleared the streets around India Gate of thousands of Kali worshippers.

"Thus far," the editorial pointed out, "Hindu nationalist politicians have not sought to exploit the situation. Doubtless because of the site's proximity to Parliament and key ministries, not to mention their own residences, they have appealed for calm."

"Think Swami-ji did it?" Tubelight asked Puri in Hindi after the detective finally arrived.

The two were standing in front of one of their favorite breakfast dhabas that served kokis. The aroma of onions, green chilies, cumin seeds and fresh coriander frying in ghee wafted over them. They both ordered one of the Sindhi-style pancakes and sipped their cups of chai. The drink seemed to perk up Tubelight, who was still groggy, early mornings being anathema to him.

"If he is the guilty one, proving as much will be a challenge, that is for sure," said Puri. "We would need someone to get on the inside of his ashram. That is the only way."

On the hot tawa, the koki mixture spat and sizzled.

"How did you get on last night?" asked the detective in Hindi.

Puri had charged Tubelight with tracking down Constable R. V. Dubey, the first police wallah to have reached the murder scene, to find out if he had seen or heard anything that had not appeared in the offical panchnama.

This was Most Private Investigators' standard procedure given that constables often failed to report key information to their superiors—either through sheer incompetence (anyone with the ability to sign their own name could become a beat cop and they received no investigative training whatsoever) or deliberately (usually because someone bribed them to keep their mouth shut or they were just plain scared).

"I befriended Constable Dubey at the liquor store," answered Tubelight, who combined a gift for getting people to talk with an ability to hold his liquor like few men could. "We enjoyed some Old Monk rum together."

"And?"

"Approaching the scene, he passed an ice cream wallah pushing his cart. He was with a rag picker. Male, twenties, black skin."

"Paagal!" bawled Puri. "That was the murderer! He just let him walk away, is it?"

"Of course, Boss." Tubelight shrugged.

Their kokis were served with a dab of fresh butter and some curd and garlic pickle on the side.

As they greedily tore them apart with their fingers, the detective asked: "Did this prize Charlie see the murder weapon?"

"Didn't see it, Boss."

"You believe him?"

"Yes, Boss. By the end of the evening he was chattering away like a parrot. Believe me, I learned all his secrets. Most of them I'd have preferred not to have heard."

"Now I've another assignment for you," said Puri, adding in English: "No rest for wicked, huh?"

Tubelight did not reciprocate Puri's mischievous smile. He had been working long hours over the past few weeks, and thanks to the heat and constant "load shedding," or power cuts, he and his family had taken to the roof of their small house at night. Sleep had been in short supply, what with the mosquitoes and the incessant arguing of the husband and wife next door. The operative badly needed a few "offs." But now did not seem the time to broach the subject; Boss had that unstoppable look in his eye.

"You know any magicians?" asked Puri.

"Jadoo wallahs?" Tubelight's eyes widened. "You want to stay clear of them."

"Why exactly?"

"They've got powers. I've known them to put curses on people."

Puri could not help but smile at his operative's superstitious nature.

"All the same I would need to talk to them," he insisted.

Tubelight regarded him warily.

"They live in Shadipur Depot, in the slums," he said. "Have their own language—a magician's language passed down father to son. No one else understands it. Not even me. But there is one old babu who might help. Calls himself Akbar the Great."

Puri's task for the day was to call on the surviving members of the Laughing Club. Before that, he planned to break into Dr. Jha's office at DIRE. The detective was certain the institute would be closed and wanted to take the opportunity to snoop through the Guru Buster's desk and files without anyone else knowing he had done so.

This was typical of Puri's approach to detective work. "Less everyone knows what I know, the better" was one of his credos.

Handbrake drove him to Nizamuddin West, once a self-contained village abutting the tomb of India's most revered Sufi saint, but now a South Delhi colony. The India of narrow alleyways filled with Muslim pilgrims, beggars cradling drugged babies and the smoke of sizzling lamb kebabs gave way to well-swept residential streets lined with houses and apartments owned by wealthy Muslim merchants, lawyers and the odd gemstone dealer.

DIRE HQ was a 1950s bungalow. There were rusting bars on the narrow windows and buddleia growing from cracks in the grime-stained walls. A poster on the gate read:

DO YOU HAVE SUPERNATURAL POWERS?
CAN YOU CURE A TERMINALLY ILL PERSON?
REPAIR A TRANSISTOR WITH USE OF REIKI?
WALK ON WATER?
READ OTHER PEOPLE'S MINDS?
FLY TO THE MOON AND BACK WITHOUT AID OF SPACESHIP?
IF SO YOU COULD WIN 2 CRORE RUPEES!
JUST PROVE YOUR POWERS IN A LOCATION

SPECIFIED BY RATIONALIST AND "GURU BUSTER"
DR. SURESH JHA.
APPLY WITHIN.
IT MAY BE NOTED: THE TWO-CRORE-RUPEES AWARD
IS NOT KEPT IN OUR OFFICE.

As he had anticipated, Puri found the front door padlocked. It was still only nine o'clock and Dr. Jha's secretary would not be along for at least an hour, if indeed she was coming to work at all, which he doubted. According to Mrs. Jha, with whom Puri had spoken briefly after her husband's cremation yesterday, the future of DIRE was uncertain. The old Guru Buster had run it more or less single-handedly and had not appointed a successor.

The detective made his way down the side of the building to the kitchen door and found it already open. The lock looked as if it had been forced, probably with a strong, metal implement like a knife.

He could hear activity inside the bungalow—drawers being opened and closed; the rustle of papers; a cough.

Puri stepped inside but had to proceed slowly on account of the squeaky rubber soles of the orthopedic shoes he wore to account for his short left leg.

He crossed the stone kitchen floor on tiptoe without making a sound and entered the reception-cum-administrative office. It was a large room, dark and musty and simply furnished with a couple of desks and chairs, and an old Gestetner stencil printer with fresh blue ink on the roller.

The door to Dr. Jha's office was on the right-hand side of the room. It was closed, but someone was moving around inside.

The detective continued on tiptoe. But as he reached the door, he felt a painful cramp shoot through his left leg. This forced him to stop, and in shifting his weight onto his right foot and almost losing his balance, his shoe squeaked like a child's bathtime rubber duck.

Puri froze, his heart beating wildly. He waited for the cramp to ease off, not moving a muscle. It was almost a minute before the pain passed. Then slowly he pushed the door to Dr. Jha's office open.

It was empty. To the right of the room stood another door that was ajar. Puri approached it cautiously. He pushed it gently open.

Just then he was hit on the back of the head with a hard object. He heard someone say, "Oh, bugger!" before he fell to the floor, unconscious.

When Puri came around, it was to a throbbing head and the sound of a woman's voice asking him if he could hear her.

Gradually, his vision came into focus. The first thing he saw was a wavering, large red dot. When his sight cleared, he recognized the face of Dr. Jha's secretary, Ms. Ruchi, who had been at the cremation yesterday. She was wearing a big red bindi.

"Mr. Vish Puri, sir, are you OK?" she asked, staring down at him.

The detective tried to respond, but his words came out slurred.

"Better take rest, sir," she said. "You've had a nasty bash. Fortunately there's no blood."

The detective felt the back of his head; a large lump had already formed.

"Whoever it was got you with this, sir," said Ms. Ruchi, holding up a cricket bat. "Knocked you for six, looks like."

Another five minutes passed before Puri was able to sit up. The floor around him was scattered with papers, the contents of Dr. Jha's desk drawers and the drawers themselves. Someone had evidently turned the place over.

"Last thing I remember . . ." said Puri, who was suffering from mild amnesia, "I was . . . crossing the reception . . . I heard . . . something inside. But after . . . it's all . . . there's nothing. It's a blank, only."

"You saw who hit you, sir?" asked Ms. Ruchi, regarding him with a caring, sympathetic expression.

He hesitated before answering. "I don't believe so . . . but . . ." he answered.

Puri had a nagging feeling, as if there was something he had forgotten to do, but he couldn't remember what it was. "Could be it will come back to me," he added. "How long I've been here?"

"I'm not sure, sir. I came five minutes back. The time is half past nine."

Ms. Ruchi helped the detective up into a chair and then went to fetch him a glass of water. Puri sat surveying the office. Pinned to a board on the wall hung a collection of photographs of Dr. Jha and a group of young volunteers working in rural India during a recent DIRE "awareness" campaign. They could be seen taking turns walking across red-hot coals, a feat performed by many traveling sanyasis to demonstrate their "supernatural powers." Watching was a group of villagers. The idea was to impress upon these illiterate peasants that India's holy men were con artists.

Could some of the volunteers or perhaps a rival rationalist have carried out the murder? the detective wondered hazily. Such types studied the tricks and illusions of Godmen, after all. Perhaps one of them had wanted Dr. Jha out of the way?

"Sir, I hope you don't mind me asking, but what are you doing here?" asked Ms. Ruchi, breaking into his thought processes when she returned with a glass of water.

"Just I was passing by and found the door open. The lock had been forced. So naturally it was my duty to do investigation."

"I suppose it must have been one of Maharaj Swami's people," said Ms. Ruchi.

"You saw him, is it?" asked Puri as he sipped the water and his head began to clear.

"I'm afraid I caught only a glimpse of his back as he climbed over the wall behind the building. He had a car waiting. I heard it drive away."

"What all he was after?" asked Puri.

"Doctor-sahib's file on the Godman, most probably."

"He found it—the file, that is?"

"Fortunately not. Doctor-sahib keeps it hidden away. I mean . . ." Ms. Ruchi dropped her gaze to the floor; she looked suddenly overcome with sadness. "I mean . . . he *kept* it hidden away."

"I'm most sincerely sorry for your loss," said Puri, who had not had the opportunity to offer her his condolences at the cremation yesterday. "Dr. Jha will be sorely missed. An upstanding fellow he was in every respect."

"Thank you, sir," she said as the tears began to trickle down her face. She dabbed them with her handkerchief, quickly regaining her composure. "Is it true you're investigating his murder?" She added quickly: "Mrs. Jha told me."

"Most certainly," he answered. "And let me assure you, my dear Ms. Ruchi, I will be most definitely getting to the bottom of it by hook or crook. Vish Puri always gets his man—or in this case I should say 'his deity,' isn't it?"

"I'm pleased to hear it, sir," she said. "I'd be happy to help in any way I can. As much as anyone, I want Maharaj Swami to face justice."

"You're certain it was he who committed the act, is it?"

"Who else could it have been?" she exclaimed, wide-eyed, as if Puri had blasphemed. "Dr. Jha was Maharaj Swami's enemy number one. He had been campaigning against him tirelessly. And recently he had been investigating a suspicious suicide of a young woman at the Godman's ashram, the Abode of Eternal Love. Her name was Manika Gill. Dr. Jha believed she was murdered.

"And there's another thing," continued Ms. Ruchi. "Yesterday Dr. Jha received a death threat. I'll fetch it for you."

She disappeared into the reception and soon returned with the piece of paper pasted with letters cut from a Hindi newspaper. Puri read it out loud: " 'Whenever there is a withering of the law and an uprising of lawlessness on all sides, then I manifest myself. For the salvation of the righteous and the destruction of such as do evil, for the firm establishing of the Law, I come to birth, age after age.'

"That is from Bhagavad Gita—book four, I believe," said the detective. "Some believe it means Lord Vishnu will appear on earth when humanity no longer understands right from wrong. It is a kind of doomsday prophecy. How this arrived?"

"It was hand-delivered—put through the letterbox the day before yesterday. That was Monday."

"Dr. Jha's reaction was what exactly?"

"He didn't take death threats seriously, Mr. Puri—he's had quite a few over the years, as you can imagine."

"Ms. Ruchi, be good enough to give me one copy of this thing and keep the original safe here with you."

"Absolutely, sir. There's a photocopy wallah under the pilu tree in the street."

"I would also be most grateful for one copy of Dr. Jha's file on Maharaj Swami, also. That is at all possible?"

"Of course, sir. I'll go and fetch it."

She went to find the file while the detective stood up, still feeling unsteady, and made his way back into the kitchen.

Getting the lock dusted for fingerprints would be a waste of time, he reasoned. But Puri wanted to see if there were any other clues: perhaps a boot mark on the floor or a thread caught on a nail.

He was examining the door when Ms. Ruchi came to find him, clutching the bulging file.

"To tell you the truth, that lock was easy to open," she said. "One time I forgot my keys and I managed to get in using a screwdriver I keep in the car. I've been meaning to get it fixed for ages. Later this morning I'll get the lock wallah to come."

"Anyone else knew it was broken?"

"Not that I'm aware. The only other people who use it are the cleaners."

Puri had seen enough and accompanied the secretary out into the street to make use of the photocopy wallah's services.

"Tell me, Ms. Ruchi," he said, "why you came into the office today? You should be taking rest, no?"

"Someone has to be here to look after the office and . . ." Her eyes started to well up again. "I suppose I wanted to be here . . . to be, well, near him. Does that sound strange?"

"Not at all. It is quite understandable."

Tears started to flood down her face.

"I just can't believe he's gone," she said, straining to keep her voice steady. "Dr. Jha was like a father to me—so calm and kind. It's like there's a big hole in my heart. What am I to do without him?"

Seven

As Puri headed off to interview the surviving members of the Laughing Club, his wife was sitting down in Lily Arora's five-bedroom house in Greater Kailash Part Two, a posh South Delhi colony.

This month's venue for Rumpi's kitty party club, the living room had been appointed with furnishings "inspired" by the ancient world. The mahogany coffee table in the middle of the room was built like a Grecian altar. The Italian sofas, with their gold arms fashioned like great curling leaves, were suggestive of Roman licentiousness. Black and gold pharaoh heads and sphinxes purchased in the gift shop of a Las Vegas hotel adorned both the side tables and the marble mantelpiece with its decorative Zoroastrian winged lions. Bunches of plastic sunflowers in replica Phoenician vases were dotted around the place—along with Chinese dragon napkin holders filled with pink paper serviettes.

The sofas' hard, slippery upholstery and curvy backs did not make them conducive to reclining or lounging. Rumpi and the fourteen other kitty party members—all housewives, most of whom she had known for years—had to sit on the edge of their seats. This suited Mrs. Nanda, who, with a straight back, a level chin and a sprinkling of gold jewelry, was a model of poise and elegance. Petite, bespectacled Mrs. Shankar, who practiced yoga and meditation and always dressed in long, loose capris and block-printed achkans, perched gracefully as well. But for the likes of Mrs. Devi, who by her own admittance had a "sweet tooth and a salty one, also" and took up a much greater portion of seating space than the aforementioned ladies, Lily Arora's furnishings were both an uncomfortable and unflattering proposition.

"What I wouldn't do for a beanbag right now," Mrs. Devi murmured to Rumpi.

Still, as the servants circulated with platters of "readymade" chai, spicy chiwda, peanut chili salad and veg samosas, the room was thick with conversation—not to mention Lily Arora's heady perfume. On one side of the room, the recent plunge in the Mumbai stock market was being discussed. In the middle, the talk was of the upcoming end-of-year school exams. And a clutch of ladies nearest the mock fireplace were making plans to attend a concert by Anoushka Shankar in Nehru Park.

Soon, though, news spread through the room that Mrs. Bina Bakshi's daughter-in-law had "fled the coop"—in other words, her in-laws' house.

Mrs. Nanda, whose husband was a high-powered accountant, had heard that "the boy" drank a lot. "Apparently he reverts tully each and every night," she reported. "Mrs. Bakshi's daughter-in-law was under depression."

Mrs. Devi, the wife of a top bureaucrat, eagerly grasped the gossip baton, passing on that she had been told by an undisclosed source that Mrs. Bakshi and "the girl" had "not hit it off from the moment she came home."

Mrs. Bansal, the only woman present to have attended the fabled Bakshi wedding at the Hyatt, spoke up next.

Mrs. Bakshi's daughter-in-law, she said disapprovingly, had "modern ideas." Not being a "domesticated person," she was trying to put off having children in order to further her career in marketing "or some such nonsense."

"Her parents must feel *so* ashamed," commented another woman. "Personally I can't imagine."

"Has she no respect?" another voice chimed in.

It was then that Puri's gray-haired mother, who at Rumpi's invitation had joined the kitty party for the first time, spoke up. "So much change in society is going on, I tell you," she said. "Relationships are getting all in a twist, na? Boys are mostly to blame. One minute wanting educated girls, next demanding stay-at-home wives. So much confusion is there, actually."

As she was the eldest in the room by some fifteen years, her words engendered a chorus of approval.

"Very true, Auntie-ji."

"Quite right."

"I totally agree."

But by the end of the discussion, the majority view still held.

"Men are not perfect, that is for sure," concluded Lily Arora, whose hot pink kurta, churidar and high heels with glittery silver straps were set off by more makeup than all the other women wore put together. "But it's a wife's role to manage. Look at what I've had to put up with. Sanjeev is a rascal, quite frankly. But running away was unthinkable. It would have brought so much pain to both families, mine and his. In these situations one has to think of others.

"As for husbands," she continued, "my dog trainer, Arti, always says to reward your pooch when he does what you ask and give appropriate correction when he doesn't. Same has worked with Sanjeev."

After the laughter had died down, Mrs. Deepak announced the birth of a fifth grandson. Amar, weight nine pounds, had been born at the Happy Go Lucky Maternity Home.

"By cesarean," she added, beaming proudly.

Mrs. Azmat then shared her news. Since the ladies had last got together a month ago, she and her husband had gone on a cruise around the Great Lakes.

"They are really *great* in every sense," she said, showing the other women some of the dozens of photographs her husband had taken of her obscuring a series of dramatic landscapes.

The conversation drifted on—the events on Rajpath were discussed, the astronomical price of gold and news of a fresh dengue outbreak in the city.

"Even the president's son got it."

"Just imagine."

"No one is safe."

At around one o'clock, Lily Arora finally brought the group to order and made various announcements. Next month's get-together was to be held at Chor Bizarre, which offered a kitty party lunch special for 500 rupees per head. Her son and daughter-in-law, who were members of one of the new "couples kitties," had been there and found it "quite satisfactory."

Next, this month's guest speaker, a physical exercise trainer called Bappi, entered the room. A diminutive but muscular young man with dyed yellow hair, he took Lily Arora's place in front of the fireplace with the portrait of Sanjeev Arora's stern-looking grandfather looming behind him. As the ladies continued to munch on deep-fried chiwda, he asked if any of them had diabetes. Eight hands went up.

How many of them exercised properly?

Again there was a strong show of hands.

"Ladies, casual walking does not count," admonished Bappi.

Most of the hands went down.

Bappi then turned to a flip chart that he had set up on a stand. The first page depicted a dumpy middle-aged Indian woman. Next to her stood an extremely athletic-looking Western lady in a leotard. GO FROM AUNTIE-JI TO MISS WOW! read a message underneath.

"You, too, can look like this with just thirty minutes' training every day at Counter Contours," announced Bappi. "Our training program is tailor-made for all ages."

He spent the next fifteen minutes demonstrating some simple exercises. When he was finished, the ladies gave him a round of applause.

"I'm sure we agree that we can all do more to stay fit and fine and Mr. Bappi has made some wonderful suggestions," said Lily Arora as the trainer packed up and left.

It was now time for the most eagerly anticipated moment of the party: the kitty draw.

Traditionally, each member of a kitty party brings a fixed sum of cash every month. The total pot is then awarded to the member whose name is drawn from a hat. Each member can only win once, so essentially the kitty is an interest-free loan system.

Lily Arora's kitty reflected the more modern values of India's middle classes in that some of the cash was given to charity and some was put aside for group vacations, like the one to Corbett National Park the ladies were planning for later in the year.

This was their fifth draw.

"Ladies, it's time to get out your cash," said Mrs. Arora, holding up a plastic bag. "I'm adding my five thousand rupees. Please, ladies, all do the same. Only exception is Mrs. Puri, who is joining us for the first time and is therefore required to add five months' total amount. Admittedly this is an unusual practice, but we are delighted to have Auntie-ji joining us."

The ladies all unclasped their handbags and took out wads of notes. These were placed in the bag.

"Today's kitty is eighty thousand. Of that, ten thousand we are donating to charity. This month Mrs. Azmat has nominated one NGO assisting slum children called Smile Foundation. Twenty goes into the holiday fund. That leaves fifty. All those ladies who have *not* collected their share in past months are eligible to draw."

A ripple of anticipation ran through the room as twelve of the ladies, including both Rumpi and Mummy, wrote their names on little pieces of paper. Once folded, these were dropped into a small plastic bucket.

Lily Arora gave it a good shake, stirred the papers and, with closed eyes, picked a name.

"And the winner is," she said, pausing for dramatic effect like Shahrukh Khan on *Kaun Banega Crorepati?* "Neeru Deepak! Congratulations!"

Mrs. Deepak, the one with the abundance of grandchildren, let out a squeal of delight and collected her money.

"Tell us. What all are you going to do with it?" asked the hostess as she handed over the winnings.

"I promised my eldest grandson a new Xbox. His birthday is coming up," she said.

"Very good," said Lily Arora, smiling. "So as per the rules you will make your contribution next month but not be eligible for the draw. Also at our next meeting you are the one responsible for providing going-away presents."

The ladies returned to their tea and gossip as they waited for lunch to be served.

About ten minutes later, Lily Arora's poodle started barking in one of the back rooms. There came a crash from the kitchen. Raised voices could be heard. Rumpi thought it was likely a servant dispute of some sort. But then two men burst into the living room wearing women's stockings over their faces.

"This is a robbery!" the taller of the two shouted in Hindi, stating the obvious. He was brandishing a country-made weapon. It looked like a poor imitation of an English highwayman's pistol. "Everyone stay sitting and do what you're told and no one will get hurt!"

A few of the women shrieked. Lily Arora stood up and shouted: "How dare you invade my home like this! Who do you think you are? Do you know who my husband is?"

"Shut up, woman!" interrupted the gunman, pointing his weapon at her. "Sit down!"

Lily Arora glared at him contemptuously with her hands on her hips. "I'll do nothing of the sort!"

"Sit down or I'll shoot!" The gunman cocked his pistol.

The click caused some of the women to scream again and bury their faces in their hands.

"Please sit down," insisted a frightened-sounding Mrs. Nanda, tugging on Lily Arora's churidar. "It's not worth it. Do as he says."

With an icy glare of contempt, the hostess resumed her place on the sofa.

"That's better," said the gunman, standing with his back to the fireplace, the most commanding position in the room, while his accomplice guarded the door. By now, most of the ladies were holding their hands up in the air although they had not been told to do so. "I want the kitty fund. Where is it? Hand it over."

"It's here, I have it," blurted out Mrs. Deepak, who was shaking. "Take it. Just don't hurt us!"

The gunman grabbed the money and sized it up. The other women exchanged confused looks but kept quiet.

"There's only fifty or sixty here. Where's the rest?" he demanded.

A calm, quiet voice spoke up. It was Puri's mother. "No need to shout, na," she said. "It's here with me."

The gunman crossed the room.

"Where?" he demanded.

"In my purse, only." By "purse" she meant handbag. He picked it up and started rummaging through the contents. Although of average size, it contained a considerable amount of stuff: her wallet, a mobile phone, a makeup kit, a bulging address book, a little plastic bag of prasad, a miniature copy of the Gita and a small canister of Mace. The gunman dropped half the items on the floor in his search for the cash.

"There's nothing here!" he exclaimed eventually.

"You're sure? Strange, na? Let me see."

As Mummy took her handbag back from him, she scratched his left hand with the fingernail of her right index finger. The gunman yelped.

"Hey, what are you doing, Auntie?" he hollered, nursing his hand.

"So clumsy of me, na," she said, smiling apologetically. "You'll be needing one bandage. Mrs. Arora must be having one."

"Forget that! Just give me the money or I'll shoot!" He raised his clunky weapon again. This time he pointed it directly at Mummy's forehead.

"It's over here! It's over here!" interrupted Lily Arora urgently. "I've got it. Leave her alone!"

The hostess picked the plastic bag up off the floor and threw it to him.

"OK, let's get out of here," said the accomplice by the door. He was evidently young; his voice sounded like it was breaking.

"Shut up! Salah! Go start the engine!"

The teenager hesitated and then backed out of the living room.

The gunman started toward the door himself, his weapon still trained on the group.

"I want all of you to get down on your knees and face the ground. Do it now!"

One by one, with varying degrees of success, the ladies did as he instructed.

"Now stay where you are for five minutes and don't call the cops! Remember, I know where you live!"

The gunman glanced around the room at the array of bottoms sticking up in the air. Then he was gone.

The ladies breathed a collective sigh of relief. All of them stayed put apart from Mummy.

"Call the police and don't touch my things," she whispered to Rumpi.

"Mummy-ji, where are you going?" asked Puri's wife, sitting up on her knees. "It's dangerous!"

Ignoring her, the elderly lady put her head around the sitting room door in time to see the gunman escaping out the back of the house.

She headed outside to the front gate, where all the ladies' drivers were sitting on the pavement playing teen patti.

"Some goondas have done armed robbery of our kitty party!" she announced. "Where's my driver, Majnu?"

"Toilet, madam," answered one of the men.

"Typical! But we've got to give chase, na? One of you must drive. Come. Don't do dillydally."

The drivers all put down their cards and stood respectfully, but none of them jumped into action. They needed permission from their respective madams before they could leave their posts, one of them explained.

Mummy went back inside and fetched Lily Arora. But her Sumo was penned in behind four other vehicles.

By the time they had been moved, the thieves had got clean away.

The police reached the house in record time and in record numbers, thanks to Mrs. Devi, whose husband was a childhood friend of the chief.

Two servants were soon discovered in the pantry, bound and gagged. Once untied, they were summarily taken away on suspicion of being accomplices to the crime.

Lily Arora's poodle was also found lying on the kitchen floor unconscious and was immediately rushed to the vet's.

A young assistant subinspector then took the ladies' statements in the living room. He was dismissive of Mummy, so she sought out his senior.

Inspector I. P. Kumar was standing by the front gate along with three gormless constables, giving the hapless drivers a grilling.

"Madam, you gave your statement?" he asked her wearily when she insisted on talking to him.

"What is point? So stupid he is, na? Got rajma for brains seems like. Now, something is there you must know. So listen carefully, na? I've some vital evidence to show."

Mummy held up her right hand; she had wrapped it in a plastic freezer bag.

"You're hurt, madam?" asked Inspector Kumar.

"Not at all," she replied. "Just I scratched the gunman most deliberately."

"Why exactly?"

"For purpose of DNA collection, naturally," she said impatiently. "That is what I have been telling. Fragments of that goonda's skin and all got under my nail. Just his fingerprints are on my compact, Gita and hand phone, also."

Mummy held up another freezer bag, which contained the other evidence she had collected.

"Madam," Inspector Kumar said with a weary sigh, "this is not Miami, US of A. For everyday robberies we're not doing DNA testing. That is for big crimes only. Like when non-state actors blow up hotels and all. Also, your fingernail does not constitute evidence. Could be you scratched yourself or petted the dog. How are we to know?"

Mummy bristled. "I will have you know my late dear husband was himself a police inspector and I was headmistress of Modern School—"

"Then better you stick to teaching and leave police work to professionals, madam," interrupted Inspector Kumar before turning away and continuing with his interrogation of the drivers.

Mummy felt Rumpi's hand on her arm.

"Come, Mummy-ji, we should be getting home," she said.

"But police are being negligent in their duties," she complained, still brandishing the evidence she had collected.

"I know. You can lead camels to water but not force them to drink. Come."

The two women walked out into the street where their cars were parked.

Behind them Kumar and the constables were chortling conspiratorially.

"Seems Miss Mar-pel is here," one of them joked.

"Bloody duffers," cursed Mummy. "No wonder so many of crimes are going unsolved."

"Perhaps we should call Chubby," suggested Rumpi.

"Why we should ask for his help, you tell me? He's no better. Just he'll do bossing and tell us don't get involved. Mummies are not detectives and all that. No need for him, na?"

"What do you mean 'us,' Mummy-ji?"

"We two. We'll solve this case together, na? Who better? It's an insider job for sure."

"You think the servants were involved?"

"Those poor fellows? Most unlikely."

Rumpi's eyes widened. "Are you saying it was one of the other ladies?" she asked, lowering her voice.

Mummy nodded gravely.

"How can you be so sure?"

"Simple, na? Those goondas were knowing how much our kitty would be. Today with my share there was some extra bonus. Also they failed in their duty to do robbery of our jewelry. So many bangles, earrings and mangal sutras and all were present. That Mrs. Azmat was wearing platinum worth lakhs and lakhs. But not one single item they took. Why?"

Eight

Shivraj Sharma, whose very first visit to the Laughing Club had ended so dramatically and in such turmoil, was first on Puri's list of interviewees. His title was superintending archaeologist; it said so on the door to his office deep in the vaults of the National Museum, a stone's throw from Rajpath.

The contents of his office also left the visitor in no doubt as to his occupation. Crates containing broken bits of pottery and fragments of idols coccooned in Bubble Wrap were stacked on the shelves. The walls were papered with maps indicating the territory occupied by the Harappan Indus Valley Civilization, which flourished between 2,600 and 1,900 BC. Pinned to a board were satellite images of the area lying between the Himalayas and the Arabian Sea, with a line indicating one of the possible routes of the lost Sarasvati River.

"I am happy to see you, but I spoke with the police yesterday and told them everything I know," Sharma explained to Puri. His tone was amiable but betrayed a boyish insouciance common amongst India's so-called creamy layer.

"As you can see I've a good deal of work to get on with,"

he added, indicating the manuscript that lay on the desk in front of him. "I do hope this won't take too long."

Sharma was pushing fifty, smartly dressed in a striped shirt, silk tie and blue blazer. He had visited the temple that morning and was wearing a fresh, rice-encrusted tilak on his forehead and a knotted kalava on his wrist. He wore thick glasses, and like so many people in Delhi today, his eyes suffered from the pollution—hence the bottle of eyedrops, which, judging from his damp eyelids, the archaeologist had used moments before the detective had been shown into his office.

"Sir, just five minutes is all that is required," said Puri.

The plump man in the safari suit and Sandown cap standing in front of Sharma's desk, business card in hand, was not the boisterous Vish Puri who had kept his son-in-law Hartosh entertained last night with generous amounts of Royal Challenge. Nor the supremely confident, tough-talking version, either. Face-to-face with a learned, well-to-do type, he was deferential.

This was an instinctual reaction. Academics were up there with ministers and virtuoso musicians, and such erudite surroundings genuinely awed him. But his deportment did his cause no harm. Obsequiousness was what Indians of such standing—barre admi, big men—were used to, and as Puri was well aware, allowing their conceit and assumption of intellectual superiority to go unchallenged often proved beneficial.

"Very well, but five minutes is all I can spare," said Sharma with a sigh, not deigning to stand or shake his visitor's hand. He motioned Puri into a chair.

"Most kind of you, sir, and quite an honor, I must say," said Puri. He glanced around the office with a childish glint in his eye. "Such a fascinating field you work in. So much of history and culture. I myself take great interest in the Mauryan dynasty. Something of a golden age we might call it."

"India was certainly a very different place in those days, Mr. . . ." Sharma referred to the detective's business card. ". . . Puri," he read, squinting down through his bifocals. "But my speciality is Harappan culture."

"Fascinating," Puri said, beaming.

"Currently my department is involved in extensive underwater marine work off the coast of Gujarat. There is every indication that we have located Dvaraka."

"The lost city of the Mahabharata." Puri's eyes widened in awe.

"This find, together with the discovery of the Sarasvati River and a good deal of other evidence unearthed in the past forty or so years, leaves no doubt as to the indigenous origins of Vedic culture," added Sharma.

The controversial nature of this statement was not lost on Puri. It suggested a Hindu nationalist bent, a rejection of the theory that Aryan tribes brought the holy Hindu scriptures to India from elsewhere. But he merely said, "Just imagine what India would be like had we not had so many of invasions. Is it any wonder everything has gone for a toss?"

Sharma met Puri's gaze in silent, meditative appraisal.

"It is undeniable that certain, shall we say, *alien belief systems* have been foisted on us that have no place here and have done considerable harm to our indigenous culture." A slight smile played across his lips. "But that's not what you came here to talk about, now, is it, Mr. Puri?" said the archaeologist.

"Correct, sir," answered the detective, fishing out his notebook and opening it to a new page. "Just a few questions are there."

Sharma gave a vague nod of encouragement.

"I would be most grateful if you told me what happened yesterday morning exactly," said Puri.

Sharma sighed. "As I already told the police," he said slowly and deliberately, "it is extremely difficult for me to answer that question."

"I understand you dropped your glasses, is it?"

"That's right, Mr. Puri. And without them I can hardly see a thing. Everything is just a blur. So I was groping around in the dark for a while, so to speak."

"What point exactly you dropped them, sir?"

"Just after Professor Pandey started telling his silly knock-knock joke and everyone started laughing again. I saw this mist forming on the ground. Where it came from I can't say—and then there was a flash. It startled me and I fell over backward. That's when my glasses came off."

"You started laughing, is it?"

"I did not. The others were all howling, though. I could hear them."

"You were able to move?"

"Perfectly able, Mr. Puri."

"And by the time you got your glasses back on, Dr. Jha was lying dead and the Kali apparition, she was gone?"

"Exactly."

"So you never saw her?"

"I saw a figure but it was blurred."

Puri asked if he had seen the murder weapon.

"Again this is all in the statement I made to the police."

"Yes, sir. Just I am cross-referencing. Sometimes these things get in a muddle."

"I did not see the murder weapon," Sharma stated categorically.

Puri scribbled in his notebook and then asked: "Sir, how you felt afterward?"

"Awful, obviously. It was a great shock. It's not every day this sort of thing happens."

"You told Inspector Singh you had a headache, is it?"

"That's right. I came home and used some Muchukunda."

"That is what exactly?"

"You've never heard of it, Mr. Puri?" Sharma tut-tutted and wagged a finger at him. "It's an Ayurvedic remedy. A paste that is applied to the forehead. Much better than aspirin. It's been used in India since time immemorial."

Puri tried making a note of it, but his pen didn't work. He chose another from the four in the outside breast pocket of his safari suit, but that one didn't work either. The same was true with the next.

"Just the humidity is wreaking havoc," he said by way of an apology.

"Here, take mine," said Sharma impatiently.

The detective wrote down "Muchukunda," checked that he had got the spelling right, and then asked: "You saw anything unusual, sir?"

"Unusual? Mr. Puri, I believe the entire incident falls under that category, does it not?"

"Yes, sir. You saw any suspicious persons around the place?"

"After Dr. Jha was murdered the place was mobbed by people. Dozens of them sprang from nowhere. It was complete chaos."

"You didn't see any ice cream wallahs, for example?"

Sharma gave him a quizzical smile. "So early?"

"Yes, sir."

"I did not."

Puri could sense that his time was running short; he got in his next question quickly.

"Dr. Jha was known to you?"

"I met him yesterday for the first time," Sharma replied briskly. "And now, Mr. Puri, I *must* get on with my work. I'm giving a lecture at the Habitat Centre this evening and I need to prepare."

"Actually, sir, one last question is there."

"Last one?"

"Undoubtedly, sir." Puri paused. "Just I wanted to ask, it was your first time at this Laughing Club?"

"That's right."

"How you came to join exactly?"

"I heard about it through somebody—a friend, I think. I'm in need of exercise so I thought I'd give it a go."

"Forgive me, sir, but you look fit already, if I may say so."

"Well, looks can be deceptive, Mr. Puri. I am in as much need of exercise as the next man. And they say laughter is good for you."

"You enjoyed it, sir?"

"Now that's four more questions, Mr. Puri, and frankly I fail to see the relevance. But seeing as you ask, I did *not* enjoy it. There's something very unnatural about forcing yourself to laugh. It didn't feel comfortable."

"You won't be continuing membership, sir?"

"No, Mr. Puri, it's not for me. And now if you don't mind, I'll take back my pen."

Second on Puri's list was N. K. Gupta, senior advocate.

Puri had no difficulty locating his house near Bengali Market, but he found the front door locked and barricaded from the inside. A big swastika had been painted in red on the doorstep to ward off evil.

"Go away! I don't want to talk to anyone!" Gupta shouted from behind the door after Puri rang the bell three times.

"But it is Vish Puri this side. I'm looking into—"

"I don't care who you are!" interrupted the lawyer. "Those media persons have been banging on my door all day. All I want is to be left alone! I've got nothing to say to anyone!"

It took the detective a good ten minutes to persuade Gupta to come to the front window.

Even then he refused to put on the lights or fully pull back the curtains. He stood a couple feet from the window, his face barely visible.

"None of us is safe!" he exclaimed. Puri caught a glimpse of his wild, tormented eyes. "*She* will return and murder us all!"

"Most unlikely," replied the detective soothingly. "What you saw was someone pretending to be the goddess, only."

"How do you know? You weren't there. I tell you that was no human being! It was the goddess herself. I looked into her eyes! She breathed fire!"

"All a trick of some sort," said Puri.

His words were wasted; Gupta could not be persuaded. And yet the advocate retained his legal faculties and, despite his ranting, provided the detective with a remarkably intelligible account of the murder: how he had been unable to stop himself laughing and felt transfixed by "an invisible force." He remembered the caws of the crows, the barks of the dogs and the mysterious mist. Kali had "materialized out of thin air" and floated above the ground.

"She was absolutely hideous! Her arms writhing, the skulls around her neck clunking together. I can't get that noise out of my head. And her voice, Mr. Puri! Her voice! Like . . . like the screams of murdered children!"

Gupta came closer to the window and looked left and right down the street.

"What about a severed head? You saw that, also?" asked Puri.

"Yes! Yes! It was dripping with blood!"

"You recognized his face—this gentleman who had been apparently deprived of his body, that is?"

Gupta faltered. "I . . . I didn't see it clearly," he admitted.

"There was no blood found at the scene apart from that belonging to Dr. Jha," Puri pointed out.

Gupta grew agitated again. "I'm telling you what I saw."

The detective asked about the sword.

Gupta said he had seen it driven through the Guru Buster's chest. But what had become of it he could not say.

"I covered my eyes. After that I can't remember much."

"When were you able to move your feet?"

"Immediately after she disappeared."

"And it is my understanding you had a headache, is it?"

"Yes, and it won't go away, Mr. Puri! It will never go away!" He gripped his hair with his hands. "Just like her voice! It's like she's here now, calling my name!"

Mr. Ved Karat lived in New Rajendra Nagar. A political speechwriter for the Congress Party, he was also at home trying to recover from the ordeal of the day before. He too was badly shaken. In his case, though, it was the shock of witnessing the murder that had affected him. The goddess herself had not scared him.

"In fact I found her quite magnificent to look at," he said, sitting in his living room still wearing his pajamas and dressing gown. In one hand he held a glass of fresh nimboo pani, to which he had added a pinch of black salt. "She had an extraordinary aura about her, an emanation of raw power. In a way it was awe-inspiring."

Karat, too, had been unable to stop himself laughing and his feet had gone "leaden." He described the mysterious mist and the severed head and a "blinding flash" before Kali appeared, "levitating high above the earth and breathing fire." The speechwriter had also witnessed Dr. Jha's death and seen the sword sticking out of the poor man's chest after Kali had "miraculously disappeared."

When Puri explained that it was yet to be found, he seemed surprised.

"Someone took it?"

"Murder weapons are often getting removed from the scene. Most probably some unscrupulous fellow took possession of it."

Karat went on to explain what had happened next: how he had stopped laughing the moment Dr. Jha was killed; how he had rushed to his aid.

"There was so much blood. I felt his pulse, but he was already gone."

"After you had any headache?"

"I felt nauseous, but no, no headache," said Karat.

"When were you able to move your feet?"

The speechwriter had to think for a moment before answering. "I believe it was soon after she vanished," he said.

Puri reached the residence of Professor R. K. Pandey, the Laughing Club instructor and organizer, late in the afternoon. A detached four-bedroom house in West Shalimar Bagh, it was surrounded by a seven-foot wall.

"Very nice to meet you!" Pandey greeted the detective at the front door with a warm, welcoming smile. "Are those rubber soles you're wearing? There's a chance of an electric shock, you see."

Puri looked down at his shoes with a quizzical expression. "They are made of natural rubber. From Kerala, I believe."

"Excellent! Then do come in."

Puri followed him through the front door and inside the house, which smelt of pipe tobacco. A collection of old computers, TVs, vacuum cleaners, electric razors, calculators and tangles of wires cluttered the place. Circuit boards, soldering irons and current testers lay on a workbench positioned against the far wall. In the center of the room stood an old washing machine that had been gutted of its innards; it looked like a robot that had suffered a nervous breakdown.

"I'm building a rudimentary thermoelectric generator," explained Pandey as he knelt next to his creation, tightening a wing nut with a spanner.

"Pardon?" asked Puri.

"It converts heat into electricity. This one creates cold air from hot! Does the job much cheaper than solar power. Think of the potential here in India. This one's for my class, to show my students. Bright young minds!"

"It's dangerous?" asked Puri with a frown, hovering by the door.

"You can never be too careful, can you? Not when you're dealing with electricity. That's why I asked about your shoes. Rubber provides insulation. Look at mine!" He lifted his right foot in the air to show Puri his boots. "See?"

"Very good, sir," said Puri, stepping tentatively into the room.

"Are you here about Dr. Jha's death?" said Pandey, beaming. He sounded positively excited by the prospect.

"I'm doing my own investigation," explained the detective, puzzled by the man's exuberant mood. "His murder should not and must not go unsolved."

Pandey looked up from what he was doing. "Good for you," he said, smiling. "And you're of the opinion nothing paranormal occurred?"

"At the present time, I am concerned with your opinion, only," he answered.

"I'd be happy to tell you what I saw," said Pandey with an ironic smile. He stood up, put the spanner on his workbench and picked up his pipe. "Frankly, it's baffling," he continued, emptying the bowl of the pipe into a dustbin and then filling it with fresh tobacco. "As an electrical engineer, I deal in data, verifiable results—in proof. But what happened yesterday . . . well, I can't explain it. Whatever that thing was—goddess, deity, apparition—it levitated three feet off the ground. That is not within the capabilities of mortal man."

"Must be a trick of some sort," suggested the detective.

"An illusion?" Pandey shook his head as he lit his pipe and the smoke wafted up over his face and hair. "I saw no wires, no stilts, no platform."

"Surely, sir, you and other members were confused, no? Something was affecting you—some narcotic or gas. Could be it had you seeing things that were not there."

"Hallucination? It's possible, I suppose. I did have a headache, which could have been an aftereffect."

"Concerning the levitation," said Puri. "What if some sort of magnetism were used?"

"An electromagnetic field? Interesting!" Pandey pondered the idea for a moment. "I suppose it would be possible for someone to levitate using such means. But nothing like that has been done before. You'd need a lot of equipment—a power supply, for example."

"What about a projection of some sort?" asked Puri.

"Another interesting idea! But no, I'm afraid it couldn't have been. Whatever killed Dr. Jha was definitely three-dimensional."

Pandey went on to relate his version of events. He maintained that the "avatar" had stood twenty feet high. Only after she had disappeared had he been able to move his feet again. The one major discrepancy was what had happened to the murder weapon.

"Again, I cannot explain how it happened scientifically. Metal cannot disintegrate of its own volition. That's impossible. And yet I saw the sword turn to dust," said Pandey, suddenly letting out a short giggle.

Puri eyed him curiously.

"Why no one else saw it happen?" he asked.

"How they missed it, I can't imagine."

And the "miraculous" appearance and disappearance of the goddess?

"The flashes could very easily have been man-made," the professor conceded. "They caused temporary blindness."

"You saw any ice cream wallah after?"

"No, but then I was busy trying to save Dr. Jha's life."

Puri referred to his notes.

"Mr. Ved Karat tells he died right away. He searched for the pulse but found none."

"That may be, but my first instinct was to get him to the hospital."

Puri changed tack.

"How long you knew him—Dr. Jha, that is?" he asked.

"Two years or so. Since he joined the Laughing Club."

"You were close, sir?"

"We became friends, yes." Professor Pandey looked up

toward heaven and raised his voice, saying, "A more courageous or generous man never walked the face of the earth."

Again, the detective found himself flummoxed by the man's lightheartedness.

"Why you didn't attend the cremation?" he asked.

"But I did, Mr. Puri. Wouldn't have missed it for the world."

"Sir, when it comes to faces my mind is better than any camera. That is because it is never running out of film. I am one hundred and fifty percent sure you were not there."

"All I can say is that in this instance you are mistaken," said the professor, apparently untroubled by the detective's assertion. "I was one of the first to offer my condolences. Perhaps you came late? I might have had my back to you."

Puri wondered if Pandey might have been the man with the video camera but decided he was too tall.

"One thing I'm getting confusion over," continued the detective. "Dr. Jha was your good friend. Yet you are not at all saddened by his demise. Very jolly, in fact."

"I can assure you that I am absolutely devastated," answered Pandey. "Suresh was a dear, dear man. But it is not in my nature to grieve. I believe in a positive outlook at all times. We only have one life and it's my opinion that we should make the most of it every minute of every day. That is why I do laughter therapy. Laughter cures all our ills. It keeps us in a positive mental state."

"There are times when crying is necessary also, no?"

"Perhaps. But laughter is so much better! It is the antidote to all the miseries of our planet. My answer to Suresh's passing is to hold a Laughter Memorial for him. I am inviting everyone who knew and loved him to come to the Garden of Five Senses day after tomorrow. Together we will enjoy a good chuckle—the best thing for our grief. I do hope you can make it."

Puri said that, regrettably, he would be "otherwise engaged."

"Very good, very good, very good," said Pandey, beaming again as he showed Puri to the door. "The best of luck with your investigation. I sincerely hope you find whoever—or should I say *whatever*—did this."

"Allow me to assure you, sir, Vish Puri never fails," said the detective in a dry, even voice. "No amount of hocus or pocus or jugglery of words will prevent me."

Pandey walked him out to the gate and opened it for him.

"One thing before you go," said the professor. "Do you know any good jokes? I haven't heard one today."

The detective was not in the mood for jokes. At best, he found Pandey's buoyant mood inappropriate.

"Nothing comes to mind," he answered.

"Next time, then," said Pandey with a grin. "Keep smiling. Remember, laughter makes the world go round! Ho ho! Ha ha ha!"

Puri hurried across the street, fleeing from the sweltering heat and humidity, and called to Handbrake to get the Ambassador's engine started. The driver, who had been trying to keep cool by the side of the road, jumped to attention and did as instructed. The car trembled into life, and within a minute or so the dashboard vents began to produce wafts of tepid but nonetheless welcome relief.

Puri sat back in his seat. His underwear was damp and was clinging to his skin. It was not the only thing making him feel uncomfortable. Something wasn't right—about Pandey, that is.

"Number one," Puri told Tubelight over the phone after they discussed plans to meet at Shadipur Depot at eight o'clock. "This fellow is positively merry. Like he is celebrating, in fact. Yet his friend has been viciously murdered. Second, why he said he attended Dr. Jha's funeral when he did not?"

Puri saw no contradiction in a man of science also believing wholeheartedly in the miraculous. That was a common Indian characteristic. Still, there was something about his version of events that did not ring true—the description of the disintegrating sword being the most obvious disparity.

"Want him tailed, Boss?"

"Night and day. This fellow is up to something. Undoubtedly."

Puri also asked Tubelight to check into Shivraj Sharma's background. "That one has skeletons in his cupboard. No doubt there are one or two in his basement, also."

Nine

Two hours later, after eating his fill of paapri chaat with lashings of tamarind chutney at a roadside stand, Puri descended underground on an escalator at Central Secretariat.

As the honking of the traffic faded and the air turned pleasantly temperate, he found himself in a cavernous, fluorescent-lit netherworld of gleaming floors and untarnished walls.

He bought a token for a few rupees at one of the efficiently run ticket counters, passed through the security check and automatic barriers, stood in an orderly line on the platform and boarded a shiny silver train.

Being whisked through tunnels more than twenty meters below the surface of the capital at fifty miles per hour was a great source of pride for the detective—as it was for most Delhiites, some of whom, he suspected, ventured underground just for the thrill of it. The construction of the Metro was a phenomenal success story. The first section had been completed to international standards within budget and ahead of schedule. The secret of the system's success lay in the fact that it was not run by politicians and bureaucrats—as was the case with the Calcutta underground, which was a disgrace—but an autonomous, for-profit entity. It bore testimony to the capabilities of India's private sector—"world-class beaters," in Puri's words.

The Metro had brought about something of a social revolution as well. Unlike on India's trains, there was only one class of travel available. Passengers drawn from every religion and caste were forced to rub shoulders and treat one another with a certain cordiality—a phenomenon unthinkable in Delhi until relatively recently and one that remained a rarity in much of rural India.

Still, Puri rarely used the Metro. The truth was he didn't enjoy traveling in what could often be cramped conditions. Nor did the anonymity it imposed appeal to him.

"Equality is all very well," he had told his friend Dr. Subhrojit Ghosh at the Gym recently when they had been reflecting upon an appeal by the chief minister for the middle classes to use public transport. "But let other people enjoy. I myself will keep my car and driver."

He had only opted for the underground this evening because he knew his Ambassador would be too wide for the narrow lanes of the slum where the magician lived.

His plan was to get off at Shadipur, where Tubelight would be waiting for him; from there they would continue their journey in the operative's auto rickshaw.

The Metro journey required one change at Rajiv Chowk, where a digital display correctly predicted the arrival of the next train.

En route, Puri found that he was able to use his mobile phone. He called a number programmed into his speed dial.

A woman's drowsy voice answered.

"I woke you?" asked Puri.

"I was just getting up."

"I'll see you tonight?"

"What time?"

"Should be nine, ten at the latest."

The detective hung up and then called home.

Monika, one of the maidservants, answered. "Madam" was out, she explained.

Puri tried Rumpi's mobile next.

She sounded distracted and was coy about where she was and what she was doing. He could hear Mummy's voice in the background.

"What are you two up to?" he asked.

"This and that, Chubby."

"More shopping, is it?"

There was a slight pause. "Yes, you caught us at it. We're picking up a few things for the twins."

"Well I would be reaching late. Tomorrow I would be going to Haridwar at crack of dawn, also," explained the detective.

This was code for, "I expect to be fed when I get home," and Rumpi knew it.

"Don't worry, Chubby," she said. "There'll be plenty of food."

The contrast between the sedate Metro and the feverish world above left Puri wondering if he had not imagined the underground journey.

It was not uncommon for him to experience such a sense of dislocation when working in Delhi these days. The India of beggars and farmer suicides and the one of cafés selling frothy Italian coffee were like parallel dimensions. As he slipped back and forth between them, he often found himself pondering the ancient Indian axiom that this world is but maya, an illusion, a collective dream.

Riding in the back of Tubelight's auto rickshaw as it bumped, shuddered and zigzagged along the turbulent byways of Shadipur quickly snapped the detective out of his reverie, however.

The slum, one of Delhi's largest, was inhabited almost entirely by street entertainers: puppeteers, snake charmers, bear handlers, acrobats, musicians, troupes of actors who performed plays with social messages, the odd storyteller and jadoo wallahs. But the view through the scratched, convex windscreen was depressingly familiar: a sooty ghetto of ramshackle brick houses smothered in cow dung patties. Plastic sheeting, chunks of concrete and twisted scrap metal were draped over roofs. Canvas tents were pitched amidst heaps of garbage, where filthy, half-clad children defecated and played.

Eyes—curious, anxious, searching, cloudy with cataracts—stared out from doorways; slit windows; smoke-filled, pencil-thin alleyways. Puri caught glimpses of dark-skinned women with half-veiled faces cooking chappatis over open fires. Families crouched on charpoys eating from shared bowls with their hands. Young men stood out in the open in their underpants, washing themselves.

Like any jungle, it was infested with animals. Mangy mutts ran snarling alongside the auto rickshaw; chickens and ducks clucked and squawked as they scurried out of the way of the oncoming vehicle; monkeys hanging from electrical cables illegally tapping the power grid screeched overhead at the intruders on their territory.

Tubelight pulled up outside a narrow, ramshackle house.

"This is the place," he said in Hindi, looking around nervously. "I'll have to wait outside." He added quickly: "To keep an eye on my auto." And then: "Someone might steal it."

"I am to face the jadoo wallah alone, is it?" mused Puri in English. "Let us hope he does not turn me into a frog."

"Let's hope, Boss."

"But he said he is willing to talk to me, is it?"

"I told him you wanted to see some magic and were willing to pay. The rest is up to you."

Puri knocked on the door. A young boy answered, looked the detective up and down and motioned him inside. They crossed a small, drab room and stepped out into a courtyard. From there, they mounted a flight of concrete stairs that curled around the outside of the house like a python.

Akbar the Great, descendant of courtly magicians, was sitting on a charpoy on the roof. His eyes were those of an anxious man, one who had lived his life by his wits and expected trouble around every corner. Still, he greeted his visitor with a respectful salaam and his right hand placed over his heart.

"Please forgive the conditions in which we must welcome such an honored guest," he said in a lyrical Urdu rarely heard in Delhi these days. Akbar the Great's wrinkled face was surmounted by an impeccably clean topi. His white beard reached his chest. "Once we entertained Mughal emperors. Babur, Humayan, Aurangzeb—all loved our magic. In those bygone days, they rewarded us with precious stones—rubies from Badakhshan, diamonds from Golkonda. But now we are reduced to performing on the streets for a few rupees, constantly harassed and beaten by the police. Earlier today we were outside the Red Fort and they chased us away and hit us with their lathis."

"There is no need to apologize on my account, Baba," said the detective, who knew only too well that India's Muslims, the largest minority in the world, were amongst its most marginalized. He sat down on a chair facing the magician. "It is an honor to meet you. I am told that you are the greatest magician in all of India."

Akbar the Great acknowledged this praise with an assuming nod.

"I'm known from one part of India to the next!" he declared with a flourish of his worn hands. "There is not a village or town where I have not performed. Ask anyone and they will have heard of Akbar the Great—he who can pull thorns from his tongue, swallow steel balls whole and bring the dead back to life!" His patter sounded well rehearsed; he delivered it as he might to an audience on the street. "But nowadays people are not interested in magic. They all want to stay at home and watch TV, an invention of the evil one, Shaitan!"

The boy who had answered the front door, one of Akbar the Great's great-grandsons as it turned out, served tea in chipped cups as the Muslim call to prayer sounded over the slum. Beyond the roof's precipitous edge lay the jutting, irregular rooftops of Shadipur—homemade TV aerials, laundry lines and plastic water tanks superimposed against the setting sun.

"I was told you have come to see me perform," said Akbar the Great, as they began to sip their tea. "My fee is five hundred rupees."

"Forgive me, Baba, but I did not come here to see your show," said Puri.

"Oh?"

"I am seeking information. And for this I am willing to pay one thousand." Puri took the money from his wallet.

"What kind of information?" Akbar the Great sounded suspicious, but his eyes were fixed on the crisp hundred-rupee notes in the detective's hand.

"Baba, I need your guidance. I am investigating the murder of Dr. Jha, the Guru Buster. You must have heard that he was killed yesterday morning on Rajpath. I believe the so-called Kali apparition was nothing of the kind. It was an illusion. I would like to understand how the levitation in particular was achieved."

Akbar surveyed him with a deep frown.

"You're a policeman?"

"No, Baba. I am Vish Puri, the private investigator."

"You're working for someone?"

"Only for myself. The victim was a friend of mine."

Akbar the Great thought for a while, stroking his long beard, and then said something in a strange language to his great-grandson. With a nod, the boy stepped forward, held out a hand for the money and took it. Then the magician said: "How it was done is irrelevant. Perhaps it was *real* jadoo! Perhaps it was only a trick. Who knows? It's what people believe that is the important thing."

"What do you mean by real magic?"

"Genuine miracles performed by those with genuine supernatural powers, of course."

"You believe such things are possible?"

"The Holy Koran is full of examples. So are the Bible and Ramayan. Water can be turned to wine. Many things happen in this life that cannot be explained."

"Do you have these powers, Baba?" asked Puri.

The old man smiled for the first time. It was a kindly, avuncular smile, the detective thought to himself.

"Alas, I'm only a humble magician," he said. "I do simple tricks and entertain people. But what the audience believes . . . well, that's another matter. When I bring a chicken back to life—as I often do—they ask me how it is done. If I tell them it is a magic trick, a sleight of hand achieved by distraction, they get very angry and accuse me of hiding something from them! To appease them I have to say that I get my powers by sleeping at the cremation ground. Then they're satisfied and stop accusing me of being a fraud!" The magician smiled indulgently. "You see," he added, "people need to believe in these things. They want to be fooled, but they do not want to be made fools of!"

A thought suddenly occurred to him.

"I will perform a simple trick for you," he said. "It's not part of my normal routine, so I don't mind explaining how it's done. It might help you understand how easily people's eyes are deceived."

Soon Akbar the Great was lying on the roof's solid concrete surface. The boy, who was regularly chopped to pieces on the streets of Delhi only to be miraculously reassembled again, announced in a loud, confident voice: "Make obeisance to the feet of Indra, whose name is one with magic, and to the feet of Shambara, whose glory was firmly established in illusions!"

Puri watched with rapt attention.

"During his travels across the length and breadth of India, my great-grandfather Akbar the Great has collected many magical objects. Rings, cloaks that can turn you invisible, a bottle that houses a terrible djinn—heaven forbid that it should ever escape!"

The boy held up a dirty blanket.

"It was high up in the Himalayas that he was given this from a man with three eyes! Now, it may look like an ordinary blanket to you. But anyone lying beneath it will float off the ground and up into the air!"

He draped the blanket over his grandfather.

"I will now make Akbar the Great, greatest magician in all of India, float up above the roof!" he declared—and as an aside, he added with the cheeky humor characteristic of

Indian street jadoo wallahs: "Let us hope Baba did not have too large a lunch or he will be too heavy!"

The boy closed his eyes, held his hands over his great-grandfather's body, moved them around as if he was divining for water and spoke the magic words, "Yantru-mantra-jaala-jaala-tantru!"

Nothing happened for ten seconds. He repeated his incantation. And then Akbar the Great's body began to shudder and rise upward.

The magician floated to a height of roughly three feet and remained there, suspended in midair.

For the life of him, Puri could not see how the trick was done. There were no wires connected to the blanket; no one was holding Akbar the Great up; no box had been slipped under him; there was no trapdoor. "You've got some kind of lifting device under there?" he asked after the magician had gently floated back down to earth.

"The jasoos is clueless!" cackled Akbar the Great with delight. "Where are your powers of detection now, sahib?"

There were hoots of laughter from the five or six other members of Akbar the Great's family who had by now gathered on the roof. Puri bristled; he did not like to be made a fool of.

"Are you going to tell me how it is done?" he demanded.

"I told you earlier, I got my powers at the cremation ground!"

The laughter reached a crescendo and then the magician pulled back the blanket.

Beneath lay two old hockey sticks, one on either side of him. A pair of shoes and socks identical to those Akbar the Great was wearing were attached to the ends.

"As the blanket was laid over me, you were distracted and didn't notice when I made the switch. Then I raised the sticks under the blanket and, at the same time, elevated my head. My feet and backside remained on the floor the entire time."

"By God! I would never have imagined it could be so simple," exclaimed the detective in English, clapping enthusiastically. And then reverting to Hindi again he said: "But whoever killed Dr. Jha yesterday was not under a blanket. The video taken by the French tourist shows Kali floating free. How was that done?"

Akbar the Great shrugged. "That I cannot answer," he said.

"Can you at least tell me who is capable of such a feat?"

Puri's question was met with a stony silence. Akbar the Great said something to the boy, who in turn told Puri politely but firmly: "My great-grandfather is getting very tired and needs to rest."

The audience had come to an end. But the detective managed to get in one last question.

"Tell me, Baba. Could a rationalist have pulled off this illusion?"

Akbar the Great shook his head. "Rationalists learn simple tricks that are done by traveling sadhus, like holding pots of boiling oil in their bare hands or piercing themselves with needles. The man you are looking for is no rationalist. He is an illusionist. Or perhaps someone who knows real magic."

Puri and Tubelight made their way back through the slum.

The meeting had proven useful but also frustrating.

"Could be Akbar the Great is knowing the identity of the murderer," said Puri. "Question is: Why protect him?"

"There's probably some kind of magician's code, Boss," suggested Tubelight in Hindi. "If they're anything like my family, they're sworn never to reveal the identity of another member of the clan. Maybe the murderer's a blood relative. In which case they'll never give him up."

It was only after the auto rickshaw had pulled into the main road that Puri discovered a piece of paper in one of his trouser pockets.

It had a name and address written on it.

"Manish the Magnificent. Hey Presto! GK1 M Block Market."

He showed it to Tubelight. "Someone slipped it into my pocket!" marveled Puri.

"Want to go to GK, Boss?"

Puri checked his watch. It was nearly eight. "Jaldi challo!" he said.

Manish the Magnificent's picture appeared on a board on the pavement outside the entrance to Hey Presto!—"magic, comedy, music and more." He was wearing a maharajah's garb: bejeweled turban, silken robes and fake whiskers. Puri recognized him instantly nonetheless. His real name was Jaideep Prabhu.

"So you've been reincarnated after so many years, is it, Jaideep?" said the detective to himself. "Takes a master of disguise to see through one, huh."

The hostess at the door led him into a restaurant-cum-bar bedecked with mirrors, rotating disco balls and velvet-upholstered booths. It was packed with good-looking young people. Laughter and cigarette smoke filled the air.

Puri sat down at a small table near the stage, where a jazz pianist and saxophonist were playing Dave Brubeck's "Take Five."

"By God! Eight hundred for whisky!" he exclaimed out loud when he read over the drinks menu. "That's for the entire bottle, is it?"

The young waiter, who had a ponytail and an overly familiar bearing, eyed the man in the safari suit, Sandown cap and aviator sunglasses with undisguised bemusement.

"Hey, man, what time are you on tonight?" he asked.

"Pardon?" replied Puri sharply.

"You're one of the stand-ups, right?"

The detective, who rarely lost his temper, could barely restrain himself. "Listen, Charlie, I am a private investigator and I am here to see your boss," he growled through gritted teeth. "Give him this." He handed the insolent young man his card.

"'Vish Puri, managing director, chief officer and winner of six national awards, confidentiality is our watchword,'" read the waiter out loud. "That's hilarious! I can't wait to see your act."

The detective banged his fist down hard on the table. "I am not an act!" he exploded. "Now go tell Jaideep Prabhu that Vish Puri is here!"

The other customers were all staring.

"OK, dude," said the waiter, holding up his hands defensively. "I thought you were . . . so you're for real. Wow! I'll give the boss your card. Relax, OK? Now what can I get you?"

"Bring one peg whisky and soda. No ice. And don't call me 'man' or 'dude'! You should call elders 'ji' or 'sir'!"

"Fine, *sir*. But just so you know . . . my name's not Charlie."

The waiter headed off to the bar to fetch his drink.

Puri sat back in his chair, fuming. Some of the other customers were still eyeing him. They looked amused. Why exactly, the detective could not fathom. Self-consciously, he checked his cap to make sure it was sitting squarely on his head.

How he hated these new "trendy" haunts! Like the malls, they were indicative of a crass materialism and hedonism undermining the family values that underpinned Indian society.

Take those females at the next table, for example, Puri thought. Baring their legs in public, drinking alcohol, using gutter language: totally disgraceful. Or those two nancy boys over there, the ones in silk shirts and big sideburns. By God, they're holding hands actually! What the bloody hell kind of place you're running here, Jaideep? he wondered.

Puri felt a letter to the editor of the *Times of India* coming on. Perhaps he would juxtapose his views with those of the late Dr. Jha. The rationalist had not been a fan of this crass, Americanized culture, either. To him education and knowledge had been all-important.

But they had held opposing views on the role of religion. Dr. Jha had often referred to dogma as the "root of all evil." The detective, on the other hand, regarded a belief in the divine as essential. Without it, in his view, society would disintegrate.

"The boss says to tell you he'll be backstage after the show, sir," said the waiter when he returned with Puri's drink.

The jazz musicians finished their set, the lights were dimmed and then a mist began to creep across the stage.

"Ladies and gentlemen," said a voice offstage. "Tonight you will be astounded and spellbound, taken to new heights of expectation and reality! Prepare your mind to travel to new frontiers, beyond time and space! Prepare to be dazzled by the greatest magician in all of India!"

A flash and a puff of smoke and Manish the Magnificent

appeared onstage. His sudden appearance engendered a round of applause and he bowed regally.

"For my first death-defying trick I will need a volunteer from the audience," he announced.

One of the leggy women at the nearby table was chosen and made her way up to the stage, sniggering and exchanging looks with her friends. The magician produced a pistol.

"I would like you to examine this and tell the audience if it is real."

She did so and agreed that it certainly looked real, and then Manish the Magnificent made a show of loading the weapon with bullets. To prove these were "live ones," he asked that a paper target on a stand be placed at the back of the stage. Once it was in position, he fired three times. The target, drilled with three round holes, was then shown to the audience.

"Now it's your turn," he told his young volunteer. "Only your target will be this tin can, which I will balance on top of my head!"

"Are you crazy?"

"Trust me, I am a professional!"

"Go on! Shoot!" a voice in the audience shouted encouragingly.

The young woman, whom Puri suspected was a plant, eventually agreed to his request. She took aim and fired. And lo and behold, Manish the Magnificent caught the bullet between his teeth.

"Next I will grow a mango tree from this pit before your very eyes."

The magician planted the pit in a pot and watered it. Soon a green shoot appeared. Within a few minutes this had grown into a miniature tree that bore fruit, which he picked and threw into the audience.

One of India's oldest tricks followed: a young boy climbed into a basket and Manish the Magnificent drove swords through it. The blades appeared bloodied, but the boy emerged miraculously unscathed.

Last came a version of the Indian rope trick.

The magician began by sitting next to a basket and playing a pungi, used by snake charmers. The end of a rope stood erect like a cobra and began to rise up into the air. When it had reached a height of ten feet, the boy climbed up the rope and, apparently out of nowhere, picked some coconuts.

After the show, Puri found Manish the Magnificent in his well-appointed office, puffing on a fat cigar. By now, he had shed his whiskers and turban.

"Mr. Vish Puri, sir," he said, shaking the detective limply by the hand and then motioning him into the chair in front of his desk. "It's been a very long time. But not long enough."

Ten years had passed since Jaideep had robbed Khanna Jewelers in Karol Bagh in broad daylight.

Posing as a customer, he had swapped fifty lakhs' worth of diamonds for glass replicas without any of the store attendants noticing. The detective, working on behalf of the owners, had caught him as he tried to sell the stones. Subsequently, Jaideep had been sentenced to six years in Tihar jail. Puri, unaware at the time that the thief was a trained magician, had never figured out how he had pulled off the robbery. Now that he had witnessed Jaideep's conjuring skills, however, the mystery was finally solved.

"I'm not going to beat around bushes," said Puri. "I want

to know your location yesterday morning between six and six thirty exactly."

The magician smiled through the haze of cigar smoke that separated them. "Ah, so that's what you're doing here. You're investigating the murder on Rajpath. And you think I'm the guilty one."

"Answer the question," directed Puri.

"I'm flattered. But, you see, I couldn't have done it."

"Why exactly?"

"Because I am a reformed individual, Mr. Vish Puri, sir. I have been successfully reintegrated into society."

"Don't do jugglery of words," scolded the detective. "Once a crook, always crooked. Now tell me where you were."

Jaideep drew on his cigar and blew a big cloud in his visitor's direction.

"Like any sensible person, I was in bed, of course. Naturally I was not alone. I think her name was Candy. She tasted sweet, that is for sure."

"Anyone else can confirm?"

"Naturally my servants will be only too happy to do so. My driver, also. I can provide you with Candy's number as well if you like. She provides a very reasonably priced home service if you're interested."

Puri did not rise to the bait.

"There can be no doubt this murder was done by a master illusionist," he said. "There are only a handful of you fellows around. So if you're not the one, must be you've a good idea who he is, no?"

"You expect me to give you names? Why should I?"

"Because I am something of a magician myself. You don't believe me, is it? Very well. Allow me to show you one trick I learned long time back."

The detective took his mobile phone from his pocket.

"This is my portable device. Nothing out of the ordinary. But see here this button? When I press it—hey presto!—one number appears. Know to whom it belongs? Inspector Jagat Prakash Singh, Delhi Police. Now there is nothing up my sleeve. Nothing hidden. See? But should I have need of pressing this green button, in seconds, only, Inspector Singh would answer day or night. Now . . . Inspector Singh is a very motivated young officer. I am quite sure he would be most interested in knowing where so much of money came for buying such a fancy club as this and what activities you are up to, also. That is aside from pulling so many rabbits from hats."

Jaideep met Puri's hard, uncompromising stare. He laid his cigar down on the lip of an ashtray and ran his fingers through his hair.

"I've got nothing to hide."

"Sitting in your bar for past forty minutes, only, I saw three crimes committed. Number one, your hostess was supplying drugs to customers—cocaine, looks like. Number two, the barman was watering down the whisky. Third, you're having so many rats in your kitchen."

"How could you know that?"

"Rats are always there, Jaideep."

The magician scowled. "OK, Mr. Vish Puri, sir, you can put away your mobile. You're right. What was done yesterday on Rajpath—the levitation, I mean—it's never been achieved before, not out in the open. It's a first. And before you ask, I have no idea how it was done. I've watched that video a dozen times and I can't figure it out. Someone worked very hard to perfect that illusion. It's a masterpiece."

"Who did it?" The detective was still brandishing his phone.

Manish the Magnificent hesitated.

"Who?" demanded Puri.

"There are only three individuals capable of pulling off something like this," said the magician. "The first is currently in intensive care, so you can rule him out. The second is a certain Bengali and he's on tour in Europe."

Puri made a note of their names all the same.

"And third?" he asked.

The magician paused, licking his lips, which had become dry.

"These days he's known to people as none other than the great, all-seeing, all-powerful . . . Maharaj Swami."

"You said '*these days*.'"

The magician looked suddenly coy. "That's not the name he's always gone by."

"You knew him before, is it?"

"Oh, yes, I knew him. But what I'm about to tell you didn't come from me. Is that understood?"

"Perfectly."

"And you'll leave after this and not come back?"

"Is that the way to treat a guest?"

Manish the Magnificent retrieved his cigar from the ashtray and blew on the tip until it glowed orange again.

"Very few people know what I'm about to tell you," he said. "But the great *Godman* grew up in Shadipur in a family of magicians. His parents were Hindu, but they died when he was four and he was adopted into a Muslim family. His real name is Aman. We were neighbors and both grew up assisting the older jadoo wallahs on the streets and learning magic tricks. When we were old enough, we became partners and started working for ourselves."

"Allow me to guess," said the detective. "You got into criminal activity and eventually there was a falling-out."

The magician eyed him warily. "Something like that. It was about twelve years ago. He suddenly disappeared one day along with a great deal of my money."

"And?"

"Naturally I tried to locate him, but he was nowhere to be found."

Some cigar ash fell into Manish the Magnificent's lap and he brushed it away.

"Life went on," he continued. "I went to prison—as you well know. Then a few years ago I was watching TV and Maharaj Swami comes on. I didn't recognize him at first. Not with all that getup. He'd made himself look a lot older. He was also changed physically—he's mastered yogic pranayamic breathing. But the moment he started conjuring objects out of thin air, I knew it was Aman. I'd recognize his technique anywhere."

Puri thought for a moment and then said: "One thing I am getting confusion over. Assuming it's true your former partner betrayed you, why you've got tension about revealing his past?"

"Haven't you heard, Mr. Vish Puri, sir? Maharaj Swami is now one of the most powerful men in India. The prime minister doesn't go to the toilet unless he okays it. He could make life very uncomfortable for me."

It was obvious to Puri that although the magician had made a pretense of not wanting to reveal what he knew about Maharaj Swami, he was only too happy to pass on what he knew.

"I take it you would not shed too many of tears in the event Swami-ji ended up behind bars," he said.

Manish the Magnificent smiled. "Not many, no."

"Then we have something in common—us two."

"I suppose so," the magician answered begrudgingly.

"Very good! So what else you can tell me about your friend Aman?"

"Only that he's the most gifted magician I've ever come across. If anyone could have pulled off the illusion on Rajpath, it's him."

"What about his character?"

"He's a perfectionist. I never knew him to give up on anything."

"Any habits—drugs, alcohol?"

"Nothing."

"Women?"

"He was always nervous around them."

Puri made a note of this.

The magician remembered something else.

"Aman had this habit of collecting things—little mementos from places he'd been," he said. "Railway ticket stubs, menus from restaurants, postcards. It was a kind of obsession with him. He used to keep a diary as well. He left it out once and I read some of it. He had written down everything that had happened to him—dates, names—along with notes and diagrams on the magic tricks he was developing."

"He kept all these things where exactly?"

"In a silver metal trunk."

Ten

National Highway 58, which ran for 334 miles northeast of Delhi, had been under construction for nearly a decade. The few sections that had been completed between Ghaziabad and the holy city of Haridwar offered three smooth lanes in both directions. Drivers reaching one of these stretches experienced instant elation, as if they had entered a vehicular promised land where there were no tedious, terrestrial speed limits.

But the euphoria was short-lived. After just a few miles, each tarmac tract ended abruptly in a rugged tear—the destructive influence of corruption and ineptitude, and not, as it perhaps appeared, an act of God. Even the most robust of vehicles had to brake suddenly and inch down sharp inclines into a purgatory of rutted, potholed tracks.

Windows were hastily rolled up as tires stirred clouds of fine white dust. Through this choking pall, drivers and passengers passed laborers with bleached faces breaking piles of rocks with chisels and crude hammers. Rows of concrete supports for half-complete flyovers appeared suddenly, giant and potentially lethal obstacles. Rusty construction equipment stood idle like tanks abandoned by a fleeing army.

That Puri was able to sleep soundly through all this—head back, mouth agape, snoring loudly—was thanks to an inherited but yet-to-be-identified Punjabi gene that endowed him with the power to snooze through almost anything. But it helped that he was exhausted from his encounter yesterday with the cricket bat in Dr. Jha's office followed by a long day of interviews.

It had been almost eleven o'clock by the time he reached the Mount Kailash Hotel, a seedy "businessman's lodge" off Connaught Place, where he had spent an hour.

Room 312 had been registered to "Miss Neena," who had an understanding with the discreet manager.

"Miss Neena" was but one of the lovely young woman's aliases. Indeed, she used so many that even Puri, who had been making use of her services for nearly five years, sometimes lost track of who she was pretending to be at any given time.

Had she ever told him her real name? he sometimes wondered.

What he knew of her past was certainly sketchy, pieced together from scraps of information.

Originally from Kathmandu, she had run away from home as a teenager to join the Maoist rebels, undergone combat training in a camp in the mountains and taken part in numerous guerrilla operations against the Nepali state. During one of them, she had witnessed or experienced something terrible. Disillusioned with the cause, she had fled and escaped to India.

For the next few years, she had rambled across northern India. She spent a year with a traveling theater troupe in Assam and worked as a bar girl in Mumbai and an ayah for a wealthy Delhi family. In between, there had been a marriage that ended disastrously.

Puri had also noted the following characteristics about her: she didn't trust the opposite sex; considered alcohol nothing short of evil; was a night owl; could handle herself in a fight better than most men.

There was a distinct possibility that she had a child (a couple of times on the phone he had heard crying in the background). But Puri had never visited her home or pried into her private life.

Indeed, despite her secretive nature, their relationship was based on mutual trust. They had met in Mumbai during the Case of the Deaf Dabawallah when Puri had saved her life. Subsequently, she had moved to Delhi to work for him as an undercover operative.

Given her talent for blending into almost any situation and "putting on so many of faces," he had dubbed her Facecream.

Now he was asking her to take on a task that would stretch even her considerable resources: to infiltrate the Abode of Eternal Love, Maharaj Swami's ashram north of Haridwar.

Last night, in the Mount Kailash Hotel, she had listened attentively to Puri's briefing.

"Frankly speaking, thus far, nothing has come to light linking Swami-ji directly with the murder," he'd told her. "But I am in possession of Dr. Jha's file on 'His Holiness' and grounds for investigation are there—no doubt about it at all. Dr. Jha spoke to three of Swami-ji's ex-associates—naturally it was off record—and seems our Godman is very much active in money laundering for politicians. This Abode of Eternal Love is also Abode of Washing Machines, we might say. Black money goes in and comes out white.

"Through Right to Information Act," Puri had continued, "Dr. Jha was endeavoring to prove Swami-ji's corrupt practices. Thus, he had petitioned for financial statements of numerous ashram bank accounts in India and Switzerland to be made public. Thus Dr. Jha had become a thorn in Swami-ji's side."

"Dr. Jha had political enemies," Facecream had pointed out. "It could have been one of them who killed him."

"Bullets delivered to the backs of heads are more their style, no?"

Puri had also briefed Facecream on what Manish the Magnificent had told him about Maharaj Swami's secret past and about his being an obsessive hoarder of personal memorabilia. He left the file with her to study.

On the journey along Highway 58 this morning, she had been reading through the information Dr. Jha had acquired about the death in April at the ashram of twenty-six-year-old devotee Manika Gill. There were press cuttings, copies of police reports, "witness" statements and affidavits from the girl's family. Dr. Jha's notes and transcripts of interviews he had conducted with some of her friends and the local farmer who had found the body lying facedown in the river were also included.

Facecream was able to glean the following:

Prior to coming to the ashram, Manika, whose father was a wealthy jeweler, had been a "rebellious type." During her late teens and early twenties, she had "entered into" a number of casual sexual relationships. At twenty-five, she had found herself pregnant. At her father's insistence, she had "gone in for" an abortion. Naturally this was hushed up; apart from her parents, only her best friend, Neetu Chandra, had known about it.

Soon after, Mr. and Mrs. Gill, who were both devotees of Maharaj Swami, had escorted their disgraced daughter to the Abode of Eternal Love and implored their guru to give her "direction." Manika had found the place "tedious and boring" at first but then had undergone a "spiritual awakening." According to several different sources, she had seen a vision during a special darshan conducted by the Godman.

Neetu Chandra said Manika "wasn't the same person" after that. All she talked about was Maharaj Swami. The two drifted apart. Seven months passed. Then on the night she died, at around eight o'clock in the evening, Neetu received a distressing call from her friend.

"She wasn't making much sense. Just babbling about how she hadn't slept in days and she'd been having these terrible nightmares. I told her to get the hell out of that bloody freak show, but she said she couldn't trust anyone. She said she'd told her parents but they didn't believe her. Told them what? I asked. She didn't answer. She sounded afraid, just broke down in tears. I told her to stay put and I'd drive up to fetch her."

Neetu Chandra had set off from Delhi early the next morning. By the time she arrived, Manika had been discovered drowned in the Ganges. The police had quickly concluded that she had gone for a swim near the ashram at eleven o'clock at night.

Mr. and Mrs. Gill maintained that their daughter had drowned by accident. But according to Manika's friends, she couldn't swim and was scared of the water.

No suicide note was discovered.

Handbrake, at the wheel of the Mercedes four-wheel drive Puri had hired in order to make the right impression at Maharaj Swami's ashram, turned off Highway 58 south of Haridwar. The single-lane road passed through waterlogged, emerald-green paddy fields fed by the mountain meltwater of the Ganges. Here and there, farmers stood in mud up to their ankles tending to their crops, and zebu, humped oxen, dragged wooden plows through the rich, oozing mire.

The holy city of Haridwar, where drops of the elixir of immortality are believed to have been spilled by the celestial bird Garuda, announced itself with a line of budget hotels with names like Disney Inn. The idyllic rice fields gave way to the all-too-familiar detritus of dusty dhabas, vegetable carts and car-repair shops with oil-stained forecourts.

Skirting to the east of the old city, the Mercedes crossed over the fast-running cobalt waters of the Ganges. A giant statue of Shiva, his neck garlanded with a spitting cobra, towered over the road. Behind the deity lay the Har ki Pauri steps, where millions come every year to bathe and cleanse their sins, and behind them the white domes and peaked rooftops of temples, shrines and ashrams. Farther on, they passed three sadhus walking barefoot away from the city into the hills. With their matted dreadlocks, loincloths and tridents, they resembled cavemen out hunting woolly mammoths.

"Would you mind if we reviewed our cover story? I'm getting a little forgetful in my old age."

The voice belonged to Mrs. Duggal, who did the occasional freelance assignment for Most Private Investigators since her retirement from the Indian Secret Service. Puri had asked her to pose as his wife for the day and she was sitting next to Facecream.

"Most certainly we can," agreed the detective. He repeated the details again: the Garodia family's home address in Singapore, the name of the school Queenie had been expelled from, the names of her paternal grandparents and so on.

Mrs. Duggal, who was expected to do a good deal of crying during their visit to the ashram, tested the menthol stick she kept in her handbag for such situations. Rubbing it beneath her nostrils quickly brought on tears.

"Most convincing," said Puri approvingly.

Mrs. Duggal patted her face dry with her handkerchief. "It is always a pleasure to work with someone as talented as yourself, Mr. Puri. I would never recognize you in all that getup," she said.

"So kind of you," replied the detective. "Actually, disguises have always been my speciality. Once I take on a role, Vish Puri is put aside and I become the character. Sometimes I don't even recognize myself. So engrossed I become."

Puri admired his disguise in his makeup mirror: stick-on henna-dyed moustache, eyebrows and wig—all a lurid orange-red—and a hawkish nose.

Mrs. Duggal and Facecream exchanged a playful glance.

The Abode of Eternal Love was spread over a vast estate in the foothills of the Himalayas. Had it not been for the bronze statues of the Hindu saints along the driveway and the comings and goings of the devotees dressed in white kurtas and sarongs, it might have passed for an American university campus. Manicured lawns dotted with shade trees and benches snuggled between new, utilitarian buildings. White picket signs pointed visitors in the right direction: DARSHAN HALL; ANANDA RESIDENCE; ABODE OF KNOWLEDGE; ATM. The well-tended flower beds around the edges of the car park were decorated with bark chips.

The main reception, with its sliding automatic doors, split air-conditioning units and computerized registration system, also contradicted all preconceived notions of modernity being at odds with spirituality.

Maharaj Swami, according to the stacks of free literature available to visitors, had attained samadhi after meditating naked in a cave high up in the Himalayas for seven years. His devotees could achieve the same while living in well-appointed dormitories, eating freshly prepared vegetarian food, attending pranayama yoga sessions in the marble-floored gazebo, listening to Swami-ji's daily discourses and following a pancha karma detox system.

For those with "health issues," the Abode of Health, a multimillion-dollar two-hundred-bed hospital, also offered treatments for every conceivable condition, including cancer and AIDS. An Ayurvedic cure was also offered for homosexuality, which Maharaj Swami considered a "sickness and disease."

While waiting in line at the front desk, the Garodia family—of Marwari stock and currently visiting from Singapore, where Lakshmi Garodia ran a multi-crore textile business—found themselves in good, middle-class company. Behind them stood a young couple from Delhi working in IT who had come to spend three days at the ashram.

"We're looking for something more to life beyond work and shopping and more work, like higher thought or something, you know," said the husband, who had paid almost a thousand dollars for the Fast Track to Yourself package.

"Lakshmi Garodia up from Singapore only," announced Puri in a sonorous tone to the young lady devotee behind the desk when it was his turn.

He placed a Garodia Enterprises business card on the counter. It listed a Singapore office address, a website and a number that Flush, Puri's computer and electronics whiz, had rerouted to the Communications Room inside the Most Private Investigators offices.

"I called one day back only to enroll my daughter, Queenie," said Puri. "We were invited to attend darshan at four o'clock."

"Yes, Mr. Garodia, we've been expecting you," the devotee said with a seraphic smile. She stood and pressed the palms of her delicate hands together in a namaste.

Puri reciprocated, as did Mrs. Duggal, aka Mrs. Garodia.

"That is your daughter?" asked the devotee.

Facecream was standing on the other side of reception with her back against the wall, listening to her iPod. It was turned up full volume. A thudding beat leaked from her headphones. She was mouthing the lyrics while looking suitably oblivious.

"Yes, that's Queenie," said Mrs. Duggal with a sigh.

The devotee regarded the young woman in the tight jeans and high heels with a curious, whimsical smile.

"Whaaat are you staring at?" squealed Facecream, pretending to have suddenly noticed the three of them staring at her. "Think I'm some kind of freak or something? Just leave me alone—*o-kaaay*?"

"That is the total limit!" shouted Puri. He stormed across reception and snatched the iPod out of her hands.

"God, Pa, what the hell's your problem anyway?"

Everyone else in reception turned and stared.

"How dare you, young madam! Think we've brought you here for nothing, huh?"

"No one asked *me* if *I* wanted to come. I *hate* this place. India's filthy and it smells. I mean, have you *seen* all the crap in the streets or what? Men just piss on the walls wherever. There are freaks with no arms begging at like every traffic light. India's a total nightmare and I hate it!"

"India is your mother country!" roared Puri. "You are here to learn about your heritage and culture, only! Think MTV can teach you anything, huh? Think you can just laze about all your life and go to so many of parties?"

Mrs. Duggal joined in: "Please, beta, try to behave. Your

papa has your best interests at heart. He's paying so much of money for you to stay here and get help. Why don't you put away the chewing gum and come and introduce yourself?"

"Nooo waaay, Ma. This is all bullshit. You're not getting me doing any yoga or stoopid crap like that. I want to go home!"

Mrs. Duggal burst into tears. "I knew we should never have gone to live in Singapore!" she wailed, addressing the devotee receptionist. "I blame myself. Had Queenie been brought up in the proper way, she'd have learned to appreciate her culture." Mrs. Duggal let out a couple of loud sobs. "Instead, she goes to . . . to nigh . . . nightclubs and . . . and dan . . . dances with b . . . b . . ." Mrs. Duggal took a gasp of air before wailing, "Boyyyyyyys!"

Queenie had to be bribed with a promise of some new Ugg boots before agreeing to accompany her parents to the darshan hall, where Maharaj Swami was due to address "his children."

Inside, chandeliers sprouted from dark pink lotus flowers, and wax effigies of the gods peered out from rows of glass cases along the walls. An enormous marble fountain spouting blue-tinted water stood in the middle of the auditorium floor, and at the far end was a stage.

Hundreds of devotees sitting cross-legged on mats were singing devotional songs accompanied by musicians on santoor, bansuri and tabla. Hundreds more were chanting Maharaj Swami's ninety-nine names. Bells rang out. Handheld cymbals clashed. Clouds of incense wafted over the congregation. The Godman's senior male disciples, recognizable by their off-white sarongs, silk stoles and intense, self-important miens, lit candles and distributed baskets of flower petals to be cast in front of their lord's feet.

The Garodia family took off their shoes outside the elaborately carved wooden doors and were served cups of papaya juice. Then they were escorted to the front of the hall, where all the other guests and visitors were seated on padded yoga mats. Puri estimated they numbered about three hundred; by the looks of them, they were mostly drawn from India's new middle class.

The man sitting next to him was in his thirties, an advertising executive from Mumbai. Like the detective, he was overweight and unable to manage the lotus position, so he sat with his short, chubby legs sticking out in front of him.

"I've been watching Swami-ji on Channel OM and I'm hoping he'll help me with my tension and high blood pressure," he told Puri. "Nothing else has worked till date."

The detective had watched Channel OM a few times; Rumpi sometimes had it on in the sitting room. Maharaj Swami's broadcasts offered a bit of everything: Vedic wisdom, Ayurvedic health advice, yoga, meditation and Deepak Chopra–style self-help guidance on how to deal with issues associated with the challenges of modern-day life—in other words, stress, wayward children and extramarital affairs. A new brand of Hinduism was sweeping India. It was highly ritualistic and steeped in the kind of pseudoscience that helped the new middle classes reconcile their use of modern science and technology with their belief, as one social commentator had put it recently, "in supernatural powers supposedly embodied in idols, divine men and women, stars and planets, rivers, trees and sacred animals." Most significantly, it also condoned materialism. "The Bhagavad Gita and Yoga Sutras have been turned into self-help manuals for making money and achieving success," the same commentator had written.

It was not Puri's cup of chai, nor that of most of his generation. Theirs was a more contemplative, philosophical Hinduism that frowned on ostentation. Besides, he hated all the appeals for donations and the slick marketing. Borrowing from the techniques used by American TV evangelists, Swami-ji sold his books, CDs and DVDs in the same cloying manner as soap powder.

"It's like 'new, improved Hinduism for the reaching of spots others can't,'" the detective had commented to his wife recently.

Lakshmi Garodia, though, was an ardent fan of the Godman.

"One can feel his presence and power through the TV, actually," he said. "I understand he's healed so many of people."

"So many!" agreed the advertising executive breathlessly. "You know, my cousin lives in Hong Kong and was dying of cancer. He was on the verge of death. Then Maharaj Swami came to him. He walked right through the wall of his hospital room and laid his hands on my cousin's head. He said he could *literally* feel the cancer being destroyed. That day only my cousin left hospital!"

A chorus of trumpets announced the arrival of Maharaj Swami. He entered through the garlanded archway at the back of the hall and then proceeded along a path that led through rows of fawning, adoring disciples, many of whom reached out to touch his feet. The guru stopped now and again to lay his hands on bowed heads. And with a seraphic smile, he sprinkled vibhuti over the congregation, the holy ash materializing in his hands.

Puri and the other visitors remained seated on the floor as the Godman approached. With hands pressed together, they grinned at him like eager children pleading for his blessings. A chosen few received reassuring, almost pitying, pats on the head.

"Swami-ji! Swami-ji!" called out the advertising executive with tears running down his cheeks. "Bless me, Swami-ji!"

The devotional singing, chanting, bell ringing and cymbal clashing reached fever pitch as Maharaj Swami walked up onto the stage, where temple priests greeted him with flaming brass diyas.

With his black beard and moustache parting to reveal a row of perfect white teeth (according to the literature Puri had read in the entrance hall, they were kept in perfect condition by Abode of Eternal Love–branded neem dental sticks), he sat down on a large silver throne. Suspended by wires behind him was a circle of blinking fairy lights that formed a halo. He held up his left hand to silence the congregation. A hush fell over the hall, and his deep, orotund voice sounded over the speakers.

"My children," he said in Hindi, "today we will consider the word 'I,' which refers to the ego born out of an attachment to the body . . ."

For thirty minutes, Puri listened attentively to Maharaj Swami's discourse, impressed by his oratory skills. Mrs. Duggal, too, appeared captivated. Facecream looked a little off color, but the detective thought nothing of it.

When he was finished giving his sermon, the Godman stood again and walked to the front of the stage.

"None of you here are yet capable of comprehending my reality," he explained. "Although I appear as flesh and blood, I exist in multiple dimensions. Time has no meaning for me. Past, present, future are but one."

Two of the senior disciples carried a brazier filled with wood onto the stage and placed it to the left of the guru's throne. This caused a ripple of anticipation to course through the congregation.

"But throughout human history, saints and avatars have

been sent to guide humanity, to reveal the infiniteness of the universe. This is done through the use of miracles. Here today I propose to reveal to you one such miracle. I propose to communicate across time and space with one of the seven rishis—Bharadwaja. It was he who came to me and revealed the ultimate Truth—who showed me the true power of God's love."

"We are truly blessed," the excited ad man whispered to Puri. "Swami-ji summons Bharadwaja rarely, usually only for special guests. They say the last time was for the prime minister. After, a date for the election was set!"

The lights in the hall were dimmed and Maharaj Swami commanded absolute silence. The hall went deathly still.

Pressing his fingertips to his forehead and temples, he closed his eyes and began to utter incomprehensible incantations. He reached out with his right hand and pointed to the brazier. With a click of his fingers, the wood burst into flames. Everyone, including Puri, gasped.

Maharaj Swami approached the burning brazier. He pushed his hands together and held them tight, muttering something under his breath. When he unclasped them again, they were full of red powder. This he threw onto the flames, causing them to leap higher.

A dense smoke began to curl upward and then, as if it had a mind of its own, made an abrupt left turn and proceeded horizontally into the middle of the stage. There it started to circle, creating a vortex. And at its center a bright white light appeared.

Maharaj Swami closed his eyes again and moved his hands back and forth over the brazier.

The white light slowly formed into a man's ghostly head.

Puri could make out his facial features—the creases on

the forehead, the crumpled nose, the sagging jowls, the ancient eyelids.

He felt a tingle run up his spine as some of his fellow visitors cried out: "He's here!" "Bharadwaja has come!"

The rishi opened his eyes and yawned, as if he had been woken from a long, peaceful sleep.

"Who dares disturb me?" spoke a deep, gravelly voice that boomed down from above.

"It is I," answered Maharaj Swami, who by now had retaken his throne.

A smile crept across the lined face. "And what is it you seek?"

"All-knowing one, I seek nothing for myself. I ask that you give guidance to my children as they strive toward the divine!"

"Not all can be helped," spoke the rishi. "Those who resist, who refuse to abandon preconceived notions, they will remain trapped forever in an endless cycle of birth and rebirth."

A timid devotee was invited up onstage and prostrated himself before the apparition. In a halting voice, he asked the rishi a question about an event in one of his past lives. He, like the six others who followed him, received answers that seemed to shock and surprise them.

All the while Puri sat, as he had done on the roof while Akbar the Great had levitated, trying to figure out the method behind the illusion.

There was no projector being used; the face was three-dimensional. It was not a hologram, either. Of that he was certain.

Was it possible there was a man onstage wearing a black outfit to camouflage his body? As if in reply to his question, the door at the side of the hall opened, casting a beam of light across the stage, revealing nothing beneath the rishi's floating head.

The detective and Mrs. Duggal exchanged a furtive, perplexed look.

It was then that Puri noticed Facecream staring blankly at the stage. She looked transfixed, as if she had been hypnotized, and there were tears running down her face.

He reached out and touched her hand. At first she didn't respond. He tried again. Facecream turned and stared at him and then, looking back at the stage, started to laugh.

Puri was unsure what to do. Was there something wrong? Was she improvising?

He decided to play along, keeping a careful eye on her.

A few minutes passed and she began to look more herself. But then she suddenly stood up and, with arms stretched wide, declared in a loud voice: "I have seen the truth and it is beautiful!"

Many of those sitting around her started to applaud. And then Facecream fainted, collapsing into the lap of the person behind her.

Eleven

"According to my dear late husband, intelligence is number one key to doing solving of cases. But two kinds of intelligence there are, na? Information and IQ, also. For proper detection both are required."

"Yes, Mummy-ji," said Rumpi wearily. "But in this case, we don't seem to have any intelligence at all—intelligence of the first sort, I mean."

It was Thursday afternoon, twenty-four hours after the kitty party robbery. Puri was in Haridwar and his wife and mother were sitting in the back of Mummy's car outside the Central Forensic Science Laboratory on Lodhi Road, South Delhi.

They had spent the past couple of hours inside the CFSL building, where the son of one of Mummy's oldest friends worked as a laboratory technician. Through a combination of charm and sheer obstinacy, she had persuaded him to lift the fingerprints from the items in her handbag and run them through the national database. The computer had not found a match. But as the young man had sheepishly admitted, such random checks rarely bore results.

"Fingerprinting comes into play when we find a murder

weapon and need to match prints to a suspect," he'd explained. "Most investigating officers don't bother collecting forensic evidence. They rely on confessions from suspects for convictions."

When Mummy had asked him to run a DNA test on her fingernail cutting, he'd responded: "Auntie-ji, I think you've been watching too much of *CSI* on Star TV, isn't it?"

Mummy had not understood what he'd meant by this; she never had time to watch television, what with all her duties as a mother and grandmother (she still lived with her eldest son, Bhupinder, and his wife and four children) and her numerous weekly social engagements and charity work—not to mention the occasional bit of sleuthing.

But she had not been put off by this setback.

"Look at bright side," Mummy told her daughter-in-law as they discussed their next move in the back of the car. "Fingerprints will come in useful once we've got hold of those goondas. Now it's time for B Plan."

Rumpi could not remember what B Plan was. Nor if there was a C or D Plan, for that matter. She was finding that detective work did not come naturally to her. It required a suspicious mind, and she was still struggling to come to terms with the idea that one of her friends had betrayed the trust upon which all kitty parties were based.

"You're sure it couldn't have been one of the ladies' husbands?" asked Puri's wife.

"You tell Chubby about your kitty, is it?" asked Mummy.

"Of course not!"

"My point exactly, na? No Indian wife is sharing such information with her husband of all people. Her private savings and jewelry worth remain top secret at all times."

"I suppose you're right, Mummy-ji."

Rumpi was still not entirely convinced that the matter

wasn't best left to the professionals. But Jaiya had gone off for the day visiting friends, so she had decided to keep her mother-in-law company—if for no other reason than to make sure she didn't get into trouble.

She had specified one condition, however. Mummy was never to tell Puri that they had worked together.

"You know how he feels about mummies doing investigations. God only knows what he'd say about wives!"

They had agreed to keep up the pretense of going shopping together.

"Where are we going now?" asked Rumpi.

"Like I said earlier, na, some intelligence is required."

"And where do you plan to find it, Mummy-ji?"

"When it comes to finding out what all well-to-do Dilli ladies are up to, there is only one place to go."

They both smiled and said in unison: "Arti's Beauty Parlor."

A French cosmetics company had set up a swish new salon called Chez Nous (known locally as "Shahnoos") across from Arti's in Khan Market. It offered the latest "cleansing systems" from Paris and a free glass of chilled white wine for every new customer. The photographs of pouting Gallic models with flawless skin in the windows extolled the benefits of laser hair removal.

By contrast, Arti's Beauty Parlor was outdated and dingy. The walls were covered in florid pink wallpaper and posters of models sporting the kind of big hairstyles that had gone out of style in the 1980s. The booking system was still done in a thick ledger with pencil-smudged pages rather than a flash Apple Mac. The beauticians wore uniforms that made them look like hospital orderlies. And the sweeper boy charged with keeping the floors clean did so on his hands and knees, weaving through an obstacle course of legs and shoes with a grimy wet cloth.

For the slim young things who arrived at Khan Market in their chauffeur-driven sedans with Louis Vuitton handbags dangling from the crooks of their arms, the choice between the two rivals was obvious.

The French establishment attracted lots of young male customers as well. They were to be spotted through the windows undergoing the latest skin-lightening techniques at the hands of academy-trained therapists dressed in black. "Because beauty *really* is only skin deep," read the slogan on the backs of their T-shirts.

Chez Nous's contrived trendiness did not appeal to Arti's middle-aged customers, but other factors guaranteed their loyalty as well. Her prices were cheaper and she offered natural Indian products and traditional techniques like henna treatment for the hair. Nationalism had played its part, a prejudice actively exploited by Arti, who was positively xenophobic about the French—"That George W. Bush had a point, no?" And there was no beating the general intimacy, in which banter and tittle-tattle thrived.

Mummy and Rumpi arrived to find the salon's reclining swivel chairs all occupied. Mrs. De Souza's daughter was getting married that week and was being fussed over by a coterie of beauticians giving her the works: waxing, threading, manicure, premarital ubtan body scrub, herbal steam and almond-meal facial. Mrs. De Souza was getting a pedicure and a chin wax. One of the bridesmaids looked as if she had fallen facedown in mud, the whites of her large eyes set off by a darkening sandalwood mask.

Arti, who wore green eye shadow, moved back and forth

across the room, giving instructions to her beauticians, fussing over her customers, making the odd bawdy joke and bestowing advice of a personal nature in a loud voice for all to hear.

"You really must go for a bra fitting!" she admonished one woman. "I'll give the number of the girl. That thing you're wearing is two sizes too big. Makes you look all saggy."

To the bride-to-be she said: "How you got so much of acne? You've been eating chocolate? Or perhaps it's all those hormones, hmmm? Must be thinking of your wedding night!"

When she spotted Mummy and Rumpi waiting in reception, Arti exclaimed in a thrilled voice: "I heard about the robbery! What a thing to happen! Arora Madam was here this morning and told me all about it. Her pooch is in a coma! Poor thing doesn't respond to its name. Who do you think did it? Probably some of those Purvanchali types. The authorities should send them packing back to their villages!"

Her attention was drawn away by a mini-crisis in the salon. A customer's wax was too hot and she had let out a yelp as it had been applied to one of her arms.

Rumpi was escorted into a private treatment room by her regular beautician, Uma.

Uma, who had been working at the parlor for some fifteen years, always told Puri Madam about her problems—the drunkard husband, the roof that let in the rain, the in-laws who demanded money, the abysmal standard of teaching at her three children's schools. Her job paid just enough to feed and clothe herself and her family. When the price of cooking gas and vegetables rose, she quickly felt the pinch.

In recent months, though, things had begun looking up and Uma was wearing a smile on her face.

Today was no exception.

"I take it your shares are doing well?" said Rumpi in Hindi as she changed into a clean but worn sleeveless smock.

"Bharti Airtel is up twenty rupees on last week!" she replied.

For weeks now, Rumpi had been hearing about the beautician's success playing the stock market. Initially, Uma had invested half her savings, roughly 10,000 rupees, in a company called InfoSoft. Only a week or so later, the company had been bought by an American firm and her shares had trebled in value. The beautician had cashed in her 20,000-rupee profit and used it to buy shares in an Indian gas company named—appropriately enough—India Gas. Less than a month later, it was awarded a contract by the Delhi government to lay domestic pipelines throughout the city. Within hours, Uma's shares were worth 35 percent more than she had paid for them.

Rumpi suspected that the beautician was getting tips from one of her clients. But Uma claimed to have made her canny investment decisions based on what the experts were saying on the TV business channels.

"So, any more good tips for me?" asked Rumpi, genuinely interested, given Uma's success.

"Yesterday, madam, I bought two-thousand-worth shares in Dr. Reddy's Laboratories. It's a very strong company. But whatever you do, don't buy any shares in InfoSoft!"

"Why?"

"You didn't see on the news what happened, madam? Two weeks back, the shares plunged seventy percent."

"How much did you lose?" asked Rumpi, suddenly concerned.

In the past, she had cautioned Uma to bank her profit in a savings account.

"A few thousand, madam. But I'm still ahead. I took your advice and put fifteen thousand in the bank."

The beautician emptied a tin full of sticky honey-colored sugaring wax into a small electric warmer.

"So you heard about the robbery?" asked Rumpi, knowing full well that it would have been the main topic of conversation in the beauty parlor since yesterday afternoon.

"Mrs. Devi was here earlier and told me all about it," said Uma breathlessly. "It must have been frightening!"

"Yes, it was. The head dacoit had a gun. He was very threatening."

"I hear they arrested the servants—and some physical trainer called Babbi from a local gym? The police think he masterminded the robbery."

Rumpi scoffed.

"You don't think it was him, madam?"

"Well, I suppose it's possible," she answered, remembering that Mummy had warned her not to tell any of the beauticians about her suspicions. "Perhaps the police know something we don't."

Rumpi sighed. "I just hope they get the cash back," she said. "Not all of us are made of money. Not like Mrs. Azmat. Her husband is a dentist from what I understand. His practice must be flourishing. Recently he took her on a luxury cruise of the Great Lakes. I saw the photographs. It must have cost a packet."

"Great Lakes, madam?"

"In Canada."

"Oh yes, that's where my cousin lives," said Uma as she spread wax on Rumpi's left leg. "She says it's a very friendly place. Lots of Indians."

Rumpi steered the conversation back on track: "Mrs. Jain is never short of money either."

"Of course not," interjected Uma. "Her husband is a high court judge. I hear he owns properties all over Delhi and a beach house in Goa as well."

After a short interruption by the tea boy, who knocked on the door asking for empty glasses and was given short shrift by the beautician, Rumpi said: "Poor Mrs. Bansal. She was very upset. She never seems to have much money."

"Ha! That one's cheaper than a Marwari!" sneered Uma. "She never tips me more than five rupees. *And* she has not paid her bill."

"Really?" Rumpi said, all innocence. "How much is it?"

"Four thousand plus. Arti Madam was talking about it only yesterday—saying how embarrassing it's getting. Mrs. Bansal keeps saying she's going to settle up but never does."

"I wonder what the problem is?"

By now Uma was finishing Rumpi's right leg, expertly spreading the warm wax with a butter knife and then whipping it off with muslin strips. She lowered her voice and said: "Last time she was here I heard her talking on the phone. Sounds like her husband is in some kind of trouble."

"Any idea what kind?"

"Where men are concerned, it's not hard to guess."

Back in the car, Rumpi told Mummy about Mrs. Bansal's unpaid bill.

"Arti was telling she paid the total amount this morning, only," said Mummy, who had got chatting with the proprietor while having her treatments in another private room.

"It could be a coincidence," suggested Rumpi, still holding out hope for another explanation for the crime.

"Assumption should not be made," agreed Mummy. "But Mrs. Bansal is suspect nonetheless."

Puri's mother then outlined what else she had learned. Arti had told her that Mrs. Devi, another member of the kitty party, was "doing hanky-panky with some toy boy."

"Anita? But she's twice my size!"

"Seems she and he meet thrice weekly."

Rumpi sat in stunned silence for a while and then said: "I suppose it just goes to show that you never really know some people. But I can't see her masterminding a robbery, Mummy-ji. Her husband's swimming in money."

None of the other women seemed to be having any kind of financial or marital difficulties.

"So what's the next step, Mummy-ji?" asked Rumpi, looking at her watch. It was nearly six o'clock, time for her to return home and start preparing the evening meals for herself, Jaiya and Chubby, who had called earlier to say that he was on the way back from Haridwar.

"Some background checking is required."

"Of Mrs. Bansal? What did you have in mind?"

"We'll do interrogation of servants. These types see and hear everything that is going on, na?"

Twelve

Inspector Singh was not in the best of moods. When his aloo paranthas were placed in front of him, he scowled at the plate and growled, "Where's the aachar?"

The Gymkhana Club waiters, a slothful bunch, had long since grown immune to the complaints of the club's members, many of whom were professional whingers. Puri had often watched people yell at them with the contempt and abrasiveness of drill sergeants, to little or no effect. In Singh, though, they had met their match. The combination of his size, police uniform and menacing snarl had them flapping around like penguins.

In double time, a bowl full of mango pickle was fetched and placed on the table before him. The inspector did not look up or say thank you, but with an ill-disposed murmur ripped off a piece of parantha, scooped up a large lump of aachar, dunked it in his curd and then crammed the food into his mouth. As he began to chew, apparently satisfied, the waiters drew a collective sigh of relief, keeping a wary eye on him from behind their serving station.

Puri, who had arrived home from Haridwar late Thursday night and then set off at seven this morning for what had been billed by the inspector as an urgent meeting, was sitting across from his guest at a table in the Gym's breakfast room.

He could tell that Singh had not enjoyed a good night's sleep. The NCR had been hit by three hours of load shedding, and the inspector, who lived in modest housing in Mustafabad, northeast Delhi, didn't have a backup inverter to run his ceiling fans.

Such systems did not come cheap. The police wallah, who had six mouths to feed, couldn't afford one on his salary and wasn't prepared to extort the price of one from the public. His ill temper, then, was a credit to him.

"I tried calling you yesterday but seems you were out of station?" he said, his mouth half full.

"Some family business was there," lied Puri, who was keeping his visit to Haridwar, and the fact that he had planted an undercover operative inside the ashram, strictly under wraps.

The detective quickly changed the subject.

"Since last we met I'd a run-in with a cricket bat," said Puri, who went on to describe how he had been ambushed in Dr. Jha's office.

"Sir, I hope you weren't breaking and entering again," said Singh reproachfully. He took a dim view of some of Puri's methods.

"Nothing of the sort. The side door was perfectly open, actually. Just I surprised some intruder engaged in going through Dr. Jha's files. How he got the better of me remains a mystery. My reflexes are like lightning."

The faintest hint of a smile flickered across Singh's face as he took another bite of his parantha and then asked: "Did you see who did it?"

For a moment, Puri seemed lost for words.

"My memory of events is something of a fog," he said. "It is like I had a dream but certain details are missing. I remember someone familiar to me saying something. Just I cannot put my finger on who or what."

"I'm sure it will come back to you, sir," said Singh helpfully. His breakfast and salty tea seemed to be improving his temperament.

"Just I hope it is not weeks or months. So frustrating it is."

A waiter arrived bearing a plate of idlis arranged on a banana leaf and placed it in front of Puri. He immediately cut off a portion of one of the rice patties, drowned it in coconut chutney and some spicy sambar and devoured it.

"So tell me. What is so urgent I had to come into town so early, Inspector?"

Singh, who had finished his food, wiped his hands on his napkin and placed it on the table. "Sir, the chief knows you're investigating the Jha case," he said with solemnity.

Puri shrugged. "That is hardly a surprise, no? Delhi is like a village with women gossiping round the water pump. Eventually everyone gets to know everyone else's business." He took another bite of his food.

"He knows I took you to the murder scene and he's furious. He ordered me to meet you this morning and warn you off."

"Then I will consider myself warned," said Puri with a grin.

Singh sipped his tea. "But tell me, sir—strictly between us. Have you made any progress?"

"Come now, Inspector, you know I don't have the habit of sharing my theories until they are tried and tested," answered Puri. The truth was, though, that he still had little to go on—just a few scraps of information and a hunch or two.

Not that Puri was worried. Not especially. He had solved

many a case in the past with less evidence available to him at this stage in the investigation. In India, perhaps more than anywhere else in the world, the methodology of undercover intelligence gathering established by Chanakya nearly two and a half millennia ago was often the only surefire way of solving a mystery. Patience was required.

"I know, sir, but is it really necessary to keep me completely in the dark?" asked Singh. "We're on the same side after all. I feel useless—impotent."

"You had the same frustrations on the 'Pickles' Sansi case. And look how that turned out."

Puri was referring to his capture eight months ago of the leader of the notorious Sansi clan, who had been wanted on murder and racketeering charges.

The official version was that Singh had single-handedly tracked him down. In fact, Flush had cloned the mobile phone signature of Pickles's mistress, an exotic dancer known as Lovely. Using SMS text messages, the detective had then lured the elusive but unsuspecting don to a midnight dalliance at the Raj Palace. Pickles had arrived at the five-star hotel expecting to enjoy, in the words of one of the detective's saucy missives, "the full thali, big boy!" Instead, he had found himself clapped in handcuffs.

Given the Sansi clan's fearsome reputation, Puri had not wanted his name associated with the case and allowed the inspector to take all the glory. The coup had helped greatly to further Singh's career.

"So tell me," said the detective as he finished his meal and pushed away his plate. "That 'ash' found at the scene? You're in receipt of the lab report?"

"It turned out to be ground charcoal," answered Singh.

If this information surprised or excited Puri, he didn't show it.

"And what about your laughing gas theory? Any progress?"

"Nitrous oxide—that's its proper, scientific name," answered Singh. "It's easy to get hold of. Doctors, dentists, all kinds of food manufacturers use it. One other thing. I talked with a chemist friend of mine and he told me the term 'laughing gas' is misleading. It doesn't make people burst out laughing automatically. But it does make them feel extremely happy. And under its influence people will *sometimes* get the giggles."

"That could explain why Shivraj Sharma was the only one not to do laughter and feel like he could not move," murmured Puri to himself.

"Oh, and I almost forgot," added Singh quickly. "People under the influence of nitrous oxide are generally susceptible to suggestion."

"Very good work, Inspector!" declared Puri before making a note of this.

Singh was struck for a brief moment by a sense of accomplishment. But this quickly passed.

While Puri was breakfasting at the Gym, a couple of Tubelight's boys were keeping vigil across the street from Professor Pandey's house in West Shalimar Bagh.

Shashi and Zia were disguised as ditchdigger wallahs, a cover they often adopted because of its simplicity and the anonymity it provided. A couple of picks and shovels and some especially dirty clothes were all that were required for props. The persona was uncomplicated, too: looking downtrodden and bored, they stared in awe at fancy cars passing by and adopted heavy Bihari accents, using phrases like "Kaisan bha?" and "Jai Ram ji ki."

The sight of such wretched, pitifully paid laborers toiling on construction sites was common across the city, and residents paid them little heed. Delhiites had also become inured to their streets and pavements being constantly dug up. There was not a neighborhood, sector or colony where new gas lines, telecommunications cables, water mains and sewage pipes were not being laid. Trenches with corresponding piles of dirt running alongside them were as common as they had once been on the Western Front, and there was no point complaining about it. As everyone knew, Delhi's three municipal corporations were utterly corrupt, and the police were in the pay of contractors who worked without proper licenses and in violation of basic safety standards. Even the wealthiest of Delhi's residents had learned to save their breath and ink.

Indeed, only one of Professor Pandey's neighbors had raised an objection when, at six o'clock yesterday morning, Shashi and Zia had started digging up the pavement outside his house. Major Randhawa—according to the brass plaque on the gatepost, formerly of the Rajput Regiment, Indian Army—had come charging out into the street in a sleeveless vest and, without so much as a "good morning" or "sorry to bother you," started cursing Tubelight's operatives as if they were a couple of street dogs. He'd also seen fit to make repeated, unflattering remarks about their mothers and sisters.

In response, Shashi and Zia had struck the right balance of crushed subservience and gormlessness, and muttered something about a water-pressure gauge and working for a local contractor.

This had prompted Major Randhawa to refer unfavorably to the contractor's mother and daughters.

"After I get hold of him he'll not father any more children!" he'd shouted.

Pretending to be illiterate, Shashi had shown the gentleman a mobile number written down on a grimy piece of paper and told him that it belonged to their employer.

Grabbing it from him, Major Randhawa had stormed back inside his house to call the contractor—and, presumably, threaten him with a swift and brutal castration.

Shashi and Zia had not heard another peep out of him after that and, within a couple of hours, dug themselves a nice, sizable hole.

They had spent the rest of yesterday tailing Pandey, who had left at ten o'clock in a car driven by his elderly chauffeur. He had reached Delhi University thirty minutes later, remained there all day, gone and done some shopping and returned home at six.

Another of Tubelight's boys had taken the overnight shift, which had passed without incident. Then at six this morning, Shashi and Zia had returned, refreshed and filthy again, for another day on the job.

By now, it was almost eight.

There was still no sign of Major Randhawa. But that was hardly surprising given that Tubelight, the contractor, had threatened to cut off his water, electricity and phone lines if he didn't simmer down.

As for Professor Pandey, he had been up for an hour and was engaged in his ablutions. The sounds of him clearing his throat and exhaling through his nostrils, which were amplified by the tiled walls of his small bathroom, could be heard clearly out in the street.

Shashi and Zia carried on shoveling some dirt, smoking bidis and discussing the physical assets of their favorite Bollywood actresses.

"Katrina Kaif is as thin as a grasshopper," said Shashi as

they kept a surreptitious eye on the house across the way. "No meat on the bones, brother. For me it is Vidya Balan. Have you seen those eyes? Wah!"

He broke into a rendition of "Tu Cheez Badi Hai Mast Mast."

From the Gym, Puri drove to Basant Lane, where he rendezvoused with Tubelight at nine o'clock.

The operative had been busy finding out all he could about Professor Pandey and archaeologist Shivraj Sharma—"putting them under the scanner," in the detective's parlance. Servants, drivers, neighbors and street sweepers had been consulted and bribed for gossip and information.

He had the following to report:

"Sharma's wife died two years back in a car accident. Son was also injured. In a wheelchair, lives at home. Sharma's a strict Brahmin: servants aren't allowed in the kitchen. He fired one last month for drinking from one of his glasses. A Brahmin cook prepares the meals. Sharma's very religious. A long-standing VHP member." VHP stood for Vishwa Hindu Parishad, a right-wing organization that sought to turn India into a solely Hindu nation.

"And Pandey?" asked Puri.

"Nothing unusual, Boss. Eccentric—obviously. Always jolly. Never married. Lived with his mummy until she died last year. One thing: his servants—cook, cleaner, driver—all left last week. No one knows why. His current driver is a replacement."

They discussed plans for breaking into Professor Pandey's house to have a look around, but decided they needed a clearer picture of his schedule first.

"Tell your boys to keep him in their sights," instructed

the detective. "This laughing professor is involved somehow. Of that much I am certain."

Tubelight's phone rang. It was Shashi, reporting that Pandey had left the house and was on his way to the Garden of Five Senses, where he was due to hold his Laughter Memorial for Dr. Jha.

"While he is so occupied, I will take a look round his office at Delhi University. See what all I can turn up," said the detective.

Puri drove through Civil Lines, where the British East India Company stationed its army before the First War of Independence of 1857, to Delhi University. He passed the British Viceregal Lodge Estate with its whitewashed pillars and rose garden, now home to the Faculty of Science, and soon reached the School of Electrical Engineering.

A gaggle of male and female students milled around outside, joking and flirting. The detective made his way up the steps of the building, catching strains of Hindi rap playing on a mobile phone and snippets of current Delhi jargon—"What's the funda, dude?" "He's one of those art frat types!" "Nice half-pants!"

Inside, the main corridor was empty save for a couple of students walking toward him. He asked them for Professor Pandey's office and was directed to the third door on the right.

While he waited for the corridor to empty, he read the notices pinned to the board. One announced the next topic of discussion at the debating society—"Can India afford to be an ally of the U.S.?"; another appealed for the "person or persons who removed the human skeleton from the biology lab to return it forthwith."

The detective, whose key chain contained a pick and a set of tension wrenches, had little trouble opening the lock to Professor Pandey's office.

The room was small but orderly, the shelves crowded with reference books and binders, the in-tray brimming with uncorrected exam papers. Puri opened drawers, searched the filing cabinet and sifted through the rubbish bin.

He then spent a few minutes reading Pandey's notes for an upcoming lecture on signal processing.

"Signals can be either analog, in which case the signal varies continuously according to the information, or digital, in which case the signal varies according to a series of discrete values representing the information. For analog signals, signal processing may involve the amplification and filtering of audio signals for audio equipment or the modulation and demodulation of signals for telecommunications. For digital signals . . ."

The detective could feel his eyes glazing over and placed the notes back where he had found them. He sat back in Pandey's chair and looked up at the photographs on the wall. One had been taken at an early morning Laughing Club session. The professor was standing with head tilted back, hands on hips and stomach pushed out.

Puri cast his eyes over the other pictures: parents, picnics, young nephews looking wide-eyed at the camera.

At the top of the wall hung an old black-and-white picture of nine men standing in front of an Indian satellite. There was a small brass plaque attached to the bottom of the frame. It read: DEPARTMENT OF TELECOMMUNICATIONS, INSAT 1A, 1981.

Puri took it down to get a closer look. A younger Professor Pandey stood near the middle of the group.

The detective recognized the man standing next to him as well. It was Dr. Suresh Jha.

The two men had known each other for much longer than two years.

"Why Pandey told me otherwise?" murmured Puri to himself.

Thirteen

Facecream didn't wake until long after it was light. She guessed it must have been around nine. Feeling groggy and dull-headed, she lay on the bedroll in the dormitory where she was staying and went over the bizarre events of yesterday in her mind.

She remembered entering the darshan hall along with Puri and Mrs. Duggal and being served a cup of papaya juice by one of the senior devotees. It seemed to her that he had handed her one from the back of the tray, whereas the others had chosen their own.

She'd sat down in front of the stage and Maharaj Swami had entered and been hailed by his adoring followers.

It had been about then that Facecream had started to feel woozy.

At first she'd put it down to all the incense smoke and the heat and noise. But soon her legs had started to feel heavy and her senses had become strangely heightened. The background din of devotional singing and chanting had faded and Maharaj Swami's words had boomed in her ears. One minute she'd felt chilled to the bone; the next, the temperature in the darshan hall had seemed unbearably hot.

Everything around her with bright colors—the canary yellow kurta of the woman in front of her, the saffron banners hanging on either side of the stage—had started to bleed and pulsate.

She'd realized with alarm that the papaya juice had been laced with some form of hallucinogen. But her fear had quickly given way to a pleasant weightlessness, a sense of blissful detachment. She'd imagined herself six years old again, playing in the front room of her grandfather's big house in Kathmandu with her old Kumari doll.

Up on the stage, the circle of lights behind Maharaj Swami's head had begun to spin around faster and faster, until they seemed almost liquid. She'd felt suddenly overcome with emotion, unable to control the tears that had streamed down her face or the impulse to laugh out loud.

But gradually the effects of the hallucinogen had started to wear off. And as Facecream had regained control of her faculties, she'd had the presence of mind to turn events to her advantage.

Her dramatic exclamations and subsequent fainting had fooled even Puri, who had given her a couple of stinging slaps and called for a glass of water.

A crowd had gathered, straining, peering, and then Facecream had started babbling excitedly about how "a kind of awesome celestial light" had "like, flooded out of Swamiji" and filled her with "such warmth and belonging."

"I could feel this energy pulsing through me. It was like I was actually part of the cosmos."

Maharaj Swami had invited her up onstage, where he had "interpreted" her vision for his congregation.

"Queenie has been given a taste of the Universal Nectar," he'd announced. "Through this experience she will come to understand her true potential and comprehend the ultimate reality. Her purpose, like all of your purposes, is to achieve moshka, unity with God.

"God is like the ocean," he'd continued. "But like raindrops taken up by clouds, you have become separated from Him. For so long you have drifted through the sky. Sometimes feeling light, other times dark and angry. But always aimless, with no purpose. Never happy. Now it is time to complete your journey. It is a long, difficult one with many obstacles. You must be prepared to go through transitions and purify yourself like water falling on the mountain and passing through rock. Those who are lazy and become distracted by worldly things will get trapped in stagnant pools deep beneath the earth. Those who overcome their own egos will join tributaries and eventually great rivers. This way leads back to the all-embracing Ocean where you will experience everlasting love."

"I had, like, no idea, Swami-ji!" Facecream had gushed. "Thank you! Thank you so much. You've opened my eyes!"

The devotional singing and chanting had struck up again. And then Maharaj Swami had made a final pronouncement before bringing the darshan to an end.

"From this day forth," he'd declared, "you will be known as Mukti. It means 'salvation.'"

Queenie had been reborn.

Facecream took a shower and changed into the white kurta and sarong that were now an integral part of her new identity as a dedicated, impressionable disciple. She forwent makeup, applied a red bindi to her forehead and pulled her long hair back into a discreet ponytail. The only reminder of the old Queenie—iPods, mobile phones and Jimmy Choos being banned in the ashram—was her Raspberry Rapture nail varnish.

She knew from the induction briefing she had been given yesterday evening that her roommates—all young Indian women—were attending the yoga and meditation sessions held every morning. Facecream decided to go and walk around the grounds in order to get a better lay of the land. But she had forgotten that silence was observed throughout the ashram until ten o'clock. And as she greeted some of her fellow devotees on the stairs with a "namashkar," they all put their index fingers to their lips and frowned.

Making her way out through the front doors of the residence hall, stunned momentarily by the bright sunshine and the sticky heat, she came face-to-face with one of her roommates. A bossy young woman, she gave Facecream a disapproving look, took her by the hand and led her over to the gazebo.

There, amidst pin-drop silence, some two hundred devotees sat meditating.

Facecream found a place at the back, seated herself on one of the rush mats and closed her eyes.

Thirty minutes of meditation was part of her usual daily constitution, and after all the clamor of yesterday, she welcomed the opportunity to declutter and refresh her mind.

She could not help but wonder, though, whether Bossy had been standing outside the residence hall waiting for her.

After the session was over, the devotees all made their way to the food hall, which was actually a big tent, and Facecream joined her roommates for a midmorning snack of curd mixed with chopped papaya, apple, pomegranate and a little spicy masala.

Conversation now being permitted, they all chatted away, introducing one another and telling their individual stories, and the mechanics of the group soon became clear.

By far the most assertive personality was Bossy, who was from Mumbai and had been living at the ashram for more than a year. Anorexic and neurotic, she spoke about Maharaj Swami as if no one else understood him as well as she did.

"You're not the only one to have been given a vision," she told Facecream. "Others have been chosen, including myself and Damayanti." She was referring to another member of the group, a nervous, pretty twenty-five-year-old. "Swami-ji moves in mysterious ways. At times he will provoke a change in someone by giving them a tiny glimpse of the ultimate reality so that others can observe their reaction and behavior and witness the all-dominating ego at work. Not everything is always as it seems."

Facecream thought it wise to listen attentively to what she had to say, at least for now, and occasionally mouthed platitudes like "Wow, that's so interesting!"

But no one else could get a word in edgewise and everyone seemed relieved when Bossy stood to go. As the spokesperson for Maharaj Swami's Committee for Poverty Reduction, she had important work to attend to.

"Come," Bossy told another of the roommates, a twenty-two-year-old. "You've got yoga in ten minutes. You shouldn't be late."

The younger woman hadn't finished her breakfast but obediently put down her bowl and said: "You're right, didi, I should get going," and the two left together.

The three remaining girls were Priyanka, Meghna and Damayanti.

Although not as assertive as Bossy, they, too, spoke of little else but Maharaj Swami and his teachings and their own spiritual journeys.

"I searched for so long for a true master," said Meghna, a southerner from Mangalore. "I tried them all: Sai, Sadhguru,

Amma, Sri Sri. So many. Unlike the others, Swami-ji wasn't so distant or boring. When I met him for the first time it was like I got an electric shock. I swear my hair stood on end. I felt totally inconsequential, this tiny speck in the universe, and yet I knew that God had brought me to his true representative."

Priyanka claimed that as a child her father had often beat her. "Then a kindly man started appearing in my dreams," she said. "I didn't know it was Swami-ji because I didn't recognize him. He told me that he would protect me and that my father was in pain and that I should forgive him. Then one day I saw a picture of Swami-ji in a magazine and I recognized him and so I came here. Later on, I persuaded my father to join me, and Swami-ji agreed to see him. He had a private audience. Apparently before Swami-ji said one word, Papa broke down in tears. Swami-ji helped him get rid of all of his negative energy and anger. Nowadays he's a completely changed person."

"Some people are saying, like, Swami-ji called on the goddess Kali to kill that guy, you know that old man in Delhi who was preaching against him. You think that's true?" asked Facecream.

"Nothing would surprise me. He's very powerful," answered Priyanka.

"No way! Swami-ji would never hurt anyone," said Meghna.

Damayanti, whose parents were also both devotees and along with their daughter often stayed in the ashram for weeks on end, had said little thus far. But now in a quiet voice she asked Facecream what had brought her to the ashram.

"It wasn't my choice," she answered. "This is, like, the last place I thought I wanted to be. My pa made me come. But now I'm really glad he did. I mean, I've never experienced anything like it. It's so awesome. It makes me feel so, like, in touch with myself, you know?"

"There is a shloka in the Bhagavad Gita that says, 'The guru appears when the disciple is ready,'" said Priyanka.

"You're very lucky. Few are blessed with so much attention as Swami-ji bestowed upon you," said Meghna with a smile that let slip a hidden jealousy.

Priyanka led Facecream over to the Abode of Health, the two-hundred-bed hospital Maharaj Swami had constructed with donations from various Indian billionaires, including the reclusive "Scooter Raja," R. K. Roy, whose company Roy Motors controlled 64 percent of India's motorbike business.

The facade of the hospital was built of pink Dholpur stone with life-size elephants holding up the arch of the entrance. Inside, everything was shiny and new and the departments were all equipped with the latest state-of-the-art diagnostic machines, like MRIs and ultrasound cardiology systems. But no surgery was available; all existing conditions were treated "naturally."

On their way to the walk-in clinic, where Facecream was due to undergo a health check, they passed a laboratory sealed behind three-inch-thick glass panels, where technicians in white coats and face masks peered into microscopes and petri dishes.

"Western drug companies have sent their spies here to try to discover Swami-ji's secrets," said Priyanka, pointing out the security cameras in the corridor outside the laboratory.

Facecream wanted to say: "Surely if Maharaj Swami is at one with the universe and knows and sees everything, there's no need for cameras!" But she held her tongue, smiled innocently and said, "This place is awesome. Can anyone get, like, treatment here?"

"People come from all over India with every kind of complaint. And if you can't afford to pay, then it's all free."

"That's amazing!"

"That is Swami-ji's way. He is here to help others. He builds wells, irrigation systems, schools. When the tsunami happened, he helped hundreds of fishermen rebuild their lives."

At the clinic, a pleasant Ayurvedic lady doctor explained that all devotees coming to stay at the ashram underwent a mandatory examination.

"For this we will check all your marma points," she explained. "There are one hundred and seven in all, and by examining them we can see what's ailing you."

"But I feel, like, absolutely fine," protested Facecream.

"I'm sure," replied the doctor with a smile, "but many of us are suffering from all kinds of conditions and don't realize it. We are here to help. Now kindly undress and put on that smock hanging on the hook."

"Undress? Like, get naked? No thanks."

"Come now, there's nothing to be afraid of. You can go behind that screen if you'd prefer."

Facecream went silent. She genuinely didn't want to have to undress. If she did, then the doctor would see the scars on her back. And then there would be questions—questions that pertained to her past that she had no intention of answering. Not for anyone.

"Is anything wrong?"

Puri's operative tried to think of an excuse for not going through with the examination, but for once she faltered. "It's just that . . ."

"Really, there's nothing to worry about," interrupted the doctor. "Now, be a good girl and do as I say. There are others waiting after you."

Facecream slowly took off her clothes, put on the smock and then lay on the examination table.

"There we are. This won't take long."

The doctor poked and prodded and made notes on a clipboard. After a few minutes, she asked her patient to turn onto her front. Facecream complied, readying herself with a story about having fallen into a thorn patch at the age of seven. Even after all these years, the scars were prominent; there were four of them, and they ran in parallel lines from her right shoulder down to her left hip. The doctor said nothing about them.

"See, that wasn't so painful, was it?" she said cheerily at the end of the examination.

Next, blood, urine and saliva samples were taken, and then Facecream was given a questionnaire to fill out. It included 150 multiple-choice questions, mostly pertaining to her relations with others and her perception of herself: "Would you say you are (a) happy; (b) sad; (c) miserable; (d) depressed?"

Facecream found herself answering honestly, curious to know how she would score. But when she returned the completed questionnaire, the doctor gave it only a cursory glance before laying it on her desk and then prescribing a number of Maharaj Swami–branded Ayurvedic "medicines" to help cleanse her system of "bile and destructive toxins and help energy flow."

"What about the test? When do I find out how I scored?"

"That's not how it works—it's not like a school examination," answered the doctor kindly. "Be patient. Swami-ji will answer all your questions in time."

After the appointment, Facecream found herself unchaperoned and, despite the heat, went for a walk around the grounds. Near the hospital, she came across the outlet for a ventilation shaft half hidden behind some bushes. There was another, identical one near the darshan hall, and yet another on the far side of the residence hall. This suggested there was a network of rooms or passages underground. But where were the access points?

Before she could investigate any further, Bossy appeared and told her everyone was gathering again at the gazebo.

The rest of Facecream's morning was spent doing yoga and repeating a mantra from the Brihadaranyaka Upanishad.

"It is designed to divert the mind from basic instinctual desires or material inclinations by focusing on a spiritual idea, such as 'I am a manifestation of divine consciousness,'" explained the senior devotee who led the session.

> Om Asato ma sat gamaya
> Tamaso ma jyotir gamaya
> Mrtyorma amrtam gamaya
> Om shanti shanti shanti
> (From ignorance, lead me to truth;
> From darkness, lead me to light;
> From death, lead me to immortality
> Om peace, peace, peace)

At lunch, Facecream helped serve the long line of poor and needy who flocked to the ashram every day for a free meal. Her task was to ladle yellow daal onto hundreds of plates.

After she herself had eaten, she decided to try to find the spot on the river where Manika Gill had supposedly killed herself.

When no one was looking, she slipped out the back of the tent and made her way toward the rear of the grounds where there were plenty of shade trees growing. It was here that she came across Damayanti sitting on her own on a bench.

"I'm going down to the river. Come for a walk," said Facecream.

The devotee hesitated. "I . . . I don't know."

"But I want to see the river and I don't know the way," she pleaded.

"I . . . I can't."

"Sure you can. Come on, it will be fun."

"What about the others?"

"Let's just go, the two of us," said Facecream, making it sound like an exciting, radical idea.

Damayanti glanced around her. "We'd better be quick," she said, and the two managed to slip away together.

A gate at the back of the grounds led to a well-worn path that wound beneath a canopy of Rudraksha trees along a sheer cliff thirty feet above the Ganges.

The river was still in its infancy here, untainted by the corrupting pollutants awaiting it along its fifteen-hundred-mile journey across the baking Indo-Gangetic plain, home to more than one-seventh of all humanity. Its virginal waters crashed and plunged over boulders, swirled around fallen tree trunks and spat at the rocks strewn along its banks.

Facecream and Damayanti passed brightly feathered kingfishers and a line of village women and girls who smelt of smoke and earth and carried bundles of kindling balanced on their heads. The locals stared at them, whispering and giggling amongst themselves, before heading higher up into the woods.

Soon the valley widened and a sandy beach appeared below them on the near bank, golden in the sunshine. A steep trail led down to it. Facecream suggested they go for a swim. But Damayanti looked suddenly terrified.

"What's wrong?"

"I don't want to go down there. Can we go back?"

"Of course we can. But tell me what's wrong."

"It's nothing. I just don't like it here."

Facecream feigned an epiphany. "This wasn't where that girl . . . she drowned, didn't she? God, that was terrible. I read about it in the papers." Facecream realized that anyone remembering the old Queenie would have found this highly improbable—unless of course the news had found its way into the Indian edition of *Hello!* "I can't remember her name. What was it?"

"Manika," said Damayanti.

"That's right, Manika Gill. She was, like, so young and beautiful. I saw her picture. Did you know her?"

The younger woman nodded.

"Oh God, I'm so sorry. I had no idea. You poor sweetie."

Facecream gave her a tender hug and the young woman began to cry on her shoulder.

"Manika didn't even say good-bye," she sobbed. "I don't understand it. She didn't say anything to anyone."

"When was the last time you saw her?"

"That night. We all went to sleep. But in the morning she was gone."

"You mean she was staying in your—*our*—dormitory?"

"Yes."

"Oh my God! That's so unbelievable. So you must have really known her well. Was she unhappy? I'm just curious, I guess."

Damayanti didn't answer. She appeared conflicted, as if there was something she wanted to say but dared not.

"I really don't want to talk about it," she said.

They walked back up the path for a few minutes and then sat down on a smooth rock listening to the susurrus of the river below. Facecream started tossing little stones over the cliff edge, watching them splash into the water.

"Can I ask you something?" she said after a while. "Have you had lots of visions like the one I had yesterday?"

Damayanti nodded.

"Did Manika have any?"

She nodded again.

"A lot?"

Just then a male voice called out Damayanti's name.

"That's my father," she said with alarm. "I've got to go."

A middle-aged man appeared. He was wearing the garb of a devotee.

"There you are," he said in a kindly yet firm voice. "I've been looking for you. Luckily someone thought they saw you coming down here."

Casting a suspicious look at Facecream, he took his daughter by the hand and led her away.

Facecream returned to the residence hall and found her other roommates preparing to go to Haridwar to watch the evening aarti ceremony. She decided to join them.

Setting off in a local bus and singing devotional songs along the way, they reached the city at dusk. The population was emerging into the streets. Along the narrow, medieval lanes, the sounds of worship spilled out from countless temples. Small petrol generators rumbled. Beggars with amputated limbs wailed for alms and showed off their deformities to frightening effect. Hardware merchants sat amidst stacks of stainless steel tiffins, baltis and enormous cooking pots that looked like imports from Brobdingnag in *Gulliver's Travels*.

Facecream's group wove through the crowd, past holy cows, open sewers and dozens of stalls selling tacky religious memorabilia like om key rings, until they reached the Har ki Pauri ghat. Thousands had already gathered at the water's edge—ordinary men and women who had traveled to the city to offer prayers of thanks to the river goddess Ganga; the odd bedraggled tourist; members of sects and cults, each in their own distinct outfit and occupying blocks of the steps like football fans in team stripes.

As darkness fell, diyas were lit and cast onto the water, floating off down the river—a miniature armada. Bells and gongs clattered. Speakers blared "Ganga Mantra." Temple priests standing at the edge of the western bank lit oil lamps, circling them in the air, casting glimmering orange reflections in the water.

Sitting there, watching this timeless, bewitching spectacle, Facecream could understand the attraction life at the ashram held for her roommates. The camaraderie, the sense of a shared purpose, was no different here than it had been in the Maoist camps. But as she had learned to her cost in Nepal, such idealism was easily preyed upon.

She found herself wondering about Maharaj Swami—what kind of man was he really?

The nineteen-year-old Facecream, the one who had fled home to join the glorious Maoist cause, might well have perceived him as a Robin Hood type, robbing the rich to help the poor. But she had learned that such men were not motivated by generosity. Building wells, helping tsunami victims—that was all done to impress others, to build a saintly reputation. Power was the only thing that motivated such men. They were intoxicated by it.

Had Swami-ji come to believe his own lie?

Facecream hoped to get a better measure of him tomorrow evening. Before she had set out for Haridwar, word had been sent that she was to be given a private audience.

Fourteen

It was Saturday morning and Puri was at home. His daughter Jaiya's godh bharai baby shower was due to start at eleven and everyone in the house was busy preparing for the festivities.

Rumpi seemed to be everywhere at once: in the kitchen overseeing the preparation of pistachio barfi and sweetened saffron milk; in the sitting room putting up decorations; and upstairs letting out Jaiya's sari blouse so that it would accommodate her new proportions.

From the sanctuary of the rooftop where he was lying low, Puri could hear his wife giving orders. It was like listening to the head chef of a restaurant.

"Malika! Don't overcook the khoya again!"

"Monika . . . Go buy one K-G of aloo . . . Then borrow some! Ask Deepak Madam. Hurry!"

"Sweetu! What are you doing? Stop being a fool and blow up the balloons properly . . . well, blow harder!"

Puri knew it was only a question of time before he was put to work himself. No excuse would be brooked: not a pressing clue that needed immediate investigation, not even a dead client.

First, though, he hoped to finish his tea and open his post.

He recognized one of the envelopes instantly. It was postmarked London: the latest catalogue from Bates Gentlemen's Hatter in Piccadilly, suppliers of all his Sandown caps. There was another from the electricity company with whom he was in an ongoing dispute over his bill. Who in Delhi wasn't? There was a circular from the Rotary Club as well.

"HIP HIP HIP HURRAY!" it read. "Rotarians of Delhi South celebrate their status as the PLATINUM CLUB OF THE ROTARY INTERNATIONAL DIST. 301. Cheers, cheers, cheers."

It included pictures taken during the gala "installation ceremony" of the incoming president and noted that "an array of Rotary District officials were present for the occasion who by their presence boosted our morale."

The circular also included an update on all the community work done by the club, of which Puri and Rumpi were active members.

His mobile rang.

"Good morning. Mr. Vishwas Puri?"

No one ever called him Vishwas, the full version of his first name, apart from salespeople. Puri had developed a deep hatred of such types. They were like a plague of leeches or locusts (or any other number of other slippery, creepy, crawly, sucking creatures that he could think of), harassing people at all hours of the day and night with offers of phone usage plans, bank loans, credit cards. Some idiot had even called him recently to ask if he was interested in buying a yacht.

"Don't call me ever!" barked Puri, anticipating another sales pitch, and angrily hung up.

A few seconds later, the phone rang again. It was the same voice. "Sir, the line got disconnect. I'm calling from—"

"Listen, bloody bastard. Why you're calling me so early, huh? Don't you know decency?"

"Sir, I'm happy to report you've—"

"Khotay da puthar! Son of a donkey!" he swore in Punjabi. "Ik thapar mar key tey moonh torr dan ga! I will break your face with one slap!"

"Sir, no need for anger. See, just I'll explain, sir. You've been preapproved for—"

The detective hung up again.

Not ten seconds elapsed before the phone rang for a third time.

"Saala maaderchod! Give me your supervisor this instant!"

"Chubby, is that you?"

Puri recognized his elder brother's voice.

"Bhuppi? Sorry, huh. Just getting some bloody sales call. Bastard doesn't understand a straightforward threat when one is made."

"Bhuppi" was how everyone referred to Bhupinder in the family.

"Do what I do, Chubby. Tell them you've got a criminal record. International credit card fraud. Very serious. They'll never call again."

"And what exactly I should tell people selling yachts?"

"Yachts? Like boats? What to do with a yacht in Delhi?"

"That is what I said only."

"And?"

Puri mimicked the sales wallah: "'Please, sir, you don't understand, sir. You can keep the yacht in the sea, sir.' 'Bloody fool,' I said, 'you've noticed any sea round these parts lately?'"

They both enjoyed a good laugh.

Then Bhuppi said: "Chubby, sorry, huh, by chance you can pick up Jassu? I'll be reaching late." Jassu was Bhuppi's wife.

"Most certainly. Any excuse to get away. I should pick up Mummy also, no?"

"Mummy's gone out. Left the house at crack of dawn."

"Where to, exactly?"

"No explanation. Last few days she's been coming and going at all hours."

"Don't tell me. She's doing more investigation, is it?"

Puri reminded him of the strict ban they and their other brother had placed on their mother getting involved with detective work.

"What to do, Chubby? Ever since Papa died, Mummy-ji's a loose cannon. No stopping her. Believe me, I've tried everything. Just be thankful you don't have to listen to her going on about her dreams each and every morning."

Puri hung up and called his mother.

"Mummy-ji, where are you?"

"Chubby? Everything is all right?"

"World-class. You're where, exactly?"

"I'll be reaching shortly, na. Just . . ." Her voice was drowned out by the clanging of temple bells and a pandit's voice chanting over a loudspeaker.

"Mummy-ji? Hello? Hello . . ."

"Chubby? Just I'm at the temple. So crowded it is. Nothing wrong, na?"

"No, Mummy, but—"

"You ate your breakfast, I hope? Tell Rumpi I'll be there soon, not to worry."

And with that, the line went dead.

Mummy was not at the temple. She just happened to be standing close to one while waiting at a bus stand in Pooth Khurd in northeast Delhi.

It was from there that Mrs. Bansal's maidservant, Naveen, took the 012 to work six days a week.

Mummy knew this because she and Rumpi had spent a few hours yesterday reconnoitering the Bansal residence.

They had also discovered that Naveen was a talkative, feisty woman who was less than enamored of her employers. At least that's what the local press wallah had said.

The plan, therefore, was for Mummy to catch the same bus, ingratiate herself with the maidservant and try to find out all she could about Mrs. Bansal's financial situation.

While Mummy waited for Naveen, a succession of battered Blue Line buses tore into the stop, the passengers all rushing for the doors and fighting their way up the steep metal stairs. Mummy began to wonder if her daughter-in-law had not been right after all. Perhaps she should have waited until Monday, when they could have traveled together. Her knees had been "paining" a lot recently and it had been a long time since she had taken one of Delhi's notoriously dangerous killer buses.

Standing there, she was reminded of how privileged she had become, what with her own car to take her around. It was certainly a far cry from the terrible conditions of the refugee train that had brought her and the surviving members of her family to safety from Pakistan in 1947.

By the time Mrs. Bansal's maidservant finally turned up, there were fewer passengers at the stand and she decided to proceed with the plan.

"I want to go to Defence Colony," she said politely in Hindi, hobbling up to the maidservant on a cane that Bhuppi had given her but that she ordinarily refused to use. "Does the bus go from here?"

Naveen, who was short and plump, said that this was indeed the right stop and that she was heading to Defence Colony herself.

"Shukkar-ey! Perhaps we could ride together? I've not been on this route before and I would hate to miss my stop. I'm on my way to a job interview—a wealthy family is in need of an ayah. They want a woman my age to look after the children and teach them proper Hindi."

The maidservant regarded her curiously, as if she didn't altogether believe her story. Mummy went on regardless. "Six months ago my husband died and left me with nothing and now I have no choice but to work," she explained.

"Your children don't look after you, Auntie-ji?"

"They don't have room," she said mournfully with eyes cast down. "Young people are so busy these days."

A bus servicing a different route roared up. One side of its front was crushed from an accident; the bonnet was peeled back like the snarling lip of a wolf.

"Super Bazaar, Sabzi Mandi, Nai Dilli station!" shouted the conductor, banging on the side of the vehicle as hapless passengers already on board stared out of the grubby windows.

"Where are you staying, Auntie-ji?" asked Naveen as the vehicle tore away with clusters of people still standing on the stairs and in the doorways, holding on for dear life.

"I'm staying with my sister. But her husband complains all the time how much it costs to feed me. That's why I'm looking for a live-in position."

The 012 bus pulled into sight.

The two women managed to get on board before it raced off again. They found all the seats occupied.

"Have you no respect?" Naveen scolded a man in the front who was eating a piece of roast corn and failed to give up his seat when he saw Mummy. "You should be ashamed of yourself. Get up this instant!"

Soon they were sitting together and discussing the foibles and failings of Indian men.

"What layabouts they are," said Naveen. "My husband sits around at home every night watching TV while I cook and clean up and look after the kids. Never lifts a finger. The other day he had the cheek to call me fat. Fat! You should see him! His face is like a giant greasy poori."

A mother of three, she lived with her family in one room and shared the toilet down the hall with four other families.

"You're lucky to have a job, so many people are without work," said Mummy.

"Ha! Lucky, am I, Auntie-ji?" she replied with a laugh. "Working six days a week, minimum ten to twelve hours every day, three-thousand-rupees-a-month salary? Our rent alone is fifteen hundred. And everything else is getting more expensive every day. How are we supposed to survive?"

"Three thousand rupees a month is not enough," agreed Mummy.

"And meanwhile, Madam"—she was referring to her employer—"is complaining that things are tight! She has no idea!"

"They're having money problems themselves?"

"Sahib's been facing difficulties the past few months."

"Oh?"

"Yes, he was charged with smuggling."

"How shocking! Was it diamonds or something?"

"Nothing like that. Actually he sells . . . hmm . . . you know that ink inside those machines that make photocopies? Turns out he's been importing it into the country disguised as something else . . . something used for making tires, which can be imported duty free. Anyhow the customs people finally got wise and seized his shipment."

"Is he out of business?"

"Nothing of the sort, Auntie-ji. He paid a big bribe and got the shipment released. Now everything is back to normal. The night before last he was out celebrating. He didn't get up until twelve yesterday. But then there's nothing new about that."

"Perhaps you should ask for a salary increase?"

Naveen laughed out loud. "Not a chance, Auntie-ji. If anything, Madam will try to reduce my salary. Then she'll go and buy herself more jewelry. She hoards it like a cowwah. You wouldn't believe how much she has hidden away. Several crores' worth. She'll never starve, that one, that's for sure . . ."

Her mission complete, Mummy got off the bus at Defence Colony, where her driver, Majnu, was waiting for her in a prearranged spot in the shade of a tree.

He was sleeping soundly on his fully reclined seat. All the car's windows were wound down and his door was open.

"Wake up, you duffer!"

The shrill rebuke from his employer and a couple of prods from her cane woke him with a start.

"How many times I've told you, na? Responsibility for the vehicle is on your head. How you can be responsible when you're dozing, I ask you?"

"But, madam—"

"Don't crib! Now sit up and drive me to Gurgaon."

Majnu mumbled an apology as he rubbed his sleepy eyes, took a slug of warm water from the bottle he kept up front and started the ignition.

Thirty minutes later, they reached Puri's house.

After a quick change from the ordinary attire she had worn for her undercover work into something more appropriate, Mummy found the sitting room already packed with women, all of them dressed in their best saris and jewelry. A few elderly uncles had slipped in as well and sat on the periphery, but strictly speaking, godh bharai was a women-only affair.

Mummy was greeted with much feet touching, hugs, smiles, banter and laughter, and then Jaiya came down to join them. She was dressed in one of her wedding saris, a lustrous red and gold silk affair, and wore a full set of wedding jewelry as well—an elaborate necklace, mini-chandelier-like matching earrings and a nose ring fit for a maharani. Her hands and feet had been decorated with paisley henna patterns. Fresh motiya flowers were strung in her hair.

After greeting everyone, the mother-to-be sat on a chair positioned in the center of the room. Rumpi lit a brass diya, circling it in front of her daughter, and applied a smudge of vermilion to her forehead. Amidst much teasing and giggling, the other women gathered round and sang, "Sola singaar karke, godhi bharaayi le. Chotu jo aawe ghar mein nani behlaawe . . . Payal pehenke nani naach dikhawe." ("Beautiful in your jewelry and makeup, we fill your lap with blessings. When little one comes, his granny will entertain him. She'll tie bells on her ankles and have to dance for him like a naach girl!")

A yellow thread was tied around the expectant mother's right wrist. And then an array of goodies was placed in her lap: fruit and sweets, betel nuts, one-rupee coins and tiny silver anklets for the babies. Blessings were also whispered in her ear.

"Jug jug jiyo," said Mummy after smearing more vermilion on her granddaughter's forehead and adding some pieces of coconut to the growing heap in her lap.

Jaiya was then hand-fed pieces of barfi and coconut, a table was placed in front of her and a feast of samosas and gulab jamuns laid out.

After everyone had eaten their fill and the singing and dancing had begun, Mummy caught up with Rumpi in the kitchen.

"Seems Mrs. Bansal's not the one," she said, keeping her voice down and explaining why. "Her husband is smuggling all the same."

"Him? Smuggling what?" exclaimed Rumpi. But before Mummy could answer she said: "Actually, Mummy-ji, I don't want to know. These revelations are proving far too depressing. Just tell me where you think this leaves us?"

"I was thinking, na. There is one lady we failed to do consideration of."

"Who?"

"Lily Arora."

"Lily? What motive could she possibly have for robbing her own house?" Rumpi shook her head. "With respect, Mummy-ji, I think this has gone far enough. It's time we told Chubby."

"Then those goondas will get away for sure," she said stubbornly. "Chubby is doing investigation of this Dr. Jha murder, na? Kitty robberies are not his concern. So busy he is. It remains for us two."

"No, Mummy-ji, I'm sorry, enough is enough. My duties are here at home. Now I'd better get back inside. I'm missing all the fun."

The scene in Puri's "den" at the back of the house was a very different one, although no less rowdy. Twenty or so men, mostly middle-aged and dressed in cotton shirts stretched tight by potbellies, stood around drinking tumblers of Royal Challenge.

The center of attention was one of Puri's brothers-in-law, who had a seemingly endless repertoire of "non-veg" jokes and stood in the middle of the room telling them one after another.

"Santa Singh was talking to Banta Singh about his love life. 'So, Santa, tell me, how's it going with the girls?' Santa answers: 'Women to me are nothing but sex objects.' 'Really?' replies Banta. 'Yes,' says Santa, shaking his head, 'whenever I mention sex, they object!'"

Before his audience could recover, he fired off another: "One doctor is examining a girl of *admirable* proportions. Holding his stethoscope up to her chest, he says, 'OK, big breaths.' 'Yes, I know,' she replies, 'and I'm only fifteen!'"

Raucous laughter followed Puri down the corridor as he went to the kitchen to tell Sweetu to bring more ice. On the way back, he bumped into his sister, Preeti.

She looked worried.

"Bagga has got himself into something again, I'm sure of it," she said.

Puri sighed. "What now?"

"This deal he was talking about the other night. You remember? Something is not right. He says the construction company wants to buy his land to build a mall. But at the same time, he's trying to borrow money."

"What for?" asked the detective.

"God knows, only," she said.

Later that evening, after all the whisky bottles had been emptied, the samosas had been eaten and the guests had finally departed, Puri received a call from Tubelight.

"Boss, you won't believe this."

He went on to explain how Pandey, dressed in a smart suit, had left his house at seven. His driver had taken him to Connaught Place, where he had stopped at a liquor store and bought a bottle of champagne. From there he had proceeded to a flower stand and purchased a bunch of red roses.

"After, his driver drove up Pusa Hill and did a U-turn," said Tubelight in Hindi. "First, I thought he was confused. But I came to know he was taking precautions. In case he was being followed."

The driver's ruse had not worked, however, and Puri's operative had tailed him to Karol Bagh.

There he had pulled in through the gates of 32 B Block.

"That's Dr. Jha's residence!" said Puri.

"Yes, Boss. As the gates closed, I saw Professor-ji putting his arms around Mrs. Jha."

The detective said nothing for a while.

"Think she's involved, Boss?" asked Tubelight.

"Could be they are just good friends. He is going there to comfort her, no."

"Or they both wanted Jha out of the way so they could be together."

"Dr. Jha had no life insurance policy or savings. There must be further motive."

"What if they're just in love?"

"Love?" scoffed Puri. "No, love is never enough."

Fifteen

Facecream's second day at the ashram proved as regimented as the first. The lights came on at five. Meditation commenced at five-thirty. Breakfast consisted of papaya, apple and yogurt.

After lunch, she managed to get to a pay phone on the main road to call Puri. He brought her up to date on Flush's efforts to hack into the Abode of Eternal Love's computer system. Apparently, the security measures were extremely sophisticated—"Some kind of fiery wall or whatnot"—and might take days to crack. They talked about trying to access the system from the inside.

Then, late in the afternoon, Facecream made an important discovery.

The roll of donors posted on the wall in the main reception included the name of Professor Pandey.

A month ago, he had given the ashram fifty thousand rupees.

Further checking with the susceptible young man on duty at the front desk revealed that Pandey had made the donation in person and subsequently spent a week at the Abode of Eternal Love.

Facecream had not yet found an opportunity to communicate this information to Puri. From reception she had been frog-marched by Bossy to yoga and from there to an hour-long om-chanting session. Then at six Maharaj Swami had made an appearance on the balcony of his private residence, which was directly behind the darshan hall. A crowd, hundreds strong, had gathered beneath him, bowing, chanting and ringing bells with their usual enthusiasm.

Facecream forced herself to join in and play the part, while in her mind she loathed their blind obedience to the Godman. But when at eight o'clock she was summoned for her anticipated private audience, she was careful to show visible excitement and nervous anticipation.

Ushered into a grand entrance hall by senior devotees, she was told to take a seat on one of the gilded settees in the shadow of a sweeping staircase.

For a man who preaches the nobility of poverty, Maharaj Swami certainly has a taste for the kitsch, Facecream thought to herself as she waited. Velvet cushions; hand-painted images of Krishna on the walls; a tinted pink chandelier . . .

The atmosphere, though, was strangely forbidding. No one spoke above a whisper, as if to do so would violate some sacred tenet. The senior devotees who crisscrossed the shiny marble floor as they went about the business of court wore solemn yet self-satisfied expressions. The two thuggish priests who guarded the door to Maharaj Swami's audience chamber observed Facecream and the two other young devotees who had been chosen to meet Swami-ji with probing stares which seemed to doubt their worthiness.

It had often struck Facecream how cults, whether of a political or religious nature, always preached equality and happiness while fostering fear. It had been the same with the

Maoists, who relied so heavily on women and children to fill their ranks. Party propaganda spoke endlessly about the Communist ideal of equality, while the hierarchy maintained strict discipline and unquestioning allegiance.

Sitting there, she thought back to the time she had been summoned to meet The Leader. The setting had been very different, of course: a simple peasant's house in a village in the rugged foothills of the Himalayas. But the sycophancy of his hangers-on and the sense of devotion they had promoted were mirrored here in the Abode of Eternal Love.

She remembered being both elated and petrified as she and her fellow cadres had filed in to meet The Leader. His presence had been overwhelming. They had hung on his every word. Yet when he had spoken to them individually, it had been as a caring father. Despite herself, Facecream had blushed.

She had gone through a lot since then, done a lot of growing up. Still, Puri's operative was not immune to fear. The tight knot in her stomach was testament enough to that. Indeed, now that she was only minutes away from meeting Maharaj Swami face-to-face, she wondered if she wasn't in over her head. One female devotee had already died in mysterious circumstances in the ashram and others were being drugged.

With half the politicians of India in his back pocket and the local police only too willing to play ball, he could do more or less what he wanted. Facecream focused her breath, as she often did before a potentially dangerous task.

Half an hour later, the door to the audience chamber opened and a suave, middle-aged man wearing a collarless black sherwani emerged. It was not Maharaj Swami, but neither did he carry himself like a minion—it struck Facecream that he would be better placed amongst a gathering of businessmen and politicians. He was no visitor either: he carried a key for the door on the other side of the reception hall, which he opened before stepping into the room beyond.

Soon one of the two other devotees was summoned into Maharaj Swami's personal chamber. He spent ten minutes inside and emerged wearing a rapturous smile and tightly clutching a silk scarf. The second one's audience lasted only five minutes and he emerged with nothing. Facecream could read the confusion on his face. Am I not worthy? Am I being tested?

Finally, at around nine thirty, her name—Mukti—was called.

A senior devotee with a shaven head and a ponytail led her across the grand entrance hall, stressing that she was "blessed" to have been granted a private audience.

"I bet if I turned up with a few crores in cash, I'd have as many private meetings as I wanted," she felt like saying.

What had Professor Pandey's fifty thousand bought him? she wondered.

The priests pushed open the tall oak doors and she found herself entering a dimly lit chamber with a desk and computer on one side and a long, ornate divan on the other. Behind the divan stood another door, half hidden behind some curtains. It was heavy, made of cast iron, and had two warded locks, she noted. Bookcases stretched along the walls.

In the middle of the room, Maharaj Swami sat in the lotus position with eyes closed, hands resting on his knees and the tips of his index fingers touching his thumb. The Godman was naked from the waist up. He had a rugged physique: hairy chest, powerfully built arms with a long scar on his right forearm. He was not especially handsome—the bushy black beard only half covered pitted cheeks, and his nose was large and crooked—but somehow this added to his powerful presence—a raw sexual energy.

Facecream stepped into the room with her hands clasped. The doors closed behind her and she stood still, not sure what to do next. The soft sigh of the air-conditioning was the only sound. There was no one else in the room.

And then his voice—a deep baritone, commanding yet somehow welcoming—broke the silence.

"Join me, Mukti," he said without opening his eyes.

She bent down to touch his feet and then knelt on the mat in front of him.

She waited. Seconds passed. And then, without warning, he opened his eyes and Facecream found herself held in his gaze. She flinched ever so slightly, then looked down. She could feel his eyes appraising her.

He said, "I know how deeply you've been hurt."

Facecream knew immediately that he was referring to her scars—that he had been told about them by the lady doctor who had examined her yesterday.

"Men never understand how deeply they are capable of hurting women," he continued. "Often it is the people closest to us who betray us. The ones in which we place our greatest trust. Tell me, my child, who did this to you?"

Facecream held her silence. She never, ever spoke of her scars—not to herself, not to anyone. And certainly not to a man who would exploit her pain for his own advantage.

She felt cornered. But this sense of vulnerability quickly gave way to anger—mostly at herself for not having seen this coming.

Nonetheless, she managed to stay calm and maintain her composure. She was there to get a look inside his inner sanctum, she reminded herself. And no matter how hard this guru, this fraud, tried to get inside her head, he would never succeed because, unlike the others, she didn't believe in him.

"Don't be afraid. I will keep your secret . . . but if you want to be free of the sadness and fear, you must tell me who did this to you."

Facecream looked up at him with sad, mournful eyes and told him that she was scared.

"Come, my child," said Maharaj Swami. He reached for her hands, and when he took them into his own, she made a mock attempt to pull them away. "Let me soothe your pain."

Girding herself, she shuffled forward, mumbling, "I'm sorry, Swami-ji."

"It is I who am sorry for you, my child, for you are starved of trust and love. You are strong yet carry so much pain inside you. It's going to destroy you one day. Your silence has bought you more time, but eventually you must allow yourself to reveal this pain to me so that I can heal it once and for all."

She met his gaze again for a moment, wondering if he had really understood something about her or if they were just words, and said, "Yes, Swami-ji."

"In the meantime you should wear this." He made a fist with his right hand and then opened it to reveal a smooth purple crystal.

Facecream gawped in astonishment. "That's amazing!" she exclaimed.

"Keep it on your person at all times. After waking up, press it to your forehead. It will help cleanse your ajna chakra. Return to me when you are ready."

"Thank you, Swami-ji! But how will I know when to return?"

"You will know," he said. "You must learn to listen to your intuition and not your mind."

Maharaj Swami closed his eyes again. The audience was over.

Facecream backed out of the chamber with her hands pressed together. In the hall, she found Damayanti waiting with her parents. The mother and father both wanted to hear about her audience. What wisdom had Swami-ji imparted? Did he perform any miracles?

But their daughter was sullen. And when the senior devotee informed them that Swami-ji had asked to see her on her own, she avoided eye contact with Facecream.

"You're not joining her?" Puri's operative asked the parents.

"If Swami-ji calls us, then we will go to him with open hearts. Today Damayanti has been blessed with a private audience."

Blankly the young woman walked toward the open doors.

Sixteen

Puri arrived early at the Gymkhana Club—on Sunday mornings there was less traffic on the road—and sat in the bar waiting for his old friend, Dr. Subhrojit Ghosh. Sometimes it was important to get away from work for purely social pleasure. And the weekend all-you-can-eat brunch buffet, a bargain at 295 rupees, was always a welcome respite.

But the Jha case was impossible to avoid. The TV was showing one of India's Oprah-style talk shows. Dr. Jha's murder had been grist to such programs for four days now. Debate over belief and superstition, a topic that stoked nothing short of hysteria in some quarters, was rife.

"Our poll says eighty-five percent of us *do* believe in miracles. Are we being fooled? That's the question we're asking on today's show," announced Kiran, the host of *Kiran!* "We'll be talking to one woman who says her baby daughter died and was brought back to life by this Godman, known as Engineer Baba." A guru with the obligatory beard and saffron robes appeared on-screen. "He's best known for his prophecies and for staying buried underground for weeks on end. He'll be taking your questions after this short break. Don't go away!"

Puri asked the barman to "reduce" the volume as his thoughts turned to the latest developments in the case.

After Pandey's liaison with Mrs. Jha last night, Puri had ordered their telephones to be bugged. A couple of Tubelight's boys had taken up position outside the Jha residence as well.

Puri had also called his researchers into the office to start picking through the two suspects' financial records.

The next step was to search Pandey's house.

Puri had ruled out doing this legally. Calling Inspector Singh and asking him to get a warrant could jeopardize the case: inevitably the chief would come to know and start demanding arrests be made. Once the lawyers and the media were involved, Puri would never see justice served.

He had decided to break in tomorrow afternoon when the professor would be teaching at the university. And if he came across any incriminating evidence . . . well, he would call in Singh when the time was right.

What else?

He opened his notebook and read through his witness interview notes.

Now that there was no doubt in his mind that Pandey was, at the very least, an accomplice to the murder, two details that had seemed unimportant during the preliminary stages of the investigation struck him as significant.

1. Pandey had told the knock-knock joke that had caused everyone to laugh hysterically before Dr. Jha had been killed.

2. Pandey had been the first to declare his inability to move his feet.

As for the professor's statement that he had seen the murder weapon turn to ash . . . Puri had doubted its veracity from the start. Pandey might well have removed the sword himself and then deposited the ground charcoal next to the body.

Something else also occurred to the detective while he was ruminating over the clues.

In the past couple of days, he had watched three magicians perform: Akbar the Great, Manish the Magnificent and, of course, Maharaj Swami. All three had performed in environments where they could make use of concealed props. Prior to putting on their acts, they could set the stage, so to speak. In Puri's book, it was called cheating, but that was an argument for another time.

What had made Dr. Jha's murder seem so baffling was that it had been done out in the open.

What if the setting for the murder, the spot where the Laughing Club always met, had been rigged long beforehand? Perhaps in a way that had not been obvious to him when he had inspected the crime scene? Had he overlooked something? Something hidden?

Puri decided to return to Rajpath and take another look.

Just as soon as his long-standing brunch date with Shubho was over.

Dr. Subhrojit Ghosh had returned from his annual two-week walking holiday in Shimla.

"What news of Shom?" asked Puri. Shom was the eldest Ghosh son, studying in Chicago.

"World-class. He's loving his internship. Getting all As. Dali thinks there's a girl, but who knows?"

"What kind of girl?" asked Puri with a disapproving frown.

"Presumably of the female variety." Dr. Ghosh laughed.

They sat down together in the dining room where the

brunch buffet was laid out—upma, poha, French toast, the works.

"How is Mummy-ji?" asked Dr. Ghosh.

"Up to her usual tricks. Such a handful, I tell you. Seems she's doing investigation again."

"Investigating what?"

"Who knows, Shubho-dada? I've not got time nor inclination to find out."

"Dada" meant older brother in Ghosh's native Bengali.

"And Rumpi?"

"Very fine. Jaiya's having twins, did I tell you?"

"Wonderful! Many congratulations, Chubby."

They made a first pass of the buffet. Puri returned to the table with an unlikely selection of poha and baked beans. From his pocket he produced a red chili carefully selected earlier from one of his plants on the roof. It was a Naga Jolokia, better known as the Ghost Chili, the hottest in the world.

The detective dipped the end in salt, bit into it and began to chew.

"These ones are not for fainthearted," he said, looking satisfied. He offered Dr. Ghosh a bite.

"You must be joking," he said. "Those things are lethal. I was reading recently they're thinking of using them in crowd-control grenades!"

A waiter filled up his chipped Gymkhana Club cup with strong, acidic black tea from a silver pot that leaked onto the tablecloth.

"So, Chubby, tell me, I'm dying to know: How's your investigation into Dr. Jha's murder going? I keep reading such conflicting things in the papers. Seems the whole country's talking about little else."

"Most certainly, it is one of the most extraordinary cases

I've come across till date," said Puri, outlining the case and his trip to Haridwar and how Maharaj Swami had conjured the rishi oracle onstage.

"Most remarkable it was. Is it any wonder people are fooled by this fellow?"

"It's certainly a very realistic trick," said Dr. Ghosh. "But by no means original."

"You've seen it before, is it?"

"When I was fourteen or fifteen. Old Professor Biswas demonstrated it in our physics class. 'Pepper's Ghost,' he called it, after the Britisher who perfected it."

Puri's enthusiastic nod was encouragement to go on.

"All that's required are a couple of silvered mirrors and a strong light source. Your subject stands hidden and his image is reflected off . . . I think it's a couple of mirrors . . . and then through a pane of glass. The image appears behind it, translucent like a spirit."

Puri slapped his thigh with a festive cry.

"Shubho-dada, *you're* the real miracle worker!" he exclaimed. "Such a mine of information you are. You should be a detective, actually."

"But then I would miss all the free trips to international conferences on things like recent advances in inflammatory bowel disease!"

They made a second pass of the buffet. Puri went for the French toast this time.

"Time for a quick game?" asked Dr. Ghosh when their plates were clear again.

"Actually, Shubho-dada, I had better make a move, huh."

"Come now, old pal, we see so little of each other. What's an hour between friends?"

"So much work is there, actually," insisted Puri, looking at his watch.

"You're sure work is not just a convenient excuse?"

"Certainly not . . ."

"I'd understand if it was. Especially after the thrashing I gave you last time."

"Listen," said the detective good-humoredly, "you are ahead by one game, only."

"I didn't know we were counting. But if you put it like that . . ."

Five minutes later, they sat facing one another across a low coffee table in the colonnaded ballroom where tea and cucumber sandwiches were served. Some of the other armchairs were occupied by elderly guests whose rheumy eyes perused the Sunday edition of the *Times of India.*

Before Puri and Dr. Ghosh lay a chessboard. They arranged the pieces but ensured that the rajas, or kings, didn't face one another—this being one of the rules of modern chess's ancient Indian precursor, chaturanga, which they'd started playing for fun in the past year or so.

The detective, whose pieces were white, opened by moving a sippoy, or pawn, and his opponent matched his move. Puri then put one of his kuthareis, or horses, into play.

As Dr. Ghosh made his second move, they began to swap Gym gossip. There was a fierce battle underway for the club's presidency. The air marshal of the Indian air force was up against the army chief.

"It's warfare of a different nature," commented the detective, who joked that it probably wouldn't be long before trenches were dug across the lawns by the opposing sides.

Dr. Ghosh put his mantri, or counselor (the equivalent to a queen, but the piece can move only one square at a time and diagonally), into play. The move puzzled Puri; it was a hugely risky one and not in character with his opponent's usually cautious tactics. But he decided to continue with his strategy nonetheless and positioned one of his yaaneis, or elephants, to strike.

The conversation strayed back to the topic of the murder.

"What saddens me is to see these Godmen types muddying the name of Hinduism," said Puri.

"The clergy is always crooked in any religion," said Dr. Ghosh.

"Hardly makes it right, Shubho-dada. They keep society hostage to superstition and nonsense. There's nothing spiritual about them. Bloody goondas, the lot of them."

By now, the detective had taken nine of his opponent's pieces and had ten remaining. But Dr. Ghosh was far from beaten and quickly launched a counterattack on Puri's left flank, taking his remaining iratham, or chariot (the equivalent of a rook). Puri's defenses suddenly crumbled and within a few moves he found his raja standing alone, signaling the end of the game. He had lost again.

"You were bluffing, is it?" asked Puri.

"Forgive me, Chubby. I've been playing with my nephew. He's brilliant, only eleven—going to give that Viswanathan Anand a run for his money one fine day. He bluffs a lot—often sets up the illusion that he's losing."

Puri stared at him blankly.

"What's wrong, Chubby?" asked Dr. Ghosh.

No reaction.

"Chubby?" prompted his friend, looking worried.

"By God!" exclaimed the detective. And then louder: "What a bloody fool I've been these past days! Of course! It is an illusion within an illusion!"

He stood up. The geriatrics lowered their newspapers and stared.

"Finally I know! I tell you, this thing has been driving me mad!"

"Know what, Chubby?"

"Who it was who knocked me for six!"

"You were knocked unconscious? When? You didn't tell me. Have you been examined?"

"Shubho-dada, I must go. No delay!"

And before Dr. Ghosh could say another word, the detective was out the door.

Fifteen minutes later, Puri reached the south end of Rajpath to find the road still barricaded by the police. A constable on duty informed him that it would not reopen until tomorrow; in the meantime, he was welcome to proceed on foot.

Frustrated but with no other option, the detective set off on his own, umbrella held aloft, retracing the steps Dr. Jha had taken five days earlier.

By now it was almost noon and the heat of the sun bore down on him like a blowtorch. He moved as fast as his left leg would allow him, the insides of his shoes squelching with sweat, until he reached the shade of the jamun tree where the Kali illusion had been staged. The police cordon around the crime scene had by now been removed, as had the incense sticks and offerings left on the ground by worshippers. On either side of the tree trunk lay a flea-bitten pye-dog and a laborer, both of whom were sleeping soundly despite the heat and the flies.

It took Puri a minute or so to recover from the walk and to wipe the salty perspiration from his eyes. And then he began to scour the murder scene.

He slowly circled around the area three times. Then he started to walk backward away from it to get a different perspective.

When he had gone about twenty feet, he noticed something odd. The grass in the vicinity where Kali had levitated was a shade darker, as if it had received more rainfall or perhaps been watered. It was a subtle difference, one that could easily be overlooked.

He hurried back to the spot, cast aside his umbrella and, with some difficulty given his girth, got down on one knee. Taking out his key chain, which had a Swiss Army penknife attached, he pushed the largest blade down into the grass. At a depth of two inches, it came into contact with something solid. He twisted the blade. It felt like metal.

"Heartiest congratulations, Mr. Vish Puri, sir!" he exclaimed out loud with a chuckle, pronouncing heartiest "hartees."

He probed with his knife in six other spots, each time with the same result, before getting back to his feet. For a minute or so, he stood looking down at the ground, contemplating whether to go and fetch a helper with a shovel and dig up the grass, but decided this would have to wait.

He still needed proof that it had been Professor Pandey who had hidden the pieces of metal under the grass.

Given that it was a Sunday, this was going to take some time.

Seventeen

Facecream was serving lunch. For an hour, she and her fellow devotees worked their way back and forth along the rows of visitors seated on the floor of the tent, ensuring that each person received their fill.

Amongst them sat a wiry young man with thick glasses, pockmarked cheeks and sharply parted hair that glistened with Brylcreem. His moustache was but a wisp, the hairs thin and fluffy like a caterpillar's legs, and his clothes served to enhance his physical immaturity, being devoid of any flair. He wore a gray Western shirt untucked over a pair of straight gray trousers. The breast pocket was stuffed with pens and marked with biro stains. From his belt hung a clump of keys and a multitool.

Facecream could not help but smile at the sight of him. It was rare to see Flush out in the field. Sitting there shoulder to shoulder with ordinary people, he looked uncharacteristically unsure of himself. His natural habitat was a darkened room where day and night were not easily discernible, surrounded by monitors, soldering irons, circuit boards and empty pizza boxes. On his days off, he read graphic novels and admired the cover girls of the Indian edition of *Maxim* magazine.

Ironically, however, the computer and electronics whiz fulfilled the first requirement of successful undercover work: to assume a persona that blended into the surroundings and didn't attract undue attention. His unmistakably yokel Uttar Pradesh Hindi helped complete the picture of a socially awkward nerd who was quickly forgettable and of no threat to anyone.

When it came to handing over the small packet Facecream had requested, he did so without raising suspicions, simply slipping it under his plate when she cleared it.

Flush then made his way back to the hotel across the road from the ashram. He had taken a room overlooking the main entrance. And from there he was still endeavoring to hack into the Abode of Eternal Love's network.

Facecream, meanwhile, went to check the contents of the packet in the privacy of a toilet cubicle: one small flashlight; a set of skeleton lever-lock keys and a small metal file; a silver pendant engraved with the om symbol, which had a USB data key concealed inside; and last but not least, a reliable watch. This was everything she needed to break into Maharaj Swami's private residence.

Until this morning, she had had serious reservations about doing so on her own. There were too many people around, and she had asked Puri to send Tubelight and a couple of his boys who specialized in breaking and entering to help.

But then chance had played into her hands.

At eight o'clock this morning, a helicopter had landed in the middle of the ashram, picked up Swami-ji and the man in the black sherwani whom Facecream had seen in the reception of the private residence and taken them to Delhi. Word had circulated amongst the devotees (none of whom seemed puzzled, let alone disillusioned, by the contradiction of their guru making use of a crude flying machine when he was supposed to be able to teleport from one side of the planet to the other) that his holiness would not return until tomorrow, and so Facecream had decided to try to get into his audience chamber tonight.

With offices closed in Delhi for the weekend and many officials away on holiday, it took the rest of the day and a good deal of cajolery to obtain the proof Puri needed.

By then it was seven in the evening and he had not eaten since brunch. Spotting a Nirulas on his way to West Delhi, he stopped for a couple of chicken frankies, which he ate with plenty of green chutney and a salty lassi. Then he called Tubelight.

"Meet me in Shalimar Bagh West in forty minutes," he said.

"Means you've solved the case, Boss?"

"Thank God the answer came to me in the nick of time, otherwise there would have been so much of egg on my face," answered the detective with uncharacteristic modesty. "For once, Vish Puri has been slow on the uptake. Must be this hot weather wreaking havoc with my brain and all. The solution has been staring me right in the face. Pandey and his accomplices have really pulled off the perfect murder, one can say."

"I should bring my pistol?"

"No need. There won't be any trouble. Of that much I am certain."

Puri bought himself a piece of Black Forest gâteau for the road and continued on his way. When he reached Pandey's house, Tubelight, Shashi and Zia were waiting for him across the street.

They reported that the professor had spent the rest of the day in his front room, apparently tinkering with his inventions.

"His driver is there, also?" asked Puri.

"Yes, Boss," reported Shashi.

"Tip-top," said Puri, who was giddy with excitement, like a little boy about to spring a trap. "I'm looking forward to this. Quite a surprise those two are going to get."

"Those *two,* Boss?" said Tubelight.

"He and his partner in crime."

"The driver?"

"Undoubtedly!"

The operatives all regarded him quizzically, clearly itching to know the truth. But they knew better than to press him further.

"Want us to watch the back of the house in case they try to get down the alley?" asked Tubelight.

"No one is going to run away. Stay in position. I would not be more than fifteen, twenty minutes maximum."

Puri approached the front gate and pressed the buzzer. A bar of "Jingle Bells" played somewhere inside the house.

Thirty seconds passed with no result. The detective peered through the narrow gap between the solid metal gate and the gatepost. He could see a light on in the front room on the ground floor. The shadow of a figure moved across the curtains. The detective tried the bell again. Still nothing. He banged on the gate with his fist.

"Professor-ji! Open up, yaar! No need for games!"

The detective's words were answered by a gunshot.

Puri spun around, disoriented. His left leg got caught on his right ankle and he toppled over onto his side.

"That came from inside, Boss!" shouted Tubelight, running across the street toward him. "Don't think it was aimed at you."

"By God, someone's shooting!" cried the detective, appalled. "How that is possible?"

Sounds of a struggle came from inside the house. Something crashed to the ground. One of the ground-floor windows was smashed. Glass tinkled onto the concrete.

Tubelight helped Puri onto his feet as Shashi and Zia reached them.

Another shot was fired. A man's voice cried out.

Zia shoved his shoulder against the front gate, but it was locked from the inside. Without a moment's hesitation, he began to scale the gate.

"You two get around back!" the detective ordered the others.

"Right, Boss!"

Tubelight and Shashi took off down the street.

A third shot rang out. About ten seconds later came a fourth.

By now, Zia was on top of the gate with his right foot balanced precariously between its crown of spikes. He managed to jump down to the other side, landing on the hood of Pandey's car.

A moment later, the gate swung open.

Zia and Puri skirted around the now dented car, keeping their heads down. They approached the front door. It was unlocked. In the corridor beyond lay a couple of pairs of shoes and a pile of old newspapers. There was a radio on somewhere inside the house playing All India Radio's FM Gold station.

They could hear laughter as well.

Cautiously, Puri made his way down the corridor and entered the front room. Professor Pandey was lying on his back in a pool of blood near the window. He was chuckling to himself as if daydreaming about something funny he had seen or heard.

In horror, Puri rushed to his side and shouted back over his shoulder: "Fetch a doctor! Jaldi karo!"

The detective peeled back the wounded man's blood-soaked shirt. He had been shot in the stomach.

"Professor, can you hear me?" He tilted back Pandey's head to keep his air passages clear. "Who did this? You saw?"

The dying man chuckled again and began to cough. Blood spluttered from his mouth. He arched his back and grimaced with pain.

"Try to relax. Help is making its way here. Tell me, who did this?"

The professor smiled, as if a lovely thought had suddenly occurred to him, and then his body went slack and his eyes glazed over.

"By God, Professor-ji, what you went and got yourself into, huh?" mumbled Puri as he moved to search the rest of the house.

Tubelight and Shashi turned into the alleyway behind Professor Pandey's house. They spotted a male figure fifty yards ahead hurrying toward them. He stopped in his tracks, turned and sprinted off in the opposite direction.

"Oi, rook!" shouted Tubelight.

Puri's operatives gave chase, soon reaching the far end of the alleyway. Here they turned right and, with Shashi in the lead, pursued the figure down the residential street that led past Modern Public School.

Three stray dogs joined in the chase. Scrambling after the fleeing man, they snarled and snapped at his heels. One of them got hold of his trouser leg, and for a moment, it looked as if the cur might stop him. But then another shot rang out and the animal yelped and collapsed in a bloody heap.

Whimpering, the other two canines hightailed it in opposite directions.

Tubelight and Shashi briefly took cover behind a parked car.

"That's five shots," said Tubelight, who was out of breath. "He should only have one more."

The killer crossed Jhulelal Mandir Marg, causing a couple of cars to come to a screeching halt, and climbed over the railings surrounding the old Mughal Shalimar Bagh Gardens.

Half a minute later, his pursuers followed him inside.

The killer sprinted down a path that passed the forlorn ornamental fountains and fruit trees once so beloved of the Emperor Shah Jahan. He reached the crumbling central pavilion and disappeared inside.

A few seconds later, a sixth bullet whizzed past Tubelight and Shashi. Instinctively they dropped to the ground.

"That should be his last," panted Tubelight. "There's only one way in and out of there. Wait here and make sure he doesn't double back."

Tubelight crept toward the small building.

"There's no escape!" he called out in Hindi, mounting the steps. "The police will be here soon. Give yourself up!"

His words echoed off the bare walls. They went unanswered. He inched past the columns at the entrance. Moonlight filtered through a window in the domed roof, illuminating the dusty interior. Tubelight almost gagged on the stench of bat droppings that littered the floor. There was no one inside.

Confused, he crept back to the entrance.

"Did he double back?" he hissed to Shashi over his shoulder.

"No, chief."

"You're sure?"

"Positive."

"But . . . that's impossible. There's no other way out of this place."

They both made another search, but the figure had vanished.

Cautiously Puri searched the back rooms on the ground floor of Professor Pandey's house.

He passed through the kitchen and into a small yard, where he noticed a couple of rubber mats, like the ones found in cars, draped over the top of the back wall.

The detective returned inside and mounted the stairs.

He found a bloodstain on the third step. Another on the fifth. He hurried up the landing and turned the corner around the banisters.

There he found another man lying facedown in a pool of blood.

Puri knew who it was without having to turn the body over.

He checked for a pulse, hoping vainly that perhaps the man could still be saved. Finding none, he slumped down on the top stair with his face in his hands.

This was where the doctor found him ten minutes later.

"I'm afraid this one's dead as well," he said after examining the body. "Did you know him?"

Puri didn't answer. His eyes were creased with sadness.

"Sir, do you know the name of the deceased?"

The detective let out a long, anguished sigh.

"Yes, I knew him," he replied. "His name was Dr. Suresh Jha."

Eighteen

"What the hell is going on here, sir?" demanded Inspector Singh when he reached the murder scene. "I thought Dr. Jha was dead. How can he be dead—again?"

"One thing at a time, Inspector," replied Puri calmly. "Just I'm attempting to retrace the killer's steps."

He was in the sitting room standing on a chair examining a bullet hole in the ceiling.

"Most probably it was a double-action revolver," the detective said half to himself, a sad resignation to his voice. He got down off the chair, squinting in the flashing blue light cast by the emergency beacon on top of Singh's Jeep, which had pulled up outside only moments earlier.

"Inspector, by chance, you could switch that disco thing off?" asked Puri, holding his hand over his eyes.

Singh went to the window and shouted through the broken pane angrily at his driver, "Off karo!"

"Most kind of you," said the detective as the order was promptly acted upon.

They walked through the kitchen to the yard behind the house. The murderer, Puri explained, had come in over the wall, having first laid a couple of rubber car mats on top of the shards of glass jutting out of the top. Finding the kitchen door open, he had proceeded to the sitting room. The professor had been sitting at his workbench—his smoking pipe was lying there, still warm.

"The murderer was already present when I rang the bell. Most probably the sound distracted him. Thus he and Pandey took to struggling and the weapon was discharged upward, the bullet getting lodged in the ceiling."

As the scuffle had continued, one of Pandey's gutted TV sets was sent crashing to the ground. The professor had been shoved hard against the window, breaking the glass. When the revolver was discharged for the second time, it had been in close proximity to his belly. This suggested that both he and the murderer had been fighting for possession of it at the time.

"See the powder burns on his shirt and fingers, also."

Puri added as an aside in a less perfunctory tone: "Inspector, when I came across the unfortunate fellow, he was laughing."

"Laughing?" echoed Singh.

"Naturally it crossed my mind maybe he was faking. Just as Dr. Jha did on Rajpath."

"Hang on a minute, sir. Are you telling me Jha faked his own death?" interjected Singh, who was growing impatient with the inordinate details about the shooting.

Puri ignored his question and continued with his reconstruction, making his way out into the hallway to the foot of the stairs.

"Dr. Jha was upstairs. Upon hearing commotion and gunshots, he came to investigate. The murderer shot at him but missed. See the round here in the wall? Dr. Jha turned and retreated upstairs. But shot number four reached him in the back."

Puri and Singh went up to the landing, where the Guru

Buster had managed to crawl before breathing his last. A blanket had been placed over his body.

"Were these killings premeditated, sir?" asked Singh.

"Seems the murderer did not intend to kill Pandey. He had ample opportunity to do so the moment he entered the house. As for Dr. Jha, must be he came down and saw the murderer. Thus his fate was sealed."

"Did you know Jha was alive—before he was killed?" asked Singh, radiating anxiety.

"I came to know this morning only during a game of chaturanga at the Gym."

"What does chaturanga have to do with it?"

"Point is it allowed me to make the connection. Suddenly I understood who it was exactly who knocked me for six. Until that moment, I had been fooled along with all and sundry to believe Dr. Jha was deceased. Thus I was unable to place his voice."

"You mean it was Dr. Jha who knocked you out?"

"Undoubtedly."

"But why?"

"Must be he imagined I was an intruder. It was an accident."

"But what was he doing there?"

"Most probably putting some papers and affairs in order. His secretary, Ms. Ruchi, will tell me for sure. She was an accomplice, also."

"So everything on Rajpath was—"

"An illusion within another illusion. Sword, blood, everything was fake. The death, also."

"But I saw the wound myself, sir! The medical officer certified Dr. Jha was dead!"

"Today I came to know the medical officer in question is one of Dr. Jha's oldest friends. A committed rationalist, also.

I traced him to his home this evening, only. He admitted to falsely issuing the death certificate. Seems the wound you saw was a fake one."

"And the cremation?"

"Dr. Jha was atheist, so no one batted any eyelids when he was cremated using CNG. Seems a real human skeleton taken from Delhi University biology department played substitute for the body. Naturally it was wrapped in a shroud from head to toe so the face was not showing."

"I can't believe they got away with it," said Singh, incredulous.

"Why not, Inspector? Just it was a question of taking advantage of our corrupt and incompetent system."

"Still, sir, you would have thought—"

"Don't blame yourself, Inspector. Even Vish Puri had the wool pulled over, no?"

Singh seemed to take a certain comfort from this. "What about Pandey? Was he involved?" he asked.

"He and Dr. Jha were former colleagues. Twenty years plus they knew one another. Definitely they were in this thing together. But Professor-ji has some connection with Maharaj Swami, also. Seems he visited his ashram one month back only. Could be he was playing a double role."

"So what was Jha's game? Was it life insurance fraud? Was he trading in his wife for a new model?"

"Not at all, Inspector. Dr. Jha was misguided in some ways. Seems he had become obsessive, also. But he never broke a single law during his entire life."

"Sir," said Singh, drawing himself up tall, "half of Delhi was closed down thanks to him. He conspired with a medical officer to issue a fake death certificate. Who knows what other laws he broke."

The inspector started to pace up and down. And then a

thought suddenly occurred to him. "Of course! He was trying to frame Maharaj Swami!" he exclaimed. "The Godman had promised a miracle, so Jha gave us all one!"

"Same thought came to me, also. But no, Inspector, I believe Dr. Jha's motives were otherwise. He was getting old, no? And increasingly frustrated with how everything is going in India. Bitter, we might say. For years he's been fighting Godmen. For what? Their popularity increases day by day. These middle-class types are hardly shunning religion. True, they love new cars and five-star holidays and all. But they are flocking to tele-yogis like Swami-ji in droves. Dr. Jha's campaign had failed, quite frankly. So before facing retirement, he decided to take drastic action. He decided to stage his own death in the most dramatic way possible. His hope was to fool all and sundry into believing a miracle had *really* happened. That goddess Kali came down to earth and killed him."

Singh was calmer now; he was listening to Puri's explanation patiently.

"That much he achieved—in aces, actually," continued the detective. "Right across India, length and breadth, people have been discussing little else these past days."

"Where did his wife fit into all this?"

"Must be she was in on the plan from day one. Quite a performance she put on at the funeral."

"So what was Dr. Jha's plan? To jump out of a cake and surprise everyone?"

"Doubtful any cake would have been involved, Inspector," answered Puri drily. "Most probably he'd have got on TV and explained how all it was done. Thus everyday people would have seen how they are ready to believe any and all nonsense."

"But then someone stopped him," cut in Singh. "Someone who knew he was alive."

"Could be, Inspector. But we cannot discount the possibility the target was Professor Pandey and Dr. Jha happened to get killed also."

A voice called from downstairs: "Inspector-ji? Star TV has reached!"

"Shit," said Singh under his breath. "What am I meant to tell them?"

"If you will take one minute, Inspector, I have got one plan hiding up my sleeve."

The plan went like this:

"Inform Star TV and all Professor Pandey was murdered. Tell them his driver was shot, also."

"His driver?"

"Dr. Jha had been posing as Professor Pandey's driver these past days. That is, after shaving his beard and putting black dye in his hair. Even I failed to recognize him when I paid Professor-ji a visit. Must be they had a good laugh at my expense."

Puri got back to the point.

"Tell them Professor Pandey's driver was wounded. Mention he was rushed to St. Stephens and his chances are fifty-fifty. Then tomorrow the hospital should announce he is very much stable—expected to make a full recovery but not conscious. Just he should be placed in a private room. No guard. Remember he is a driver, only, an everyday person."

"But . . . who is *he*?" asked Singh.

"One of my boys will play the part of Dr. Jha and we two will be present, also."

"You're expecting the killer to come?"

Puri nodded.

"But surely he'll know that we know the driver is really Dr. Jha and suspect a trap."

"That is a risk he will take, no, assuming Dr. Jha saw his killer."

Singh smiled. "That's ingenious, sir," he said.

"Let us hope, Inspector," replied Puri briskly.

His thoughts turned to Facecream. She had called him earlier in the day to say that Maharaj Swami had left the ashram, apparently for Delhi, and that she was planning to break into his private residence.

Perhaps she would be able to establish what the connection was between the Godman and Professor Pandey. It was the only piece of the puzzle that still didn't fit.

Nineteen

Facecream lay on her bedroll staring up at the ceiling fan—it was a good two hours after the lights had been switched off in the dormitory. The mantra in praise of Shiva, which she and her fellow devotees had spent most of the evening repeating over and over again, was playing back in her head.

"Om namah Shivaya. Om namah Shivaya. Om namah Shivaya . . ."

According to Maharaj Swami's philosophy, repetition of such mantras would help awaken her spiritual life force, her Kundalini, as well as stimulate her chakras.

So far, though, all she had got out of the exercise was a splitting headache.

She tried to focus her mind on other things: her adopted eight-year-old son, Momo, who was being looked after by her ayah; her flat in Delhi, where the three of them lived together; the hungry street cats that perched on her wall and meowed and yowled until she fed them.

She sang herself one of her favorite Hindi songs, "Paani Paani Re." But nothing worked. The mantra kept cutting back into her thought processes like a traffic update on FM radio. "Om namah Shivaya."

Aaaagh! No wonder so many of the devotees wore eerie, passive-aggressive grins, she thought.

At three in the morning, Facecream crawled out from under her mosquito net and, chappals in hand, tiptoed silently from the dormitory.

The corridor beyond was dark and empty. Facecream made her way to the stairs and crept down to the ground floor. Upon reaching the bottom and hearing footsteps approaching, she ducked under the stairwell. One of Maharaj Swami's senior devotees shuffled past, clicking his bead necklace between his fingers, and exited through the front door of the residence hall.

Puri's operative stepped out from her hiding place and made for the emergency side door, which was propped open and, like all such doors in India, never alarmed.

It was cooler outside. A light breeze played in the topmost branches of the Himalayan maple next to the building. Crouched beneath it, Facecream took several deep breaths to calm her nerves and surveyed the surrounding terrain.

The wide lawn in front of the tree ended at the edge of the driveway, which was lined with lollipop streetlights and statues of Hindu saints. To her left lay the car park and, far beyond, the main gate, where nighttime chowkidars were sitting around playing cards. Above the din of chirping crickets could be heard snippets of conversation and laughter.

Off to the right stood the main reception building and behind this the darshan hall and Maharaj Swami's residence, where there were only a couple of lights on.

Facecream spent ten minutes under the maple tree making sure that the coast was clear. Then she made her way to the darshan hall, keeping to the shadows and meandering between plinths, benches and trees. She reached a side door that was warped and didn't close properly and slipped inside the building.

Although the lights were all off and no moonlight filtered in through the stained glass windows, there were still enough candles burning under the effigies for her to see her way up onto the stage.

There, she had to switch on Flush's pocket-size flashlight in order to search for the trapdoor behind Maharaj Swami's silver throne she was sure must be there. Facecream soon came across its outline but in the process bumped her head into something hard—a large pane of thin glass about ten feet across and at least twenty feet high suspended on ultrathin wires from the ceiling. Hanging at an angle of forty-five degrees over the trapdoor, it touched the stage at its base.

Puri's operative felt her way behind the glass and discovered a second, smaller trapdoor. This one had a latch.

It lifted easily to reveal a set of concrete stairs.

At the bottom, Facecream found herself standing at the beginning of a passage.

On one side stood a door.

The room beyond was roughly ten feet square and twenty feet high. Its ceiling was the underside of the larger of the two trapdoors. Now she could see that it was designed to open downward on quiet rubber-lined tracks. A switch on the wall operated a mechanical pulley system like those used on automatic garage doors.

In the middle of the room stood a plinth with a light projector on top of it. The front of the projector was raised up on a block. It was pointing at a wooden platform built against the wall at the back of the room. The platform stood about six feet off the ground and could be reached by a ladder.

On the wall opposite the platform hung a large silvered mirror positioned at an angle of forty-five degrees.

There were only two pieces of furniture in the room: a chair and a dressing table. In a drawer of the latter, she found a rubber mask. Its face was that of a wizened old man with a thick, bulbous nose and pronounced frontal lobes.

Facecream recognized it instantly: it was the rishi oracle.

She spent a few minutes trying to make sense of how the illusion worked and thought she understood. An actor wearing the mask stood on the platform and the light projector was switched on. His brightly lit profile appeared in the silvered mirror and was reflected up to the pane of glass on the stage through the trapdoors, which opened on demand. Somehow—science was not her strong point—this created a ghostlike image. The smoke was an extra touch to make the illusion all the more spectacular.

The room also contained a hydraulic lift, which, according to the instructions on the control panel, could be raised to a height of twenty-five feet. Facecream wondered if perhaps this was the secret behind Maharaj Swami's levitation.

Venturing farther down the damp and musty passage with her flashlight's feeble beam catching glimpses of the odd rat, she soon came to an intersection. The passage to the left, she guessed, led to the Abode of Tranquility; the one to the right, back to the residence hall. Facecream took neither of these, pressing on through puddles of water, until about a hundred yards farther on, she reached another set of stairs.

These led up to yet another door.

Switching off her flashlight, she pushed it open an inch and peeked through the gap. The room beyond was dark, but she recognized the desk with the computer on top of it by the window and realized with glee that she had found her way into Maharaj Swami's private audience chamber.

The door was a secret one disguised amongst the bookshelves.

She opened it a little wider so that she could get a better look.

The Venetian blinds were drawn and the only source of light was coming from beneath the main door to the room, which was on her right.

Suddenly she heard male voices and footsteps beyond in the echoey entrance hall and stepped back, pulling the secret door almost shut.

For several minutes she waited, not daring to venture into the room. Finally the voices faded and the light was switched off.

Silence.

Facecream slipped off one of her chappals and lodged it between the door and the wall. Risking her flashlight again, she stole across the room to Maharaj Swami's desk. Following Flush's instructions, she turned on the computer and, by holding down the escape key, ensured that it booted up in DOS.

She drew the om pendant from around her neck and pulled it apart to reveal the USB data key inside. This she inserted into one of the computer's ports, typed the word "copy" and pressed the return key.

The process took only a few minutes. Then she retrieved the key, put it back around her neck and switched off the machine.

Opening the metal door that she had spotted during her private audience with Swami-ji did not prove as easy. The two warded locks were both different, and she had to make subtle alterations to two different skeleton keys in order to get them open.

Finally, however, the second of the locks let out a satisfying click.

Fully fireproofed, windowless and meticulously organized, the room beyond was a veritable Aladdin's cave—not of jewels and coins but of information.

Manish the Magnificent had been right. Maharaj Swami—Aman in his former incarnation—was an obsessive hoarder. Stacked on the shelves along both walls were boxes and silver metal trunks. The room was an archive of memorabilia collected from an early age.

It read like an autobiography.

All the props the young Aman had used in his teens and early twenties as a traveling street magician were there—dusty old wicker baskets, aluminum swords and a bed of nails. There were bottles of chemicals, some with still legible labels: "Potassium Permanganate," "Glycerine," "Yellow Phosphorous." And Facecream came across photographs taken of him performing for tourists in front of the Taj Mahal when he was no more than seventeen—skinny, pencil-thin moustache, suit two sizes too small.

Aman had evidently traveled the length and breadth of India. And then, at the age of twenty-seven, he had left the country. In one box marked "USA," she discovered souvenir postcards, ticket stubs, brochures and a crude diary detailing his travels. Far from sitting in a cave attaining nirvana as he claimed to have done, Maharaj Swami had traveled to Las Vegas, where he had won nearly nine thousand dollars on blackjack and watched David Copperfield perform!

"To Aman with love, David," read the dedication scrawled in marker pen on a glossy headshot of Mr. Copperfield. Attached was the pink flamingo drink stirrer that had dressed the Long Island iced tea he had drunk at Caesars Palace after the show.

From America, Aman had traveled across Europe, Russia and the Far East, seeking out the world's greatest magicians and working for some of them as an understudy.

Finally, at the age of thirty-four, he had returned to India and dedicated two years to mastering yoga. It was during this period that he had come to meet the man in the black sherwani. His name, according to Aman's diary from this period, was Vivek Swaroop, and he was a graduate of Harvard Business School. At the time of their first meeting, he had been working for another internationally successful guru in Pune, marketing his books and health products and running his ashram, which catered to Western, spirituality-seeking tourists.

Aman and Swaroop had teamed up, and a year later, Maharaj Swami had emerged from his long years of isolation high up in the Himalayas to establish the Abode of Eternal Love in Haridwar.

The room was well stocked with the everyday accoutrements he needed to be a successful miracle worker—"sacred" stone eggs that he claimed to produce from his stomach; fake thumb tips into which he concealed pellets of condensed vibhuti; camphor tablets that burned harmlessly on the skin or the tongue.

In one of the metal trunks, Facecream also came across a collection of notebooks in which Aman kept meticulous notes on how his illusions were performed. There were a couple of pages illustrating how he levitated in the darshan hall (as she'd suspected, he sat on a Perspex stand; this in turn was mounted on the platform of the hydraulic lift). And she discovered diagrams pertaining to new miracles he was in the process of developing. The most ambitious involved producing hundreds of fish from a single specimen. He was also working on walking on water.

Facecream could find no reference to the Kali illusion, but there was a file on Dr. Suresh Jha. Much of the information it contained had been gathered over the past few years by a private detective in Delhi, one of Puri's rivals. Bank details, names and addresses of family members, a short biography of his secretary, Ms. Ruchi, even pictures of the Laughing Club taken on a telephoto lens. There were transcripts of telephone conversations, which indicated that DIRE's phones had been tapped, and a special dossier on whom the Guru Buster had talked to during his investigation into the death of Manika Gill. A letter to Vivek Swaroop marked confidential and dated a month earlier warned that Jha had gathered "a great deal of information" on the case and was planning to "petition the Supreme Court to order a murder investigation."

Facecream returned the file to the shelf and noticed some video equipment at the back of the room—a recorder and a monitor. These, she soon discovered, were linked to a hidden camera inside Swami-ji's audience chamber. A cabinet also contained a collection of mini DV tapes.

"Manika" was written on one tape dated two days before she died. Damayanti's tapes took up an entire shelf.

There wasn't time to watch any of them: it was nearly four-thirty. She had stayed longer than she had planned. So Facecream grabbed Manika's tape and one of Damayanti's and headed for the door.

The moment she opened the fireproof—and apparently soundproof—door, she knew she was in trouble.

Maharaj Swami's audience chamber throbbed with a thudding noise.

The helicopter had returned.

The light came on in the entrance hall.

Voices.

Tucking the tapes into the elastic of her underwear, she made for the secret door, retrieved her chappal and hurried down into the underground passage.

She had gone only about thirty feet when the overhead lights in the passage were switched on.

Footsteps.

She broke into a run.

Reaching the darshan hall exit, Facecream scrambled up the stairs and pushed up the trapdoor.

Standing onstage with a revolver trained on her was Vivek Swaroop, the man in the black sherwani.

Twenty

"Please don't kill me! I was just trying to see Swami-ji again. I swear!"

Facecream had put on a look of exaggerated terror.

"He said that when I was, like, ready, I should come to him and then I heard his voice calling to me in my dream . . . I *know* I shouldn't be here, but I couldn't stay away."

Vivek Swaroop, still holding his revolver on her, said in a camp Indian accent: "I suppose in this dream of yours Swami-ji told you where to find this trapdoor and how to get into his chambers, did he?"

"That's right!" she replied, sounding relieved. "He told me exactly where to come! That's how I knew! You see, I—"

"Enough!" he snapped angrily. "You can drop all the spiritual bullshit. I'm immune. I want to know what you were doing down in the tunnels and up in the private residence."

"But I just told you!" said Facecream, all innocence. "Swami-ji promised to cleanse my chakras."

"If that's the case, then what are you doing with this?" He stepped forward and snatched the om pendant from around her neck. "I've got the exact same one. They sell them at the airport."

Gripping one end between his teeth, he pulled it apart to reveal the USB data key inside.

"Somehow I doubt Swami-ji gave you this."

Swaroop dropped both sections of the pendant on the stage and crushed them beneath the heel of his shoe. Then, with his revolver pressed against Facecream's temple, he frisked her and found the tapes.

"I've warned him before about these falling into the wrong hands," he said, stomping on them as well. "But he doesn't listen. That's the trouble with Godmen. They come to believe they're infallible, like they actually *have* supernatural powers."

He cocked the pistol.

"Now, madam," he continued. "I'm going to ask you one last time: What's your game?"

Facecream's eyes narrowed and she regarded him with contempt.

"I'm an officer with the CBI," she said.

"Oh, please!" Swaroop's voice was half-mocking. "The CBI wouldn't *dare* set foot in here. Besides, their agents don't play James Bond. They come knocking on the door with warrants."

"I work for a special section," she said. "It's covert, just been set up. We're investigating corrupt Godmen. You wouldn't have heard of us."

Swaroop regarded Facecream askance.

"My colleagues know exactly where I am," she added in a calm, even voice. "They're outside. And if you don't want kidnapping added to the charges of rape, money laundering and murder you're facing, then you'd better let me go now."

A slow grin suffused his features. "You're really very good, do you know that? For a moment you actually had me going."

"I'm telling you the truth." Facecream looked him straight in the eye. "Our office address is first floor, block number four, CGO complex, Lodhi Road, Delhi, area code 110003. My boss is R. K. Narendra. If you shoot me I guarantee you'll hang for it later."

Swaroop turned his head to the right, keeping one eye on her.

"What do you think?" he asked over his shoulder.

Maharaj Swami stepped out of the shadow at the back of the stage. His eyes were cold, his face expressionless.

"Take her to the river," was all he said before descending down through the trapdoor.

Swaroop smiled. "You heard the Godman. Let's go." He motioned with the pistol toward the front of the stage. "Keep your hands up where I can see them."

Soon they were outside, where it was still dark. In slow procession, they walked to the back of the grounds and passed through the gate that led to the path along the river.

"Shooting me isn't going to solve anything," said Facecream.

"Shooting wasn't what I had in mind—although don't get me wrong, I'll shoot you if I have to," said Swaroop. "With a bullet there's always so much explaining to do. Whereas someone slipping off a cliff in the dark—well, that happens from time to time, doesn't it? Especially around here. Very narrow and treacherous, the pathway up ahead. Someone really should put up a sign warning people."

"Is this what happened to Manika Gill?" asked Facecream. "She met with one of your *accidents*?"

"Manika Gill, Manika Gill," said Swaroop, mulling over

the name. "Oh, *her*? Don't tell me that's what you're investigating." He sounded disappointed.

"Aman seduced her, didn't he? She told her parents, so you murdered her."

"Just keep moving."

"Aman only chooses the ones whose parents are die-hard devotees, doesn't he? He must really get off on that. Knowing that his victims are terrified of telling their parents. What a sense of power it must give him."

Swaroop gave her a shove. Facecream stumbled forward. "Did you bring Manika down here yourself and hold her under the water?" she asked, recovering her balance.

"Didn't have to. Poor little Manika was so scared that she came and jumped in all on her own." He let out a short, psychotic chuckle. "I don't suppose you'd be prepared to save me the bother and do the same? A suicide note would come in very handy as well. 'Farewell, cruel world!'"

Facecream walked on in silence. They reached the cliff edge. Below the waters of the Ganges crashed and swirled around rocks and boulders. She turned to face him.

"Last chance," he said, brandishing the revolver. "Tell me who you work for."

"All right, all right, you win!" she said, glancing back at the precipice. Facecream sounded frightened for the first time. "I work for a private detective. We're investigating the murder of Dr. Suresh Jha."

"So that's it!" Swaroop shook his head as if in pity. "I should have known. And what's the name of this private detective you work for?"

Facecream didn't answer.

He took a step forward. "Well?"

Just then a twig snapped behind him.

In the second that Swaroop was distracted, Facecream

struck, delivering a swift kick to his wrist and then another to his left kneecap.

He stumbled and fell back on the ground, firing off a shot into the air.

"Bitch!"

Facecream sidestepped him and hurled herself toward Flush, who had been trying to sneak up on Swaroop.

"Run!" she shouted.

Together the two operatives sprinted up the path.

Three rounds whizzed over their heads. The sounds echoed and re-echoed off the cliffs, half drowning out their pursuer's curses.

"Get back here! I'm going to kill you, you bitch!"

They turned a bend in the path and Facecream stopped. Picking up a branch, she motioned for Flush to hide behind a bush and readied herself.

Her baseball-style swing could not have been better timed. It caught Swaroop square in the face, sending him reeling backward, bloody and unconscious.

"That was incredible!" marveled Flush as Facecream kicked the revolver into the undergrowth.

"Save the congratulations. Let's go."

As they reached the gate and reentered the ashram grounds, the sun was coming up and the devotees were beginning to make their way in silence to the gazebo. The two operatives returned their nods and smiles, walking slowly past the darshan hall.

Out of the corner of her eye, Facecream spotted Maharaj Swami emerging from the main reception building.

Spotting her at the same time, he turned to the senior devotees accompanying him and pointed in their direction.

"Hurry!" Facecream urged Flush, grabbing him by the arm. "They're coming."

They ran through the car park, watched by a group of bewildered-looking devotees, and pushed past the chowkidars on duty at the main gate.

A local bus bound for Haridwar happened to be passing along the road and they jumped on board.

Looking back as it pulled away, Facecream saw their pursuers sprinting after them, shouting for the driver to stop, but getting left behind.

"We'd better jump off at the next bazaar," she suggested. "I'll get a change of clothes and we'll hire a car."

They took a minute to catch their breath. Then Flush said: "I waited for you on the side of the residence hall at five like you told me to do, but the helicopter landed and I had to hide. Who was that lunatic with the gun?"

"That's Maharaj Swami's number two," explained Facecream.

She went on to describe in a whisper what she had found in the Godman's room.

"But Swaroop smashed the data key and the tapes, so now we've got nothing."

Flush grinned. "Have faith," he said.

Twenty-one

Rumpi rose at five-thirty the next morning. She checked in on Jaiya, who was still sleeping soundly in her room, and then went downstairs to make herself the glass of warm water with lemon juice and black salt that constituted an essential part of her morning ritual.

The photographs from the godh bharai party had come back from the shop yesterday evening and for a while she had sat at the kitchen table looking through them again with a contented smile. Monika joined her from the servant quarters, admired the pictures herself, giggled about funny things people had done and said during the baby shower and started making the tea. While the milk, cardamoms and black Darjeeling leaves boiled, she talked excitedly about the Saif Ali Khan movie she had watched the night before. Naturally the plot sounded extremely convoluted and the actor had taken off his shirt at almost every opportunity.

Rumpi switched on the radio and listened to the headlines on All India Radio as she started to prepare aloo paranthas, Jaiya's favorite.

First, she added jeera, chili and turmeric powder to the boiled aloo and then mixed the atta in a bowl with a little water until it turned into dough. Then, while Monika mopped the floor, Rumpi heated her tava and retrieved the ghee from the fridge.

Puri's wife often found that she did her best thinking while cooking. She had never completely understood why—there was something about preparing food that was relaxing, therapeutic even—but often, while she stood chopping ginger or stirring the paalak paneer, some name she'd had trouble remembering earlier would suddenly pop into her head or a solution to a problem would miraculously bubble up to the surface.

This morning, it was the act of making little dough balls, stuffing them with a potato mixture and rolling them out into flat disks that led—not immediately, it should be said—to the identification of the mastermind behind the kitty party robbery.

When this eureka moment came, Rumpi stopped what she was doing, quickly washed her hands, told Monika to finish preparing breakfast and then reached for the phone.

First she called Arti of Arti's Beauty Parlor and asked for Uma's number, saying that she needed to ask her about some recipe.

It took Rumpi more than five minutes to get Arti off the line. Then she called her beautician.

"Uma? That's you? This is Puri Madam this side. Hello? Hello? Can you hear me?" She had to raise her voice. "I said this is Puri Madam. Yes, that's right. Good morning. Sorry to call you so early. Tell me, you'll reach work at what time? Hello? Hello?"

Practically shouting now: "Uma? You'll reach work at what time, exactly? It's your off? I see. Actually, something important has come up. You'll be at home? What's your address, Uma, I need to see you. No, no, nothing bad, I promise. Something I want to ask you. I would need only five minutes of your time . . ."

Next Rumpi called her mother-in-law.

Yesterday, Mummy-ji, who had refused to give up the investigation, had spent the day following Lily Arora around Delhi.

The kitty party hostess had lunched with a handsome young man who wore expensive shoes and had driven her to a luxurious farmhouse in Najafgarh, where the two had spent a couple of hours.

Expensive Shoes had turned out to be a party organizer who was helping Lily Arora plan her husband's surprise sixtieth birthday party. The kind of money she was spending on the function was far in excess of the amount that had been stolen and Mummy had concluded that the Aroras could not be facing any kind of financial difficulties.

"Something we've overlooked is there, na," she'd told Rumpi in the evening. "One lady is hiding something, that is for sure."

Rumpi had reminded her mother-in-law that she was no longer involved in the investigation.

Now she had to backtrack.

"I think I know who it is," she said. "Last night I was watching the news and there was a story about how an accountant who audits several big companies has been accused of profiting from insider information. Then this morning something Uma told me the other day suddenly clicked."

"It came to you while cooking, is it?" asked Mummy.

"While I was preparing the paranthas."

"That is always the way."

Uma lived in Chhatarpur, a vast warren of three-story apartment blocks. Although "completed" in the past three years, they looked half-finished—bare brickwork, missing window frames, loose cinder blocks in place of missing steps leading up to missing front entrances. The heat, humidity, pollution and monsoon rains, together with the streaks of paan spit and urine on the walls, also conspired to make the buildings look twenty years older.

Twenty-five hundred rupees a month, almost half her monthly salary, rented Uma three small rooms. The living room—all of ten feet across—doubled as a bedroom for her husband, herself and their three children. The kitchen was half that size and comprised a two-ring stove and a fridge that stood idle because the electricity supply was too sporadic and too expensive. There was also a toilet and a small washing area, but water had to be brought from a bore well in the street, which was shared by three buildings—twenty-seven families altogether.

The rooms, though, were clean, with the TV lovingly draped in a piece of fabric to keep off the dust and the family's shoes stacked on a rack next to the door.

A metal cabinet with glass doors contained a few effigies and her three children's school textbooks. Pride of place was given to a china tea set, a Diwali gift from a nice Swiss client who had been going to Arti's Beauty Parlor for years.

As Mummy and Rumpi sat squeezed together on the two-seater settee, Uma carefully retrieved the teapot and, cradling it in one arm, carried it into the kitchen.

When she returned, the spout was steaming and she filled three cups with hot milky chai. A plate of biscuits was also placed on the small coffee table.

Uma sat down on a stool, making all sorts of apologies for not having something more substantial to serve them, or more comfortable furniture for them to sit on, and for how hot it was (the family relied on an overhead fan, which thankfully was on).

Recognizing Uma's embarrassment and awkwardness at having to entertain well-to-do guests, Rumpi and Mummy sought to put her at ease, admiring the cups and saucers, complimenting the tea and repeating that it was they who were sorry for imposing upon her on her one day off.

Small chat ensued. Where are the kids? Off at school. Is that Doll in the picture? Yes, she's already nine and very bright; recently she came in at the top of her class in English. How is the rest of the family? Everyone is well. And work? Ticking along.

But Uma was not her normal relaxed, chatty self. Clients never came to visit her at home. It had to be serious for one of them to suddenly turn up like this.

"Madam, I was very surprised to receive your call this morning," she said in Hindi with a nervous giggle, replenishing their cups.

"The reason I came is because I believe you might be able to help us," replied Rumpi.

"Of course, if there's anything I can do . . ."

"We need some information," said Mummy in Hindi. "It's about one of your clients."

"Uma, before we ask, I want you to understand that anything you tell us will remain"—here she used the English—"top secret," added Rumpi. "We would never reveal you as our source of information. Please understand we don't want to get you into trouble. You can trust us."

"Our lips will remain totally sealed," added Mummy in English.

By now, the beautician was looking extremely worried. "Did someone make a complaint about me?"

"No, no, nothing like that," said Mummy with a reassuring smile. "Everyone is very satisfied with your work."

Uma's eyes widened as a thought suddenly occurred to her. "Then it must be about *her*!" she declared. "Now I understand. Well, I don't mind telling you that *everyone*'s been saying the same thing. That she was behind it. You are talking about the kitty robbery, aren't you?"

"Yes, but—"

"Arti said that it seemed strange she had all that money in her handbag. Big wads of notes and all five hundreds."

"Who?" asked Rumpi.

Before Uma could answer, there was a loud knock on the door and a man's gruff voice said: "Open up! I'm hungry!"

"My husband," Uma said apologetically, getting up from her stool. "He's working as an overnight security guard. His shift finished at seven."

The beautician opened the door a crack, explaining to him in a whisper that she had guests and telling him to go and have breakfast at the dhaba.

Rumpi caught a fleeting glimpse of his unshaven face and bleary eyes and then the door was closed.

"So sorry," said Uma.

"There was really no need to send him away," said Rumpi. "The poor man must be tired and needs his sleep."

"Oh, don't worry about him," she said, rolling her eyes. "I'm sure he got plenty last night." Uma offered them the biscuits. "Now where were we?"

"You were saying you thought you knew who was behind the robbery," said Mummy.

"Oh yes, Bansal Madam. So what's going to happen to her? Are you going to call the police?"

"Uma, Mrs. Bansal was not behind the robbery."

"You're sure, madam?"

"Quite sure," said Mummy in English.

The beautician looked disappointed. "Then what did you want to talk to me about?"

"Your share dealing," answered Rumpi. "I think one of the ladies has been giving you stock market tips. Or perhaps you've overheard her talking on her portable device. Either way, you have done extremely well out of it. And who can blame you? Believe me, I would have done the same. But while you have been sensible and not gambled all your winnings, greed has got the better of your client. She owned stock in InfoSoft—must have been a considerable amount—and as you told me during my last treatment, the company recently crashed."

Rumpi took a sip of tea. Uma could not decide where to look.

"The lady in question is married to a senior accountant—he audits a number of big corporations, including InfoSoft, as I confirmed earlier this morning," continued Puri's wife. "So, she's getting her insider information from him—possibly without him realizing. Perhaps he leaves his papers lying around or talks in his sleep. Who knows? The point is that after this lady lost so much, she could not go to him and confess. She had to find a way to cover her losses but without letting anyone know."

There was a brief silence.

"Now, Uma, I'm going to say this lady's name, and if I'm right and she is the one who has been giving you tips, I would like you to nod your head."

Rumpi named the woman in question, but the beautician neither confirmed nor denied her theory. She sat staring at the wall in stunned silence, as if something terrible had just occurred to her.

Twenty-two

Puri reached the DIRE bungalow in Nizamuddin West at ten o'clock. It was the earliest he could expect Ms. Ruchi to come to work under the circumstances.

She answered his knock with a tear-stained face and a red nose.

Unlike her remarkable performance last Wednesday, her grief today was genuine.

"They've come?" asked the detective, who had broken the terrible news to her last night over the phone.

"Everyone is present," she said in a sad, quiet voice.

It took the detective's eyes a minute to adjust to the dimly lit interior.

In the reception area of the front room, he was pleased to find the three young men he had asked to be present waiting for him.

All in their early twenties, thin, gangly, plainly dressed and palpably earnest, they, too, bore the shock of their mentor's murder in their eyes and the stains of their anguish on their cheeks.

The tallest of the trio was the first to speak. His name was Rupin, a philosophy student at Jawaharlal Nehru University.

"It was you who played the part of Kali, is it?" guessed Puri.

"Yes, sir, it was my honor," he answered with obvious pride, standing respectfully with hands held in front of him.

"And one of you played the ice cream wallah?"

"That was my duty," said the youngest, introducing himself as Peter. "Our colleague Samir was the backup person. He waited at a distance in case something went wrong."

As Rupin went on to explain, they were DIRE volunteers and, during the past few years, had often traveled with Dr. Jha to towns and villages in rural India to participate in "awareness workshops" aimed at educating the public about how so-called miracles were done. This had involved mastering a repertoire of magic tricks.

"I know how to eat lightbulbs and put my hands in boiling oil," explained Peter.

"And I could show you how to drive a skewer through your cheek," volunteered Samir.

Puri could see why Dr. Jha had chosen these idealistic young men to help perform the Kali illusion. They were bright, confident and fervently dedicated to the cause. Rationalism had become something of a religion to them. It provided purpose, structure and philosophy without all the bells and incense or blood turned to wine.

The detective asked them to resume their seats and pulled up a chair.

"We will have to save skewering cheeks for another time," he said. "For now, it is vital you tell me everything that occurred that day, including how the miracle was performed. Some clue might be there that would help find the murderer."

"Sir, we are ready to cooperate in any way," Rupin said ardently.

"We would give our lives three times over to see the killer brought to justice!" added Peter.

"Very good," said Puri. "Now first thing I want to know. When Dr. Jha was planning to let all and sundry know he was alive and well?"

"Today, only," answered Rupin.

"Why he waited almost one week?"

"To maximize the media coverage."

"It was then you planned to release the video footage, is it?"

The trio exchanged surprised looks.

"Video footage, sir?" responded Rupin with a frown.

"Come, let us not waste time, no," scolded the detective. "From my investigation I came to know you recorded video footage of the entire illusion."

There was a brief, awkward silence and then Peter said: "How could you know? Only sir"—he was referring to Dr. Jha—"and the four of us present in this room were involved."

"I am a detective of many long years' standing—that is how," replied Puri pompously.

This did not satisfy the DIRE team as an explanation and Puri had to elaborate.

"Firstly, some holes were drilled into one tree adjacent to the murder scene," he said. "Obviously some bracket had been attached. For what? Yesterday afternoon, only, when I did two and two and came to understand Dr. Jha had faked his own death, I concluded a video camera had been secured to the bracket for purposes of recording the event. Later on, one individual was present at Dr. Jha's CNG funeral for purposes of video recording, also. That individual was you, Samir."

He continued: "Dr. Jha's intention was to show this video

footage on TV to the entire world and appear very much alive as proof that his murder was a fraud. Thus he hoped to create awareness of his cause."

Rupin, Peter and Samir said nothing; their eyes appealed to Ms. Ruchi for help.

She was hovering beside them, clutching a damp handkerchief with which she kept dabbing her tears.

"Mr. Puri, sir, please understand one thing," she said. "The video material is under lock and key. Dr. Jha gave strict instructions for the tapes not to be touched in case they got lost or damaged. I cannot release them to you."

"Where did he keep them?"

She hesitated. "They are locked away."

"Where exactly?" he pressed her.

"Please understand, sir. He trusted me to guard them and I must honor his wishes."

"You intend for the tapes to remain unseen, is it?"

"Sir, we have not yet had the opportunity to discuss how to proceed. I would need to ask Mrs. Jha for her wishes and she is totally indisposed at the present time."

"Come now, Ms. Ruchi," said Puri gently but firmly. "There can be no doubt Dr. Jha would want the tapes released to media persons as intended. It is my suggestion you should carry out his plan in the coming days. Meantime, allow me to view the footage. I assure you with hand on heart, and on my mummy-ji's life also, I will keep their existence and whereabouts top secret. Not another soul will come to know."

The DIRE team went into a huddle to discuss his proposal.

Ten minutes later Puri found himself seated in Dr. Jha's office in front of a TV and VCR.

"Sir, planning for the operation began one year back," explained Rupin before playing the first tape. "It took months of preparation and rehearsal to get it right. Like magicians or Godmen, we had to practice the illusion over and over again to ensure it was believable and worked faultlessly. Everyone had to be fooled into believing they had seen a real apparition."

"You see, sir," added Ms. Ruchi, who was standing with the others behind Puri, "Dr. Jha was planning to retire next month. But before withdrawing from public life, he wanted to stage a spectacular event, something that would gain the attention of the whole of India. His idea was to make the TV channels work for our cause for a change, instead of those of Godmen and other so-called miracle workers."

The first sequence showed Rupin donning a Kali outfit: black cloak, hideous wig surmounted by a crown, garland of skulls, and a frightening mask complete with long red tongue. The volunteer also strapped on an extra pair of arms, which worked mechanically, seemingly of their own accord. One of the fake hands gripped a latex head complete with bloody neck and popping-out eyes.

Dr. Jha appeared in the frame, smiling and chatting, as he timed Rupin taking off all the regalia.

The sight of him caused everyone to fall silent. Ms. Ruchi started sobbing again.

"You'll have twenty seconds to get the arms off," the Guru Buster could be heard saying.

In the next sequence, Rupin fastened a voice distorter with a mini amplifier around his neck.

The picture abruptly cut to Peter standing next to an ice cream cart. The camera revealed that it had been customized. The sides came off and there were two compartments inside.

"One of them held the canister of liquid carbon dioxide and a theatrical fog-making machine," explained Samir.

"And the other?"

"We'll come to that, sir," said Ms. Ruchi.

More footage followed of Rupin fire-breathing using paraffin, then a sequence in which he and Dr. Jha practiced the moment of death using a stage sword with a collapsing blade.

"That was purchased in the USA," explained Rupin. "Nowadays such props and tricks are available by mail order. We often come across traveling 'holy men' using them. Recently we met a fakir who made coins float in the air. He was using a kit sold by an American magician called Kris Nevling."

Another tape was inserted into the machine. A static shot of the spot where the illusion had been performed appeared—evidently the view from the camera mounted on the tree. There was no one in the frame—the Laughing Club members were yet to arrive. A couple of crows hopped around in the foreground. A pye-dog sauntered behind, stopped and yawned. Beyond, Rajpath was shrouded in mist. The time code read 05:43.

"Sir, the camera was disguised inside a bird box and attached to the side of the tree on a bracket," explained Rupin. "We placed it there the night before. It sent a remote signal to the recorder. That in turn was inside Dr. Jha's car at India Gate."

At 05:55, Professor Pandey appeared, smiling as usual, along with Ved Karat. Mr. Gupta was next. Then Mr. Sharma. Last on the scene was Dr. Jha, who stood in profile to the left of the camera.

At 06:33 all the members apart from Sharma started to laugh uncontrollably at Pandey's knock-knock joke.

The detective asked if laughing gas had been used.

"No, sir, Professor-ji used the power of suggestion. Over

many months, he had conditioned the other members of the club to laugh whenever he laughed. One of the exercises he did was called Knock-Knock Laughter."

"And when the fog appeared and both Professor Pandey and Dr. Jha said they couldn't move their feet . . ."

"Same thing, sir. The suggestion made the others think they were rooted to the spot. It worked like post-hypnotic suggestion."

"But on Mr. Sharma it had no effect."

"It was his first time at the Laughing Club."

"You were not expecting him?"

"No, sir."

"Must be you got worried he would ruin everything, no?"

"Not really, sir. We attracted all the stray dogs and they surrounded the group and that kept everyone from running away. There was always a possibility some newcomer might turn up."

"Actually, sir, we were expecting more members to come, maybe another four or five, but it turned out a lot of people were away or busy, so it was a low turnout," added Peter.

The tape started again. The fog formed on the ground. There was a bright, blinding flash, the work of a customized fountain firework. Sharma fell back and dropped his glasses. And then Rupin, aka Kali, appeared, floating through the air.

It was no wonder the other members had been so convinced by the illusion, Puri thought to himself.

"When questioned by my good self, Professor Pandey denied magnetism was used," the detective said after asking for the tape to be paused. "But yesterday, only, I probed the ground with my trusty Swiss Army knife and detected some metal hidden under the grass. Now tell me: How all the levitation was done?"

Puri's question was met with silence and more anxious looks. Eventually it was Ms. Ruchi who answered.

"Sir, this is something we cannot reveal at the present time. The levitation was Professor Pandey's department," she insisted over Puri's protests. "The invention he used was his own. The rights now belong to his sister. It will be up to her to decide whether to go public or not. You are welcome to her number if you like."

She wrote it down for him as they watched the last few minutes of the tape—the climactic moment when the sword was "plunged" into Dr. Jha; the second flash in which Kali disappeared; the pandemonium that followed.

"So while others were distracted, you slipped away," he said to Rupin.

"Yes, sir," answered the volunteer. "I was able to take off the arms, boots and costume in under one minute. Then we wheeled away the ice cream cart, using the tree trunk as cover. Naturally, my face was still black, but it did not attract any undue attention. I easily passed for a rag picker."

"You took the bird box and camera, also?"

"That we retrieved later once the crowd had formed."

"Ved Karat told me he felt Dr. Jha's pulse but could not find one. How was it done?" he asked.

"Simple, sir." It was Rupin speaking again. "Dr. Jha had a golf ball taped to his underarm. As he was playing dead, he squeezed it against his chest. The pressure slowed his pulse enough to be undetectable. It's an old guru trick. They use it during yoga to prove they have reached an elevated state."

Puri asked that the tape be rewound.

"Concerning the ice cream cart—you said two compartments were there. But you failed to tell what all was kept in the second."

"It was a small petrol generator," answered Ms. Ruchi, hesitating. "But—"

"What all it was used for is a question for Professor Pandey's sister, is it?"

"Yes, sir."

The detective nodded. "Why no one heard it? The generator, that is. Those things make quite a racket, no?'

"Two reasons, sir," volunteered Rupin. "One, the ice cream cart was sound insulated. Two, we made all the dogs howl using a high-frequency emitter."

"What is that exactly?"

"A dog whistle, sir. In some of the members it caused headaches."

"And the crows? On the tape so many of them can be seen flying overhead."

"I threw down some pieces of mutton on the ground," answered Peter. "They attracted the dogs and the crows. Eventually they all got gobbled up."

Puri watched the tape again. As he did so, nothing in his demeanor indicated that he had noticed something significant.

"Heartiest congratulations all round," he said when he was finished. "There can be no doubt Dr. Jha was proud of each and every one of you. The operation was most remarkable in every respect. Ms. Ruchi, allow me to compliment your acting skills, also. Vish Puri is not easily fooled. But such a perfect performance you gave."

"Sir, if it's any consolation, Dr. Jha felt terrible about knocking you out. He mistook you for a burglar. And what is more, he was worried you would crack the case before long. He said there wasn't anything you didn't miss."

Puri swelled with pride. "Most kind of you, Ms. Ruchi. And now I better be going."

He made his way back through the reception, but stopped short of the front door.

"Actually one final thing is there," he said, turning around. "Concerning Professor Pandey. Why he stayed at Maharaj Swami's ashram last month?"

"How could you possibly know that, sir?" asked Ms. Ruchi.

"I, too, have secrets, no," replied the detective. "Fact is it has come to my attention Professor Pandey made one donation for fifty thousand bucks."

"Yes, sir, he has been to the ashram on several occasions, posing as a devotee of Maharaj Swami. He made the donation in order to attend a private séance."

"Why exactly?"

"Sir, Godmen, like magicians, are constantly coming up with new tricks for their acts. We have to keep abreast of the latest ones. Now and again, Professor Pandey visited ashrams and temples on our behalf in his capacity as an engineer to try to figure out how certain illusions and miracles were being performed. Then we would publish his findings and expose the truth. In this case, he went to see how Maharaj Swami was conjuring the spirit with which he claims to be able to commune."

"He got it figured out, is it?"

"I believe it was the professor's conclusion that the Godman was using mirrors reflected off one another. But he had not yet written up his findings."

The detective gave a satisfied smile.

"Ms. Ruchi, once the case is getting over, I will introduce you to a certain individual who will explain precisely and exactly how it is done," he promised.

Twenty-three

Back in his Ambassador, Puri called Professor Pandey's sister, offered his condolences and stressed how important it was that they meet. Although in mourning and busy making preparations for the funeral, she invited the detective to her residence at six PM.

Next, he phoned Ved Karat and asked to see him immediately—"a matter of some great urgency, actually."

The speechwriter was at home, working on the prime minister's Independence Day address, but said to come straight over.

Puri immediately set out for New Rajendra Nagar. En route, he rang Inspector Singh.

"Haan ji, haan ji. So what progress is there?"

"Everything's going to plan, sir," Singh reported. "In two hours we will announce that Professor Pandey's driver has survived the shooting and is expected to make a full recovery. I've arranged for a private room at St. Stephens. It's on a busy corridor where people come and go all the time."

"Tip-top. My man will be there in one hour," said Puri, referring to Tubelight. "My guess is the murderer will do the needful after dark. Therefore I will reach St. Stephens at seven-thirty. You will be present also, is it?"

"Yes, sir. Are you sure the murderer will come?"

"Has to, Inspector. He cannot and will not take the chance Dr. Jha could identify him. It is not a question of whether the plan will work, only a question of who it will work against."

"What if he sends someone else—a hired killer?"

"Let us cross that bridge should it rise up."

"Speaking of which, sir, I am reliably informed that Maharaj Swami was in Delhi last night," said Singh.

"He touched down at Safdarjung Airport at 12:07 yesterday. Then this morning he reverted to Haridwar. That was in the wee hours," said Puri.

"You're having him followed?"

"Unfortunately, that is not possible. He travels VVIP with security escort. I came to know by checking the airport log only."

"You think he's our man, sir?"

"Inspector, allow me to assure you, by hook or crook His Holiness Maharaj Swami will face arrest," said Puri. "Please have your handcuffs on standby."

Ved Karat worked in longhand on legal pads; the floor surrounding his desk was strewn with screwed-up pieces of yellow paper.

"I could not sleep last night after hearing about Professor Pandey's murder," he said as Puri took the basket chair in his office. The story had made the morning news. "What is the world coming to? The TV said he was shot in his own house?"

"Yes, sir."

"Terrible!" exclaimed Karat. "What has happened to

our Dilli? There was a time when my front door was open twenty-four/seven. People dropped in whenever they liked. No need for security persons. But now? Only recently some of my neighbors were murdered. Husband and wife and one fourteen-year-old boy. Perhaps you read about it in the papers? These terrible crimes occur every day. In this instance, some Bawarias broke in and clubbed them to death. And for what? Some jewelry and a couple of lakhs they kept under the mattress. Animals! Worse than!"

A servant brought cups of tea and pinnis.

"I have rarely met such a warm, kindly and giving person," continued Karat, referring to the late professor. "Did you know that when I had my heart attack last year, he visited my bedside each and every day? And he always came with a joke to cheer me up. Such a jolly fellow. A few of us are organizing a memorial on Rajpath this evening. We plan to light some candles, tell some jokes and have a thoroughly good laugh. It's what he would have wanted. I understand even as he lay dying he was chuckling to himself."

"Yes, sir, I was the one to witness his last moments, actually."

"You, Mr. Puri? What were you doing there?"

"I've been investigating Dr. Jha's death."

"The two are connected in some way?"

"Undoubtedly! That is the reason I am here, actually. I wanted to ask you about this Shivraj Sharma. Seems to me you know him, is it?"

"Naturally; we were neighbors for many years, his family and mine."

"You faced any problems with him?"

"Personally, no, but . . ." Ved Karat lowered his voice, as if someone might overhear them. "He's not the most tolerant of gentlemen. He often complained about the types moving into the colony. He took particular exception to a Muslim family living here. Tried to start a campaign to get them out. When it didn't work he sold up and left. Now I understand he lives in one of those new colonies where minorities aren't openly banned, but if your surname happens to be Khan, you get the brush-off."

"You were surprised to see him that morning. Is that not so?"

"Very surprised. He's not the type to join a laughing club."

"He's not one for doing laughter," suggested Puri.

"Exactly. Takes life too seriously."

"You're one hundred percent certain it was his intention to join, is it?"

Ved Karat thought for a moment. "Well, now you come to mention it, Mr. Puri . . ."

As Puri suspected from having watched the DIRE footage, Ved Karat had spotted Mr. Sharma two minutes after Dr. Jha had reached the Laughing Club.

The speechwriter had first stared and squinted; then his expression had turned to one of recognition.

"Finally you waved to him, isn't it?" asked Puri.

"Yes, I believe I did," replied Karat. "You've certainly done a thorough job at re-creating the scene."

"What all he was doing? Walking toward you?"

"Yes, but slowly. In fact, now that I think about it, he had stopped next to one of the trees and was watching us."

"Then you walked toward him and what?"

"I greeted him, naturally, and then asked him to join us."

"He agreed?"

Again Ved Karat had to think hard and then concluded: "Seems to me he was reluctant. I believe he said something about having to get back home. But I insisted."

"Why?"

"I thought that of all people he could do with some laughter."

"He was enjoying?" asked Puri, remembering Sharma's pained expression during the exercises.

"Not at all. He looked uncomfortable throughout."

The detective nodded. "He said anything to you after?"

"Nothing," said Karat. "He was as shocked as all of us."

There was a pause.

"Now I have a question," said Karat. "Why all the suspicion?"

"Most probably it is nothing," replied Puri. "Just I am trying to clarify everybody's movements. In my profession, no stone should go unturned. Sharma being an archaeologist, that is one thing we share in common."

Puri was hungry—it was almost two. Finding it hard to think clearly on an empty stomach and knowing that Rumpi had packed his tiffin with kale channe, one of his favorites, he returned to the office.

Door Stop, the tea boy, heated the food and brought it to him at his desk. He ate on his own in silence with a napkin tucked into the top of his safari suit jacket.

Only after he was finished and had washed his hands, cleared his nasal passages and sat back at his desk drinking a cup of chai did he give the day's developments any further consideration.

What had Sharma been doing on Rajpath at six in the morning, apparently spying on the Laughing Club members? he wondered.

Puri reached for the file he had started on the Jha murder case and took out the photocopies of the death threats Ms. Ruchi had provided him.

Had Sharma sent them to Dr. Jha? Had he been planning to kill him?

For the archaeologist to be the murderer, he would have to have known that the Guru Buster had faked his own death and then traced him to Professor Pandey's house.

Puri found it hard to picture the bespectacled, oh-so-respectable Brahmin scaling the wall and shooting down men in cold blood.

On the other hand, when it came to fanatics and psychopaths, there was no telling.

Puri reached for his mobile; called Tubelight, who was just reaching the hospital; and asked him to assign Shashi and Zia to tail Sharma.

"Tell them to get hold his garbage, also. Let's see what all he is into," instructed the detective.

Puri's sister had phoned twice this morning, but he had ignored her calls. He was dreading having to hear more about Bagga-ji's latest mess. But when she called him again at three o'clock, he felt compelled to answer.

"Chubby, thank God!"

Preeti was at home in Ludhiana. She sounded panicked.

"You've got to help me. He's planning to put up the house against a loan of one crore with some lowborn money-lender!"

"What is that bugger up to exactly?"

"He won't tell me, Chubby. He's so blinded by the profit he says is to be made. But a crore! And the high interest to pay! It can be our ruin."

Puri sighed. There was nothing for it; he could not stand by and watch his sister lose everything.

"What is his current location exactly?"

"He's up in Delhi."

"I'll talk to him," the detective promised.

"Sir-ji! Kaha-hain?"

"Haa! Mr. Sherluck! Kidd-an?"

"Very fine, sir-ji! I want to see you. Something urgent."

"Fine, fine, fine, fine."

"Sir-ji, where are you? Hello? Hello?"

"Haa!" Bagga Uncle was somewhere noisy—a background din of laughter and raised voices.

"Sir-ji?"

"Haa!"

"You've been drinking or what?"

"Haa!"

The detective felt like he was about to explode but managed to contain his fury. He said in sharp, staccato Punjabi: "Baaga-ji, tell me where you are!"

"Mr. Sherluck? Hello? You're asking me?"

"Of course I'm asking you!" He refrained from adding: "Saala!"

"I'm at the adda. What do you want?"

"Adda" translated as "joint." Puri knew the place: Bagga-ji's favorite haunt in Delhi, a carrom-board and illegal-drinking den in Punjabi Bagh.

"I'll be reaching in forty minutes."

"Fine, fine, fine, fine."

Puri had mixed feelings about Punjabi Bagh. It was the neighborhood where he had grown up, and every street, every corner, held a memory for him.

Returning there, as he did from time to time to visit near or dear, always stirred strong feelings of nostalgia—

especially for Papa-ji, who had built his house in the Moti Nagar subsection in the early 1960s. But nowadays the detective found the old neighborhood a stifling place. Although he always told everyone he had moved to Gurgaon to escape the noise and pollution, the truth was that he had also sought to distance himself from Punjabi Bagh's boisterous inhabitants.

He was, after all, India's Most Private Investigator. And when everyone was constantly coming in and out of your house at all hours, asking for favors and the odd loan of a thousand rupees for some uncle's heart medicine, it was impossible to keep your affairs confidential and not become embroiled in everyone else's problems.

Punjabi Bagh was not an especially noteworthy address, either. Not for a member of the Gymkhana Club and the son-in-law of a retired army colonel with a penchant for oxford shoes. Gurgaon fitted the bill better—although, admittedly, for the son of a local police officer there was no competing with the old elite.

The constant gridlock had been another reason for leaving. Some bloody Charlie was forever stopping his Tempo in the middle of one of the narrow streets and off-loading a consignment of live chickens, thereby turning the entire neighborhood into a solid, honking traffic jam.

Today was no different. But instead of live chickens, it was rusty barrels with skull-and-crossbones stickers plastered all over them.

The fact that they were being carried into someone's house by a gang of laborers who looked as if they had tuberculosis did not strike Puri as odd. Suspicious, perhaps, but by Punjabi Bagh standards, definitely not odd.

The detective decided to abandon the car and told Handbrake to park as close as he could to Bagga-ji's adda.

"I'll give you 'missed call' when I'm in position, Boss," said the driver in a combination of Hindi and English.

Feeling the heat rush at him like the thermal radiation of a forest fire, Puri stepped out of the Ambassador, narrowly avoiding a cowpat underfoot.

He kept to the shady side of the street, making his way along a busy pavement where children played hopscotch and carpenters sawed, sanded and hammered made-to-measure mango-wood furniture for one of the residents of the kothis. A door-to-door salesman of mops, brooms and dusters passed down the middle of the street on a bicycle bristling with his wares. It looked like a kind of punk porcupine. "Jharu, ponche! Saste! Brooms, mops, cheap!"

Puri turned the next corner, looking up at all the brightly colored laundry hanging overhead and the paper kites up in the hazy sky, and almost ran straight into an old school chum whom everyone knew as Mintoo.

"Oi! Chubby! Kisteran?"

They chatted for a couple of minutes and then Puri made his excuses and hurried on. Farther down the street, he met Billa, a former next-door neighbor who owned a shop selling galvanized-steel buckets in Jawala Heri. Master-ji, the local tailor, waved and called out greetings from his shop, which had once been four times the size, but thanks to family property disputes was now little more than a cubicle. And inevitably, Bhartia Auntie (who had bad hips and walked with her feet splayed like a circus clown) appeared and reminded him, as she always did, how, at the age of six, he had burned his lip eating some of her homemade gulab jamuns.

"You couldn't wait and just shoved it in your mouth!" she cackled, pinching his cheek. "Greedy little bacha!"

Bagga-ji's adda was housed in the basement of a doctor's

private clinic, Dr. Darshan being the owner and a regular himself.

The entrance was down the side of the building behind a door with a notice on it that read CLINIC IN SESSION.

In the poorly lit room beyond, through a haze of cigarette smoke, Puri counted nine tables with carrom boards. Around each sat four men with chalky fingers.

The sight of the boards and the sound of the strikers hitting the pucks and ricocheting off the buffers immediately aroused in Puri a desire to join in. As a teenager, he had been a carrom fanatic; to the detriment of his homework, he had played for hours on end. But it was rare that he got in a game these days, chess and bridge being more the Gymkhana's speed.

Indeed, when he located Bagga-ji at one of the boards in the middle of the room—"Mr. Sherluck, what you're doing here?"—and one of the players offered to give up his seat, Puri could not resist.

"I'm drinking Aristocrat." Bagga-ji grinned. "Aristocrat" came out "aa-rist-row-krAAt." "Instant relief! You want?"

"Most certainly, sir-ji!" declared Puri. "How often I get to drink with my favorite brother-in-law, huh?"

Bagga Uncle was too drunk to be suspicious of the detective's disingenuous chumminess and poured him a large glass from the bottle he had under the table. Then he called to the eleven-year-old boy who fetched packets of cigarettes and fresh paan from the stand across the road and plates of murg saharabi tikka and "chutney sandwitch" from the local restaurant.

"Oi! Soda bottle laow!"

The black and white pucks and the red queen were arranged in the middle of the lacquered board. One of the other two players at the table flicked the puck with his index finger, sending it crashing into the pack. A black shot into one of the corner pockets.

When it came to Bagga's turn, he potted five pucks in a row; if there was one skill the man possessed, it was as a carrom player.

"You've still got it, sir-ji!" said Puri in Punjabi as he took his turn and, being out of practice, only managed to pot a single white.

Bagga Uncle showed Puri his index finger.

"This is one in a billion!" he declared.

"Just like you, Bagga-ji!" bawled one of the opponents to roars of laughter.

The banter, drinking and play went on. And after Bagga had won the game and declared himself "vorld champion!" the detective told him there was something he wished to discuss.

"Not for others' ears," he said.

They went and sat to one side of the room against a wall that was decorated with red-brick wallpaper.

By now Bagga's eyes were bloodshot and he looked like he might pass out.

"Sir-ji, I've been thinking," said Puri.

"Haa?"

"Sir-ji, I'm talking to you."

"Haa."

"This business proposition of yours sounds like a sure thing."

"Huh?"

"You said a construction company wants to build a mall on your land. It sounds like a very good thing!"

"Oh yes, that! Well, it is!" declared Bagga Uncle, finally cottoning on. "Chubby, I will soon be the richest man in all Punjab! People will treat me with respect!"

"You of all people deserve it, sir-ji. I have always thought you to be a canny fellow. You've just had bad luck, that's all."

"Exactly! Unlucky, that is all!" agreed Bagga Uncle.

He replenished their glasses.

"Sir-ji, I want to make you a business proposition," lied the detective. "I will loan you the one crore you need so that your deal goes through. In return, I want only two percent of the profit. And you can pay me back the money when you can. How does that sound?"

Bagga Uncle stared at him blankly and blinked.

"I could draw the money for you from the bank in the morning. No need to borrow from some stranger you don't know and risk your house. Let me take care of it."

"You would do that for me?"

"Of course, sir-ji!" The detective gave him a hearty slap on the back. "What is family for?"

Tears formed in Bagga Uncle's bloodshot eyes.

"Mr. Sherluck, you are number one!"

"So you accept?"

They shook on it. More Aristocrat whisky was consumed. And then the detective said: "Sir-ji, there is one thing I don't understand. Why do you need this money if you are selling your land?"

Bagga Uncle leaned in. "You promise not to tell anyone?"

"They would have to gouge out my eyes!"

"I can trust you?" Bagga Uncle suddenly regarded Puri as if he were a stranger.

"Have you ever had any reason not to?"

"There was that one time you called me 'saala,'" said Bagga Uncle with a wounded expression.

"For that I apologize unreservedly, sir-ji. I was angry, but it was uncalled for. Besides, now we are business partners."

That seemed to do the trick.

"OK, I'll tell you. In order to build the mall, the developers need the land next to mine as well," said Bagga Uncle.

"Go on."

"That land is owned by that son-of-a-whore bastard motherf—"

"What's his name, yaar?" interrupted Puri.

"Jasbir Jaggi."

"He does what exactly?"

"He's into transportation. Lives in a big farmhouse off Ferozepur Road. Laad sahib!"

"And?"

Bagga Uncle leaned in farther, looking pleased with himself.

"See, Chubby . . . when the construction company approached me they mentioned they would need that other land as well."

"And?"

"I told them I could get it for them. No need to talk to that son-of-a-whore bastard motherf—"

"And so you offered to buy it from this Jasbir Jaggi?"

"Exactly!"

Puri stood up abruptly and pushed back his chair

"Saala!" he roared, and stormed out, leaving Bagga Uncle staring after him in bewilderment.

Twenty-four

Rumpi had a big lump in her throat as she sat in Mummy's car across the street from the white villa in C Block, Greater Kailash Part One, in South Delhi.

"You realize I have known this woman for near on twenty years?" she said to her mother-in-law. "Her children and mine used to play together. I was present at her son's wedding. I still can't believe she went and did this. What was she thinking? Now her whole reputation will lie in tatters."

"Some people are lacking in moral fibers, na," said Mummy. "Rich or poor—doesn't matter."

They sat in silence for a while, watching cars and auto rickshaws and the occasional bicycle rickshaw pass by in the gathering darkness.

Majnu was restless in the front seat.

"Madam, my duty is getting over," he said grumpily.

It was a quarter to six. But the driver had arrived an hour late for work, making some excuse about a headache, so by Mummy's reckoning, he still owed her an hour and fifteen minutes.

Weary of scolding him, she simply let out an irritated tut

and then said to Rumpi: "It is nearly time, na? Think others are coming?"

"I do hope so. It would be much better if we all confronted her at once."

Presently, Lily Arora's Sumo turned into the space in front of Mummy's Indica. Mrs. Shankar, who rode a scooter, was next. A minute later, Mrs. Bansal pulled up in her BMW.

"I'm afraid Phoolan isn't coming," she called from her window with a long face. "Something about a root canal."

They gave it another five minutes and then gathered at the gate. There were three no-shows, bringing the total to nine plus Mummy.

"Madam is expecting only myself," Rumpi told the security guard. "So don't tell her I have come with friends. Or you will ruin the surprise."

He wobbled his head in an understanding kind of way and stepped into his sentry box to use the intercom.

When word came back that Rumpi was to be shown up, she led the way past the cars in the forecourt and into the house.

Mrs. Nanda, as straight, tall and elegant as ever, was waiting in the sitting room. She stood to greet Puri's wife with a smile and both hands held out in welcome.

"What's wrong, my dear?" was her reaction to Rumpi's cold response. And then, still smiling: "What's this? Ladies, what a surprise! How nice of you all to come. Please make yourselves comfortable. I'll ask for more cups."

In silence, they all stood in a row just inside the room looking either pensive or embarrassed, and in Lily Arora's case, enraged.

Mummy, who had been elected by a quick vote at the gate as official spokeswoman, said: "We won't be staying long, na. Just we came to say we have come to know everything."

Lily Arora suddenly interjected angrily, pointing a finger at Mrs. Nanda. "How could you have done this, Sona? You realize my poor baby's lying in a coma? He might not live and the vet says even if he does he will probably never walk or talk!"

"I'm sorry, Lily, I don't know what you're talking about. I—"

"Oh, don't lie to us, Sona." Lily Arora had her hands on her hips now. "That will only make it worse for you, believe me."

"Ladies, I think there's been some kind of misunderstanding," said Mrs. Nanda calmly. "Are you suggesting I was involved in the robbery somehow? Is that it?"

The silence answered well enough.

"Well, that's ridiculous!" She looked incredulous. "What reason would I have for doing something like that?"

"Same reason anyone does dacoity, na," said Mummy. "You needed paisa."

"Forgive me, Auntie-ji, but you obviously don't know me very well. I can assure you I have no need of cash. My husband—"

"Is doing accounting. Yes, we're aware. He's a topper, handling so many of big companies. Thanks to that he's getting information on stock market and takeovers and such."

"Insider information, which is illegal to share, by the way!" bawled Lily Arora.

"Unbeknownst to him, you've been acting on what he's told you and buying your own shares," said Rumpi. "You did well at first, but then a couple of weeks ago, disaster struck. InfoSoft crashed and all your money was wiped out. You suddenly found yourself heavily in debt."

"Problem was, na, last person you could ask for help was

your husband," said Mummy. "So furious he would have been. Naturally selling your jewelry was out of the question, also. He would have noticed. That was when you decided to go the criminal way."

Mrs. Nanda shook her head testily. "Ladies, I'm shocked you think that I would be capable of such a thing. I have considered some of you friends for many years."

"Oh, shut up, Sona, you're not going to talk your way out of this! We know all about that security guard!" shouted Lily Arora.

"What security guard?"

"The nighttime security guard you got to do the robbery, of course!"

Mummy had been hoping to play their trump card at a more opportune moment. But now she had no choice but to identify the thieves.

"One month back, only, you gave Kishan, the husband of Uma from Arti's Beauty Parlor, one job as nighttime chowkidar," she said. "Later you requested him to do robbery of our kitty party. Being totally lacking in moral fibers, he complied. Unfortunately, he brought along his nephew of fourteen years."

"Kishan was behind it? I had no idea!" declared an apparently shocked Mrs. Nanda. "He must have overheard me talking about the kitty party on the phone. Or perhaps some of the other servants told them. We should call the police!"

"Police can certainly be called. But these two"—Mummy was referring to Uma's husband and his nephew—"will say they were working for you, na?"

"Well, that's a lie! I had nothing to do with this."

Mummy paused before saying with an edge of triumphant power: "That is strange, na? Earlier, we got him to do a call to you and recorded every last word."

Mrs. Nanda froze.

"There's no getting away with this, Sona," said Rumpi. "Now here's what we're going to do . . ."

They did not plan to involve the police for the nephew's sake, she went on to explain, but they had made sure Lily Arora's servants and Bappi the physical trainer were in the clear. Mummy had spoken with the boy and found him to be decent and repentant. Kishan had surrendered his weapon, which had been thrown into the Yamuna, and then Uma had kicked him out of the house.

"And as for you, *Sona,*" Lily Arora cut in again, "we want our money back! So if you're not going to tell your husband, we will!"

"You have until this time tomorrow to deliver the total amount or we will have no choice but to go to the police," said Rumpi.

Slowly Mrs. Nanda sat back down on her couch. She looked as if she was in a trance.

"That is all, na?" said Mummy to the other ladies. "Challo?"

"Challo," they replied.

One by one, they all filed out of the room. All apart from Lily Arora, who took a final parting shot.

"Sona, I want you to know one other thing," she said. "I'm going to make sure you can *never* join another kitty again. I'm going to make sure everyone knows what you did. You have broken the sacred trust upon which kitties were founded! Consider your face blackened!"

Mummy and Rumpi were soon on their way to Gurgaon.

"You don't think she'll do something to herself, do you? Something rash? It seemed like she went into shock."

"Not a chance," answered Mummy. "That one is hard, na? Hard as marble."

"But she'll never be able to show her face anywhere in Delhi again. Lily will see to it, that's for sure."

They both got lost in their own thoughts for a few minutes and then Rumpi asked: "Mummy-ji, do you think we should do something about her husband? If we're right and he's sharing insider information, then we should tell someone."

"Definitely it is our duty to report our suspicions. Problem is: Why proper authorities should listen to us two? Who are we, after all?"

"Just a couple of housewives," said Rumpi.

"Exactly. What is required is proof . . ."

"Oh no, Mummy-ji, now I'm going to have to stop you there. We've done what we needed to do."

"But it's our duty, na?"

"We have plenty of other responsibilities as well. And chasing after a crooked accountant is not one of them. Don't worry, he'll get unstuck eventually. It's not for us to deal with."

Mummy looked disappointed but conceded.

"You are right," she said. "So many things I have to do, actually. But we made a good team, na?"

Rumpi laughed. "Yes, Mummy-ji, we made a good team. You know something? I didn't think I had much of a brain for mysteries. How would Chubby put it? I amazed even myself!"

Twenty-five

Puri entered St. Stephens hospital through a back door and climbed the emergency stairs. By the time he reached the fourth floor, where Inspector Singh was waiting for him, he was out of breath and his face was glistening with sweat.

"Did anyone see you arrive, sir?" asked the police wallah.

The detective was unable to answer straightaway.

"I . . . I . . . don't . . . believe so," he panted. "Coast was . . . clear."

"Sir, what is that you've brought with you?" Singh pointed at the plastic bag Puri was carrying. "It's not takeaway, is it?"

The detective held up a hand to indicate that he needed a minute. When he had recovered his breath, he said: "Might be we will be here until the wee hours. Hunger could definitely set in."

"With respect, sir, this is hardly the time to be thinking about your stomach."

"Don't worry, Inspector," said Puri. "There will be no thinking involved."

Singh cracked open the door that led from the emergency stairs onto the ward and peeked through the gap. The corridor beyond was busy—patients, nurses, a couple of doctors coming and going.

"Sir, your man is positioned in the second room on the left," the inspector explained over his shoulder. "I have arranged for us to be in the first room, which has a connecting door to the second. But I can foresee one problem. The murderer could easily be here already, out there in the corridor, and is watching to see who comes and goes."

"Might be he'll recognize me when we cross the corridor," agreed Puri.

"Exactly, sir."

"So, what all you're proposing?"

"Here, I brought a doctor's coat for you to put on," said Singh, who had changed into civilian clothes himself.

"Very good, Inspector," said the detective, donning the white coat over his safari suit.

"You might like to wear this, also," said Singh, who, knowing that Puri never took off his Sandown cap (at least not in public) had brought along a surgeon's elasticized cap to put over it.

Without a word, the detective slipped it on.

The room where Singh had arranged for them to hole up was large enough for a bed, a side table and a cupboard. It had bare, damp-stained walls, an overhead fan and a naked bulb hanging by a wire from the ceiling.

Puri looked into the second room through the connecting door and could see that it was similarly basic, except there were two beds and one of these—the one farthest from the door near the window—had a privacy curtain drawn around it.

"Baldev, you're there?" whispered Puri.

"Yes, Boss," answered Tubelight.

"You're fine?"

"I'm getting hungry."

"You didn't eat, is it?"

"There wasn't time."

"Then let us hope the wait is not long."

"Yes, Boss."

Puri pulled away from the door, leaving it open a fraction.

"How we'll know when the murderer arrives?" he asked Singh.

"I propose we keep the light off and position a chair here by this connecting door. If we leave it open a little, we can take turns keeping vigil."

The detective, who had brought along his .32 IOF pistol, agreed to this plan and asked that the inspector take the first watch—"Otherwise my food will be getting cold."

By the moonlight coming in through the window, Puri then went about unpacking his takeaway on the side table next to the bed. Soon the room—and no doubt the room beyond—was filled with the heady aroma of Hyderabadi biryani and the sounds of his munching.

It was ten past eight when Puri's mobile phone, which was on silent mode, vibrated inside his pocket. He looked at the screen. "Zia."

"Ji?" answered Puri in a whisper.

"Fossil has left home, Boss. We're in pursuit," reported Zia, who watched a lot of American cop shows and liked to use the lingo. "Fossil" was code for Shivraj Sharma.

"Very good, send update," was all the detective said before ending the call.

"Who was that?" whispered Inspector Singh, who was still keeping vigil.

"Some of my boys," said Puri, sitting down on a chair next to him.

"And?"

"They're following one suspect."

"A suspect in the Jha-Pandey murder?"

"Correct, but I am doubtful he's the one."

"When were you going to tell me about him?"

"Inspector, you know me, huh. I don't like to declare before end of innings."

For a couple of minutes, the only sounds came from the squeaking fan overhead and the beeping of the ECG in Tubelight's room.

"Are there any other suspects?" asked Singh.

"Two exactly."

"Two!"

"Inspector, please keep down your voice."

"OK, sir, but are you going to tell me who they are?"

"One of them will enter that room before long and then you will have your answer."

There was another long silence.

"Sir, I want to know one thing . . . When did you conclude there were two suspects?"

"This evening at six o'clock I met with Professor Pandey's elder sister and came by certain information that convinced me of as much."

Just then, his mobile vibrated again and he returned to the other side of the room to answer it.

"Boss, Fossil isn't heading your way," reported Zia. "He's crossing the Jamuna."

"Fine. Keep him in your sights."

"Ten-four."

Puri lay down on the bed to have a rest, but found it incredibly hard and uncomfortable. Curious, he checked under the mattress, only to discover that it was resting on a heavy steel-plate support.

He concluded steel had been used as a deterrent to thieves, who would make easy pickings of, say, springs or wooden slats.

Presumably that meant all the beds in the hospital were the same.

In his mind, an idea began to form.

It was almost eleven. Puri was beginning to regret that he had not bought himself some kheer when the door to Tubelight's room opened a crack. A thin streak of light shone on the wall. A head appeared, the face masked by shadows. It withdrew. A moment later, the door opened a little wider and a male figure slipped inside.

Puri stood up slowly, his pistol at the ready, and signaled to Singh.

The figure closed the door behind him, and as his eyes adjusted to the semidarkness, he sized up the room. Silently he approached the first bed and picked up a pillow. Then he made his way across the room to the second bed. He found a gap in the curtain and looked inside. Puri saw him tug out a pistol tucked beneath his belt. He cocked it, buried the muzzle in the pillow and sidled in behind the curtain.

A moment later, there came three dull thuds.

Singh, who was by now standing to one side of the connecting doorway with his revolver drawn, shouted out: "Put down your weapon! You are under arrest!"

Suddenly there came sounds of a struggle. Someone went "Aaaagh!" The killer's pistol clunked to the ground. And then Tubelight, who had ensconced himself under the bed's steel-plate support, called out: "I've got him!"

Singh charged into the room and tore back the curtain.

He grabbed the shooter by both arms and shoved him up against the wall.

Puri switched on the light.

Roughly, Singh turned his captive around.

"Gentlemen, allow me to introduce you," said the detective. "This is one Jaideep Prabhu. Better known as Manish the Magnificent."

Cursing, the magician lunged at Puri, his features suffused with malice and hatred, trying to kick at him like a wild mule. Singh kept a strong grip on his captive and pulled him back, giving him a hard slap across the back of the head.

"That's enough out of you, bastard!" he shouted. "From now on you speak only when I tell you to speak."

Manish the Magnificent cursed Singh as well. "Who the hell are you, anyway?"

"As far as you are concerned, I am God!" The inspector handcuffed the magician. "I am placing you under arrest for the double murder of Dr. Suresh Jha and Professor R. K. Pandey."

The magician scoffed. "You can't prove anything."

By now Puri was holding Manish the Magnificent's double-action revolver with his handkerchief wrapped around it.

"You have been good enough to supply all the evidence required," he said with a smile.

"That's not mine. I've never seen it before!"

Singh gave Manish the Magnificent a hard slap across the face. "I told you to shut up!" he bawled, shoving the magician down onto a chair. "Don't make me tell you again!"

Manish the Magnificent glowered at him.

Singh raised his hand again as if to strike. "Oi harami!"

he swore. "Keep your eyes down or I won't just break your bones, I'll grind them to dust!"

This time the magician had the good sense to do as he was told.

"Better," said Singh. He turned and addressed Puri: "Now before I take this son of a whore to the station, would you mind telling me what the hell has been going on?"

"Most certainly, Inspector."

They stood by the main door to the room, leaving Tubelight closest to the captive.

"I told you I met Professor Pandey's sister, no?"

"You mentioned it, yes."

"It was she who told me how her brother invented one revolutionary method by which levitation can be achieved," said Puri. "He built a pair of extraordinary boots with metal soles made of some substance called"—here Puri had to refer to his notebook—"pyrolytic carbon. Attached to these boots were some whatnots called"—again he had to read the name—"servo mechanisms. They are responsible for maintaining stability."

"So these boots just float in the air?" asked Singh, sounding dubious.

"Not at all, Inspector. Extremely powerful magnets were buried under the grass. This was achieved some months in advance by Dr. Jha and his team. Afterward, they diligently kept the grass watered and seeded so no one noticed the ground had been disturbed." Puri went on to explain as much as he knew about how the rest of the illusion had been done.

"So how did this bastard become involved in all of this?" asked Singh, referring to Manish the Magnificent.

"He watched the French tourist's video of goddess Kali's miraculous appearance. But he did so with different eyes. Being a magician, he saw a levitation illusion likes of which had never been achieved before. Thus he wanted to know how all it was done. He visited Rajpath as we two did. Guessing the stage had been set in some way, he thought to probe under the grass. Thus he discovered the magnets."

Here Puri added an aside: "Inspector, yesterday only I discovered them myself using my trusty Swiss Army knife."

"But what led him to Professor Pandey, Boss?" asked Tubelight, who was listening in on the conversation.

"Naturally he guessed Professor Pandey, being one inventor and electrical engineer, had invented the means by which levitation could be achieved. What is more, Manish the Magnificent understood such levitation technology was worth many crores. Must be he planned to sell it to fellow magicians the world over. A Godman like Maharaj Swami would have paid him handsomely for it, also."

"So he planned to steal the boots?" asked Singh.

"Correct. He went to the house to demand them from Pandey. Only his plan did not go to plan at all."

"And what became of these . . . these *magic* boots?" asked the inspector.

"Unfortunately for Manish the Magnificent, Vish Puri and others were on the scene, so he was forced to flee, failing in his duty to find them. Now they are very much safely out of reach."

Singh shook his head in wonder. "You've done a first-rate job, sir. It's amazing how you figured it all out."

"Most kind of you, Inspector," said Puri, beaming.

"But there's one thing I still don't understand."

"What exactly, Inspector?"

"You said your boys chased him into Shalimar Bagh Gardens, but he disappeared. How did he do it?"

"It is said there is a secret passage built by Shah Jahan that connects those gardens to the Red Fort," said Puri. "But who is to know? Manish the Magnificent is not about to share his secret, that is for sure."

Singh went to fetch his prisoner.

But as he reached down to lift him up by the arm, the inspector suddenly found himself handcuffed to the chair.

Manish the Magnificent slipped past him and, catching Tubelight unawares, knocked him down and rushed for the door. There he found Puri blocking his way with pistol drawn.

"Not another move or I will shoot," said the detective. "And believe me, *these bullets* are not the variety you can catch between your teeth."

Puri made a quick stop at his office to put his pistol in the safe and then asked Handbrake to drive him home.

They had just pulled out of Khan Market when a cream-colored Ambassador with a Government of India license plate and a cluster of antennas on the roof pulled them over.

A smartly dressed peon alighted, approached the detective's car and knocked on his window.

"Sir, your presence is requested at Nineteen Akbar Road," he said politely.

That was the health minister's residence.

"Just I was on my way home, actually," said the detective. "It is nearly midnight, no? Thank sir for the invitation and I would be pleased to pay him a visit tomorrow morning."

"That would not be at all convenient, sir," said the peon. "You are required on an urgent matter, sir."

Another man got out of the Ambassador. Tall, angular, with sharply parted hair, he was wearing a gray safari suit.

In one hand, he held a military-issue walkie-talkie with an antenna almost the length of a fishing rod. It crackled with static and conversation.

There was nothing for it but to comply.

"You think sir will offer me a peg or three?" Puri asked the peon, knowing full well that the minister was an avowed teetotaler.

"Sir, that I cannot say," answered the lackey, smiling awkwardly. "He is not in the habit. But maybe I could arrange something."

"Most kind of you. Then challo. Lead the way."

They passed through the silent streets of New Delhi—the same streets that only a few days ago the ingenious Dr. Jha had brought to a standstill with his antics.

Border Security Force soldiers stood on guard behind sandbagged positions at the entrance to 19 Akbar Road. One of them checked the undercarriage of Puri's Ambassador with a mirror attached to a long pole, while another searched the trunk. Puri was then asked to step out of the car to be frisked.

His license plate was entered into the logbook and then the property's gates swung open. Beyond lay a wide expanse of lawn as smooth and green as Lord's cricket ground. At the far end stood a classic Lutyens bungalow with a whitewashed facade and columns lit up by spotlights.

The driveway, which was edged with flowerpots bursting with plump marigold blossoms, led to a parking area to the right of the building.

Handbrake stopped the car, got out and opened the door for the detective. The peon then led the way to the front entrance, where an ancient St. Bernard lay snoring on the stone floor of the veranda, a wet patch beneath his quivering jowls.

The main doors parted and Puri was ushered into the reception, where a liveried servant stood to attention. He showed the detective to one of the armchairs and asked what he could fetch him.

"Two pegs, ice, soda," said the detective.

The servant nodded and went out through a nearby door.

The peon, meanwhile, took a seat on the other side of the room and checked his watch. Then he folded his hands and placed them in his lap.

When the servant returned a couple of minutes later, it was with a glass of chilled water. He placed it on a coaster on the coffee table in front of Puri and, without a word, withdrew.

Under normal circumstances, the detective would have expected a long wait. But given the hour he knew sir would be anxious to get off to his mistress's bed. Thirty minutes would probably be about right; any less would be a sign of weakness.

In the event, it was thirty-five.

Another peon, who could have been the first one's twin, emerged from the adjacent room and signaled to the detective to enter.

Puri found Vikram Bhatt, India's health minister, dressed in his customary collarless waistcoat and immaculately pressed white kurta pyjama sitting behind an expansive antique desk lit by a lead-crystal lamp. He was not alone. On one of the settees in front of the fireplace sat none other than His Holiness Maharaj Swami. Behind him stood Vivek Swaroop, his left eye blackened and his nose swathed in bandages.

The two men glared at the detective, sizing him up, while the minister continued studying his papers.

"You're Puri?" he asked, looking up after the requisite thirty seconds.

"Vish Puri, Most Private Investigators, at your service, sir," answered the detective cheerily. He produced a business card and laid it on the desk, adding, "Confidentiality is our watchword."

The minister could not have looked less interested; indifferently, he indicated one of the chairs in front of him.

"You're sure your name isn't Lakshmi Garodia?"

"Garodia? No, sir, quite sure."

"Strange. Because a man who looks just like you going by that name visited Haridwar recently. He said he was from Singapore. I have a photograph of him here. Would you like to see it?"

The minister slid the picture to the front of the desk.

It was a still captured from CCTV footage of Puri in disguise standing in the reception of the Abode of Eternal Love.

"Sir, evidently this gentleman has a healthy appetite, as I do," said the detective, putting the photo back on the desk. "Otherwise I fail to see any similarity."

"Well, I'm glad to hear it, Mr. Puri," said the minister. "We have very strict laws in India against fraud, you know. The police look on it very seriously. I would hate to come to know that you were engaged in such illicit activity."

The minister took off his glasses, breathed on one of the lenses and began to clean it with a cloth.

"But let us leave that aside—at least for the time being," he continued. "What is important is that this man Garodia arrived in Haridwar with a beautiful daughter. A very unusual and, shall we say, spirited young woman. One night during her time at the Abode of Eternal Love, it seems she broke into a restricted area and attempted to steal property belonging to His Holiness Maharaj Swami."

"I am sorry to hear that, sir," said Puri. "Naturally the police were called."

"Actually, I believe Swami-ji wished to deal with the matter internally. Our Indian police can sometimes be heavy-handed with such matters and he wanted to give the woman a chance to reform."

"Most considerate of him."

Puri could sense that the preamble was coming to an end.

"Unfortunately this young woman absconded before Swami-ji was able to help her," continued the minister. "He brought the matter to my attention and I did a little checking of my own. And then I thought, well, why not hire Vish Puri, the famous detective, to find her."

"Most kind of you, sir," said Puri. "Truly I am honored."

The minister checked his glasses and began to polish the other lens.

"All we require is an address where we can find this young woman. That and an assurance that anything she might tell you will remain confidential. Assuming you are willing to take on the case, I can assure you that you will be well compensated."

Puri was thoughtfully silent.

"And if I say no, sir?" he asked.

"No, Mr. Puri?" replied the minister with a quizzical smile. "That's not a word I hear very often."

"No doubt. But I take it you still understand its meaning, sir."

"I can honestly say that I do not. You see, Mr. Puri, on the very rare occasion someone says no to me, they find out very quickly that what they really mean is yes."

The detective nodded. "It might take me some time to find the girl in question," he said.

The minister looked over at Vivek Swaroop, who gave a slow, uncompromising shake of his head.

"My friend here is very anxious to see this young lady again."

"It is late, sir. She will take time to locate."

Bhatt thought for a moment. "You have until noon tomorrow," he said. With that he returned to his papers. The interview was over.

Puri made his way out of the room, wished the peons a good evening and walked calmly to his Ambassador.

"Get me back to the office—double fast," he instructed Handbrake.

Twenty-six

The next morning, Elizabeth Rani reached Most Private Investigators at nine, put her tiffin in the fridge, turned on the air-conditioning in reception and then arranged herself behind her desk.

She was in the process of removing the plastic cover from her computer when Door Stop arrived bearing the stainless steel milk pail he was charged with filling at the nearby Mother Dairy stand every morning.

"Namaste, madam," he said before heading into the kitchen to make the first batch of tea.

Mrs. Chadha came next, greeting Puri's secretary with the usual pleasantries before making her way into the Communications Room, where her job was to answer phone lines using various fronts and assumed names—and where she managed to get a lot of knitting done at the same time.

"Mrs. Chadha, before I forget, I've got a note here for you," Elizabeth Rani called after her. "You should be getting a ring on line one sometime this morning for Madam Go Go—it's in connection with the ongoing Kapoor matrimonial case."

The office sweeper (who did her work at the end of the day for fear of brushing away the good fortune precipitated by the goddess Lakshmi) soon appeared at the top of the narrow stairs that led from the street into reception. She had never had cause to complain about Elizabeth Rani, but society as a whole treated her with the same disdain as the interminable dirt it was her lot to sweep, making her as timid as a mole.

A light tap on the door frame indicated her presence and then she advanced gingerly toward the desk to collect her weekly wage of 200 rupees.

Soon after the sweeper had retreated back down the stairs, the lights, computer and air conditioner all simultaneously switched off, signaling another power cut. Elizabeth Rani had to tell Door Stop to activate the backup UPS battery.

While she waited, it was strangely quiet in reception—so quiet in fact that she noticed a noise coming from the next room. It sounded a lot like her pressure cooker when it was coming to a boil: first a rattling as the steam built up inside and then the volcanic release accompanied by a high whistle.

She went and put her ear to the door. The noise came again. It was her employer snoring.

"Sir, are you in there?" she said, having returned to her desk and speaking quietly over the intercom.

The response was groggy. "What time you've got, Madam Rani?"

"Nearly half past nine, sir."

"By God! Why no one woke me!" he exclaimed.

"Sir, I—"

The automatic security latch on his door opened. Elizabeth Rani took this as a signal that she was wanted and hurried inside.

The office was a shambles. Every surface was cluttered with takeaway boxes, soft drink cans and Styrofoam cups. An ashtray on the windowsill was overflowing with cigarette butts. Evidently, the detective had had a number of visitors during the night.

Puri was looking equally disheveled. His mien betrayed both exhaustion and anxiety.

"This thing is not turning on," he grumbled as he pressed the TV remote control.

"There's load shedding, sir. I told the boy to put on the UPS."

"Well, tell him to get a move on. Should be the story will air at ten."

"Story, sir?"

"Ask him why my chai is taking so long also."

"Yes, sir."

"And after, send him for some aloo parathas."

The lights suddenly went on, as did the TV.

An anchor on one of the news channels was talking about cricket. Puri flicked to one of its rivals, which was airing a feature about a Bollywood actor's on-set tantrum. The channel after that was covering the usual humdrum politics.

"Our three national obsessions—and all in the usual order of priorities," he commented sarcastically to Elizabeth Rani, who had given Door Stop his orders and was in the process of cleaning up the office.

"Yes, sir," she said, distracted by seeing him in such a state. "Is everything all right?"

"No, Madam Rani, everything is certainly not all right. But God willing, everything will be all right. I have hardly slept a single wink, actually. Round the clock we have been working. But it is nothing a cup of tea and something hot and tasty should not fix."

Two cups of chai, three aloo parathas and some of Rumpi's homemade garlic pickle—a jar of which he kept in his desk drawer—did indeed work wonders for his temperament.

After a cat wash in his private bathroom with some cold water from the fridge, Puri was more or less back to his normal self.

By ten o'clock, his office was also spick and span and smelling of mountain-pine air freshener.

"Madam Rani, be good enough to come and watch this," said Puri, back behind his desk with the TV tuned to *Action News!* "If all has gone to plan, it will be dynamite."

She came and stood next to him as the headlines rolled.

"This morning we have an exclusive that is going to shake the whole of India," said the young anchor. "The footage that you are about to see was released to us in the past few hours. We have been able to verify that it is not a hoax. What you are about to see is authentic and has been independently verified."

Puri quickly checked the other channels to see if they were carrying the same story. On Bharat TV a graphic screamed: WORLD EXCLUSIVE.

Only government-controlled DD News, and SATYA, which was owned in part by the Foundation for the Promotion of World Consciousness, a Maharaj Swami mouthpiece, were not airing the story.

He returned to *Action News!*

It was running grainy CCTV black-and-white footage of Maharaj Swami sitting on the floor of his private audience chamber.

"It's our understanding the Godman recorded this footage himself with cameras hidden inside the room where he has welcomed thousands of people privately over the years—including at least two prime ministers," said the lady presenter.

The video showed a young female devotee entering the audience chamber, stopping to touch Maharaj Swami's feet and then sitting before him.

"The pixilation effect you're seeing around her face has been added by our technicians in order to protect her identity," continued the presenter. "Some of the images we are about to show you have had to be disguised as well because of their graphic content. But what you're watching here is this young lady performing favors of, well, an oral nature for the pleasure of Godman Maharaj Swami. Again, this footage was taken inside his private audience chamber on a hidden camera placed there for—and here we can only speculate—Swami-ji's own purposes."

A male co-presenter appeared on the screen and said: "In an extraordinary development, the woman who appeared in the video has come forward this morning. We cannot show her face, but she tells a harrowing tale of systematic sexual abuse at the ashram."

A silhouetted profile of Damayanti, newly liberated from the Abode of Eternal Love, appeared. In a hesitant, at times choked voice, she described how the Godman had emotionally blackmailed her into performing sexual acts in his audience chamber.

"Swami-ji used to say that like Lord Krishna's gopis, or milk maidens, it was my duty to show him unconditional love," she said. "I was terrified of telling my parents because I knew they would never believe me and I thought they would disown me."

After the clip, the male presenter appeared again and said: "We're going live now to Haridwar for the latest developments in this breaking story from our reporter Smeeta. Smeeta, what can you tell us?"

The screen divided. On the left, the CCTV footage played on a loop; on the right, Smeeta stood in front of the main gates of the Abode of Eternal Love, which were being guarded by police.

"Yes, dramatic developments here in Haridwar," she said excitedly. "We've learned that at eight o'clock this morning, police, led by Delhi inspector Jagat Prakash Singh, entered Maharaj Swami's ashram with a warrant for the Godman's arrest. Apparently, Inspector Singh and his men did encounter resistance inside the ashram. This was of a passive nature. Hundreds of devotees lay down on the ground in front of the entrance to the Godman's private residence and Singh had to call for reinforcements before they were able to get inside."

"Was Maharaj Swami there at the time?" The question came from the anchor in the studio.

"My sources tell me he had been in Delhi overnight but arrived back at his ashram this morning at around six by helicopter," answered Smeeta. "But police say when they . . ."

Her words were drowned out by a flurry of activity behind her. The camera zoomed in on a scowling Inspector Singh emerging through the gates on foot.

"Sir, sir, sir!" cried the reporters, rushing toward him.

The police wallah stopped as the cameras gathered round and the questions came all at once.

"Have you arrested Maharaj Swami? What are the charges? What's that smoke we can see rising above the ashram?"

Singh's gruff voice broke in. "I have a statement to make,"

he said. "This morning my men and I entered the Abode of Eternal Love with the intention of arresting the man known as Maharaj Swami on charges of sexual assault, manslaughter and fraud. Our progress was severely hampered by his followers, who blocked our entrance. We were only able to gain access to his private residence a short while ago. So far we have been unable to locate Swami-ji, but we are now conducting a thorough search of the area."

The reporters started shouting all at once again.

"As to the smoke you can see rising over the buildings," Singh continued, "a fire started in a room adjacent to Maharaj Swami's private audience chamber minutes before we entered the building at approximately half past nine. It has since been extinguished, but the contents of the room were destroyed. We have reason to believe the fire was started deliberately."

More questions were fired at him. Ignoring them, the inspector finished his statement: "One Vivek Swaroop, Maharaj Swami's number two, is also wanted on the same charges. So far, he is absconding. We will be issuing a photofit of both him and Maharaj Swami within the hour. Anyone seeing these two gentlemen should contact the Delhi police immediately."

Singh turned and walked back inside the ashram and the gates were slammed shut in the reporters' faces.

Puri muted the TV and sat back in his chair. "Seems Swami-ji got word about the video footage being released in advance. But his goose is definitely cooked, that is for sure," he said. "My only regret is Dr. Jha did not live to see the day."

"He would have been overjoyed, sir," Elizabeth Rani said, smiling. "But how did you get hold of that shocking material?"

"It was not I, Madam Rani. For that we have Flush to thank."

"But I read in Facecream's report that she got no information. Her USB key was destroyed by that thug Vivek Swaroop."

By now Elizabeth Rani was standing in front of the detective's desk.

"That was a masterstroke!" said the detective, beaming. "Unbeknownst even to my good self, the USB key contained a virus. Thus when Facecream inserted it into the Godman's computer it was delivered. Afterward, Flush was able to penetrate the protection system of the network—"

"I believe it is known as a firewall, sir," interjected his secretary helpfully.

"Exactly. So this fiery wall was penetrated and thus the system was accessed. Flush got hold of all the secret accounts. Even Maharaj Swami's private computer was not immune. That is where the video clip and many more besides were located."

Elizabeth Rani, looking disgusted, said: "What kind of a man could do something like that to those poor young women?"

"One without any moral compasses. One who is ready to take full advantage of any and all people for his own benefit."

A philosophical look came over the detective's face. "Actually, Madam Rani, we Indian people believe that in life a spiritual guide is required, that we cannot find all the answers on our own," he said. "Like children learning ABC, we need a teacher. This is a belief I hold to be true, also. If we are to escape the cycle of birth and rebirth, a guru must and should be there to show the way. But that does not mean one should follow any Tom, Dick or Harry, no?

"Problem is so many people these days are following these con men without question, ready to believe anything they say and do," he continued. "If any old Charlie like this Swami-ji can make a watch appear from thin air, they are ready to worship him. But that is not genuine spirituality. Just it is so much hocus-pocus."

"I agree, sir, people are all too gullible these days," said Elizabeth Rani. "I suppose that is what Dr. Jha was trying to teach them."

Mention of the Guru Buster reminded Puri that he needed to bring his file up-to-date with last night's developments and he asked his secretary to fetch her laptop so she could take dictation.

When he was finished and Elizabeth Rani had saved the file, she said: "Sir, there are a few things I don't understand. While you were waiting in the hospital room you told Inspector Singh there were two suspects. Who was the other one?"

"Allow me to tell you a little secret, Madam Rani," answered the detective mischievously. "At that time exactly, I strongly suspected Professor Pandey had been killed for his magical boots. I suspected, also, Manish the Magnificent could be the one. He is a charge sheeter, after all. But other miscreant persons came to mind, also. Those who would have liked the invention for themselves—Maharaj Swami being one other."

"I see, sir," said Elizabeth Rani, but she was still frowning.

"There is something else I can help you with?" asked Puri.

"Yes, sir. What was the role of Dr. Jha's widow in all this?"

"Naturally she knew from day one her husband was not dead, that the Kali murder was totally fake."

"So the wine and flowers Professor Pandey bought that

night he went to visit Mrs. Jha—those were actually from Dr. Jha?"

"Correct, Madam Rani. Dr. Jha was posing as Pandey's driver so as to get around unrecognized. He was in disguise, actually. Naturally when Tubelight saw the good professor giving Mrs. Jha one embrace, he was not aware her husband was also present."

It took his secretary a few seconds to decipher Puri's syntax before she nodded and said: "I think I understand, sir."

"The truth is, Madam Rani, Vish Puri was slow on the uptake," he said with a mournful shake of his head. "Moment I saw that picture in Pandey's office—the one of him standing along with Dr. Jha—I should have known the two were in this thing together."

Elizabeth Rani took her cue. "But how were you to know, sir?" she said.

"It is my business to know, no?"

"Sir, the plan was so elaborate and perfectly executed," she stressed. "Who could have ever guessed that Dr. Jha's cremation was staged? What with all his near or dear present."

"Most kind of you, Madam Rani," said Puri, shaking off his self-pity. "As usual you are quite correct."

She sighed. "What a remarkable case it's been," she commented.

"Undoubtedly, Madam Rani. One of the most remarkable till date. And even now, as we speak, it is not seen the curtains go down."

There were two loose ends.

Puri decided to deal with them both before heading home to catch up on some sleep.

The first was Shivraj Sharma.

He called Shashi to get the latest on the archaeologist's movements and asked him in Hindi: "Where did Fossil go?"

"B Block, Sector Forty-four, Boss. It's a church."

"He went inside?"

"He put an envelope through the letter box."

"And after?"

"He went home, Boss. Then this morning, very early, he returned to NOIDA. This time to a different address in B Block. The Christian priest who works at the church lives there. Fossil followed him for half an hour and then drove to work.

"One other thing, Boss," continued Shashi. "We got hold of his garbage this morning. It contained some copies of *Dainik Bhaskar*. They were in tatters, lots of pieces cut with scissors. Looked like rats got at them."

Puri immediately called the church and asked to speak with the priest. Father James confirmed that he had received a strange note in his postbox that morning—the Hindi letters all cut from a newspaper.

"What it said exactly, Father?" asked Puri

"It was a quote from a Hindu text—something about how all unbelievers would be purged."

"Whenever there is a withering of the law; and an uprising of lawlessness on all sides; then I manifest myself," quoted Puri.

"Yes that's it."

"You called the cops, Father?"

"Why bother? We get threats all the time and they never show any concern, let alone investigate."

"It is most important you keep the note safe—and the envelope, also," the detective told him.

Puri decided to hold off from calling Singh and briefing

him about Sharma. It could wait until tomorrow. The archaeologist was a hatemonger aspiring to be a murderer and not an immediate threat to anyone.

He checked his watch. It was nearly twelve. Time to contact the health minister's secretary—the last loose thread.

"Vish Puri, Most Private Investigators Ltd., this side," he said politely when his call was answered. "Sir asked me to revert this morning. You were made aware? Exactly. You'd be good enough to pass on my answer? Fine. Be good enough to tell him following: It is with regret I must decline his generous offer. Actually, I am very much engaged in getting my shoes polished."

Twenty-seven

Vish Puri was at home in his sitting room laughing so hard the tears were rolling down his face. His mother, who had come to visit, was also having convulsions.

"What a total duffer!" she guffawed. "There's daal in that head of his or what?"

Jaiya, who was by now six weeks from her due date—it being a week after Maharaj Swami's disappearance—waddled into the room with a quizzical smile.

"What's so funny?" she asked, lowering herself into one of the armchairs.

"Sorry, na," said Mummy through a grin she could barely control. "Just we're talking about Bagga-ji."

"Oh God, what's he done now?"

"Go ahead and tell her, Chubby," prompted Rumpi as she returned from the kitchen with a tray of tea and chillas. "Jaiya, you've got to hear this. Even by Uncle's standards, well, it . . . *bagga-rs* belief!"

Everyone burst into laughter again. It was a good minute before Puri was able to pull himself together and let his daughter in on the joke.

"Beta, you remember Baggage-ji was here the night you arrived, no? Talking about some money-minting scheme?"

"I remember." She did an impression of him in a strong yokel accent: "'I'll soon be richest man in *aaall* Paannjaaab!' Didn't some construction company want to build a mall on his land?"

"Correct."

"Let me guess. The company is a bogus one."

"No, no, company is bilkul real."

"So?"

Puri went on to describe his visit to his brother-in-law's drinking den in Punjabi Bagh and how Bagga had admitted that he was planning to buy his neighbor's land for one crore, hoping to sell it to the construction company at a profit. The detective also described the priceless expression on Bagga's face when he had cursed him and stormed out.

"Papa, I don't understand," said Jaiya. "What was so wrong about Uncle buying the other land?"

"Obviously its owner, a most cunning gentleman by name of Jasbir Jaggi, was giving Bagga the squeeze."

"How?"

"See . . . Mr. Jaggi wanted to sell some land adjacent to Bagga-ji's. But it had market value of maximum *half* crore. So the fellow devised one plan. He asked his friend and associate working at the construction company to contact Bagga and make him one offer. 'Tell him you want to build one mall on his land. Mention you require the adjacent land also.'"

"The adjacent land being owned by Jasbir Jaggi?" asked Jaiya.

"Correct. Knowing his greedy and idiotic nature, Jaggi was certain Bagga would try to buy it for himself."

"With the idea of selling it to the construction company at a profit . . . now I see." Jaiya shook her head in disbelief. "So presumably Bagga went to Jaggi and asked to buy his land for one crore and of course he accepted."

"Exactly. That is why he required one crore. I got him to admit to the plan by offering to loan him the amount. Naturally I never intended to give him the money."

"So did you warn him about Jaggi, Papa?"

"Naturally I told Preeti and she in turn tried to convince Bagga-ji," answered Puri. "But he refused to believe."

"He went ahead anyway?" asked Jaiya, wide-eyed, with her hands half covering her face.

Puri smiled. "What happened was this," he said. "Bagga visited the construction company. There he begged Jaggi's associate to build a smaller mall on his land. You know what this fellow told him? That he would not build even one public urinal there. Then he abused him and told him, 'Get out!'

"Later Bagga-ji came home and told Preeti that he believed he was the victim of one conspiracy. 'That is what I was trying to tell you earlier!' she said. 'No, no,' he answers. 'Just they're trying to trick me into believing my land is worthless so I will sell cheap! But I am no fool! A better offer will come and then I will be . . .'"

Everyone in the room joined in: "'Richest man in *aaall* Paannjaaab.'"

Rumpi and Jaiya went to the kitchen while Puri and Mummy sat back enjoying their tea.

The TV was now on and one of the channels was repeating the video footage that DIRE had released to all the channels a few days earlier, shocking the nation with the truth about the Kali illusion.

Dr. Jha appeared on the screen. He was sitting in the hospital after faking his own death. There was fake blood around his mouth and a remarkably realistic wound on his chest. But he was smiling and laughing and chatting with his friend Professor Pandey.

The channel went live to Haridwar where Bossy was standing in front of the darshan hall at the Abode of Eternal Love. In the past few days, she had taken over as the spokesperson for the charitable trust administering the ashram. The CCTV sex videos were fakes, she claimed. Anyone who believed they were real was not worthy of Swami-ji's teachings.

"He is testing all of us," Puri heard Bossy say before pressing the mute button on his remote control.

"So many people are getting totally angry at what Dr. Jha did, na," said Mummy. "Makes you wonder if the whole thing hurt his cause after all."

"No one enjoys being made fools out of, that much is certain," said Puri. "But I myself cannot help admiring what he did. Absolute genius it was, actually."

"What about this Swami character? His whereabouts are known or what?"

"He we'll not be seeing for a very long time—if at all," said the detective. "Same goes for his cohort, Swaroop. Must be they stashed away so many of crores."

"And what about that goonda health minister? I was reading he could be facing money-laundering charges."

"*Could be facing,*" emphasized Puri. "But it will be a dry day in Patiala before a neta finds himself behind bars."

Suddenly there came a yell from the kitchen.

"Chubby, come quick!" screamed Rumpi.

The detective ran into the room to find Jaiya slumped on the floor. She was bleeding.

"By God! Jaiya!"

"Call an ambulance, na!" cried Mummy.

The ambulance, a little van that had to come from a private hospital twenty minutes away, took thirty minutes to arrive—by which time Jaiya was complaining of severe abdominal cramping.

The van was just large enough to hold one patient, a doctor, a nurse, a driver plus one relative on the passenger's seat.

Rumpi got inside and it raced out of the gate, siren wailing and emergency light flashing.

Few vehicles gave way for the ambulance en route and it was another half hour before it reached the entrance to the emergency ward.

Puri and Mummy, who followed together in the Ambassador, pulled up in time to see Jaiya being wheeled inside.

Soon, they were gathered with Rumpi anxiously awaiting news.

Another twenty minutes passed.

Then a doctor in a green smock and mask came out to tell them that Jaiya had gone into preterm labor.

"We'll do everything we can for her twins," he said before returning to the operating theater.

By now, Rumpi was crying and clinging to Puri.

He remained calm and collected as he comforted and reassured her. But after ten minutes, the detective stood up to leave, asking Mummy to take care of his wife.

"I must go," he said. "Call me when the outcome is known either way."

"I understand," said Mummy, taking a hundred-rupee note from her purse and handing it to him.

Back at the car he instructed Handbrake to drive as fast as he could to DLF City.

"Never mind usual rules," he said.

"Yes, Boss."

They covered the distance at breakneck speed, soon screeching to a halt outside the Ganesh temple in Phase Four.

At the gate, Puri bought some offerings—a coconut, a few bananas and a packet of some candied nuts—as well as incense sticks. Having removed his shoes, he climbed the steps and hurried inside.

The temple was quiet, it being a weekday afternoon. Just a few worshippers sat in prayer or contemplation. Puri approached the effigy of the elephant god in the temple's main shrine, bowed and sat on the floor before it. A priest received his offerings and Mummy's one-hundred-rupee note, listened to his plight and began to say prayers asking for the protection of Jaiya and the safe delivery of her twins.

With head bent devoutly, eyes closed and the palms of his hands pressed together in supplication, Puri silently beseeched God's mercy.

Handbrake soon joined his employer, sitting to one side of him and making his own offerings.

The two men barely stirred for nearly three hours despite the oppressive heat.

When Mummy finally rang, it was dark and the temple was packed with worshippers and the sound of ringing bells.

Puri returned to the hospital to find Jaiya weak but in stable condition and the twins lying in separate incubators.

He stood watching them through the observation window of the maternity ward, their tiny, frail bodies still purple and wrinkled.

"It was really touch-and-go, Chubby," said Rumpi as she and Mummy gathered next to him, mesmerized by the latest additions to the Puri clan. "The doctor said they nearly didn't make it. But something—who knows what?—pulled them through."

"It's a miracle, na," declared Mummy.

Puri smiled, his eyes brimming with tears.

"Yes, Mummy-ji, it is a miracle," he said. "This time a real one."

Glossary

AACHAR — a pickle. Most commonly made of carrot, lime, garlic, cauliflower, chili or unripe mango cooked in mustard oil and spices.

AARTI — Hindu fire ritual, often performed daily, in which a plate holding a flame and offerings is circled in front of a deity or guru while devotional songs are sung.

ACHKAN — a close-fitting high-necked coat, slightly flared below the waist and reaching almost to the knee, worn by men in India.

ALOO — potato.

ALOO TIKKI MASALA — spicy fried potato patties.

AMBASSADOR — until recently India's national car. The design, which has changed little since production started in 1957, is similar to the British Morris Oxford.

ANGREZI	adjective; Hindi for English or British. "Angrez" is the noun form.
ART FRAT	a member of the artistic community or fraternity.
ATTA	a kind of wheat flour dough commonly used in South Asian cooking.
AYAH	a domestic servant role combining the functions of maid and nanny.
BABU	a bureaucrat or other government official.
BACHA	a child.
BAKSHEESH	a term used to describe tipping, charitable giving and bribery.
BALTI	a bucket.
BANSURI	a flute.
BARFI	sweetmeat made from condensed milk and sugar.
BETA	a son or child; used in endearment.
BIDI	Indian cigarette made of strong tobacco hand-rolled in a leaf from the ebony tree.
"BILKUL"	"of course," "certainly," "for sure."
BIRYANI	rice-based foods made with spices, rice, meat, fish, eggs or vegetables. With Hyderabadi biryani, the marinated meat and rice are cooked together.

CHALLAN — literally a receipt for a payment or delivery, but generally slang for a traffic fine.

"CHALLO" — Hindi for "let's go."

CHARGE SHEETER — a person with a criminal record.

CHARPAI — literally, "four feet." A charpai is a woven string bed used throughout northern India and Pakistan.

CHAVAL — rice.

CHAWL — a tenement building.

CHILLA — a flatbread made from black chickpea flour, onions and spices.

CHIWDA — a variable mixture of spicy dried ingredients, which may include fried lentils, peanuts, chickpea flour noodles, corn, chickpeas, flaked rice and fried onion. This is all flavored with salt and a blend of spices.

CHOWKIDAR — a watchman.

CHURIDAAR — a style of leg-hugging drawstring pajamas.

CHUSKI — crushed ice and flavored syrup on a stick.

CHUTTRI — an elevated, dome-shaped pavilion used as an element in Indian architecture. "Chhatri" means umbrella or canopy.

COWWAH	crow.
"CRIB"	Indian English; to complain or grumble.
DAAL	spiced lentils.
DACOITY	criminal activity involving robbery by a groups of armed bandits. A dacoit is a member of an Indian or Burmese armed robber band.
DARSHAN	a Sanskrit term meaning sight (in the sense of an instance of seeing or beholding). It is most commonly used for "visions of the divine," i.e., of a god or a very holy person or artifact. One can "receive darshana" of the deity in the temple or from a saintly person, such as a guru.
DHABA	an Indian roadside restaurant, popular in northern India, playing loud music and serving spicy Punjabi food.
DHARMA	a Sanskrit term that refers to a person's righteous duty or any virtuous path.
DHOKLA	a fast food from the Indian state of Gujarat made with a fermented batter of chickpeas.
DHOTI	a traditional men's garment. It is a rectangular piece of unstitched cloth, usually around seven yards long, wrapped around the waist and legs and knotted at the waist.

DIDI	a sister.
DIYA	a lamp usually made of clay with a cotton wick dipped in vegetable oil.
DJINN	a genie.
FAKIR	an ascetic or mystic.
"FUNDA"	from "fundamentals"; Indian English slang for situation or understanding.
GHAT	a descending path or stairway to a river or landing place.
GHEE	clarified butter.
GOONDA	a thug or miscreant.
GORA/GORI	a light-skinned person; the term is often used in reference to Westerners.
GULAB JAMUN	a dessert made of dough consisting mainly of milk solids in a sugar syrup. It is usually flavored with cardamom seeds and rosewater or saffron.
"HAAN-JI"	Hindi for "yes, sir/madam."
"HAI!"	an exclamation indicating surprise or shock.
HAKIM	a Muslim physician.
HALF-PANTS	shorts.
"HARAMI"	"bastard."
IDLI	a South Indian savory cake popular throughout India. The cakes are usually two to three inches in diameter

and are made by steaming a batter consisting of fermented black lentils and rice. Most often eaten at breakfast or as a snack.

JADOO — magic.

JASOOS — a spy or private detective.

JAWAN — a male constable or soldier.

JEERA — cumin seeds.

KADI — a spicy, sour curry made from gram flour fried in butter and mixed with buttermilk or yogurt. Served with chaval, rice.

"KAHA-HAIN?" — "where are you?"

"KAISAN BHA?" — "how are you, brother?"

KALAVA — the sacred Hindu thread also called mauli in Hindi. It is worn while performing rituals.

KALE CHANNE — black chickpeas.

"KARO" — "do it."

KHEER — rice or vermicelli pudding made with milk and sugar and topped with slivered almonds or pistachios.

KHOYA — milk cooked slowly until only the solids remain; used in desserts.

"KIDD-AN?" — Punjabi for "how are you?"

"KISTERAN?" — Punjabi for "how are things?"

KOKI — a spiced Indian flatbread from Sindh.

KOTHI — a stand-alone, multistory house.

KSHATRIYA — the military and ruling order of the traditional Vedic-Hindu social system as outlined by the Vedas; the warrior caste.

KURTA — a long shirt.

LAAD SAHIB — bastardization of "lord sahib," meaning spoiled or arrogant.

LADOO — a sweet that is often prepared to celebrate festivals or household events such as weddings. Essentially, ladoos are flour balls cooked in sugar syrup.

LAKH — a unit in the Indian numbering system equal to 100,000.

"LAOW" — "bring."

LASSI — a drink made from buttermilk. It can be plain, sweet or salty, or made with fruit such as banana or mango.

LATHI — length of bamboo or cane often used by police or schoolmasters to lash people.

LIZER — Indian English; derived from "liaiser."

MANGAL SUTRA — a symbol of Hindu marriage consisting of a gold ornament strung from a yellow thread, a string of black beads or a gold chain.

MARMA POINTS	an anatomical site where flesh, veins, arteries, tendons, bones and joints meet up. Resembles the acupressure points.
MIXIE	Indian English for a food processor.
MOONG DAAL HALWA	dessert made from milk and lentils.
"NA"	"no?" or "isn't it?"
NAMASHKAR/ NAMASTE	traditional Hindu greeting said with hands pressed together.
NANI	maternal grandmother.
NEEM	a tree in the mahogany family.
NETA	a politician.
NIMBOO PANI	lemonade, salty or sweet or both.
PAAGAL	crazy.
PAALAK PANEER	spinach with Indian cottage cheese.
PAAN	a betel leaf, stuffed with betel nut, lime and other condiments and used as a stimulant.
PAAPRI CHAAT	a North Indian fast food. "Chaat" means lick; "paapri" refers to crispy fried-dough wafers made from refined white flour. The paapris are served with boiled potato, boiled chickpeas, chilis, yogurt, tamarind chutney and chaat masala.
PAGRI	a traditional Indian turban.

PAISA	one hundredth of a rupee.
PANCHA KARMA	an Ayurvedic cleansing and rejuvenating program for the body, mind and consciousness.
PANCHNAMA	first listing of the evidence and findings that a police officer makes at the scene of a crime.
PANDIT	a Hindu, almost always a Brahmin, who has memorized a substantial portion of the Vedas, along with the corresponding rhythms and melodies for chanting or singing them.
PARANTHA	flat Indian wheat bread pan-fried and served with yogurt and pickle. Often stuffed with spiced potatoes, cauliflower or cottage cheese and eaten for breakfast.
PATKAS	head coverings worn by Sikh children in preference to the bigger turban.
PINNI	a Punjabi sweetmeat usually topped with cashews, almonds or pistachios.
POHA	a breakfast dish made from flattened rice traditionally cooked with peanuts, mustard seeds and curry leaves.
POORI	puffy wheat bread deep fried in oil.
PRANAYAMA	a yoga term meaning learning to control the breath.

PRASAD — offerings of fruit or sweetmeats sanctified in front of deities during prayer and then passed out to devotees to consume as blessings.

PUJA — a prayer.

PUKKA — Hindi word meaning solid, well made. Also means definitely.

PUNGI — also called a "been." A wind instrument played by snake charmers in India.

RAJA — a king.

RAJMA — red kidney beans cooked with onions, garlic, ginger, tomatoes and spices. A much-loved Punjabi dish eaten with basmati rice.

RISHI — a poet-sage through whom the Vedic hymns flowed; credited also as a divine scribe. According to post-Vedic tradition, the rishi is a seer or shaman to whom the Vedas were originally revealed through states of higher consciousness.

"ROOK!" — "stop!"

SAALA — slang. An expression of disgust.

SADHU — a holy man who has renounced the material world to devote himself to spiritual practice. He wanders from place to place and owns nothing. A female sadhu is a sadhvi.

SAHIB — an Urdu honorific now used across South Asia as a term of respect, equivalent to the English "sir."

SAMADHI — a higher level of concentrated meditation.

SAMBAR — a South Indian spicy and sour lentil dish.

SANTOOR — an Indian trapezoid-shaped hammer dulcimer.

SANYASI — a Hindu who has renounced all his material possessions and adopted the life of begging for survival.

SARDAR — a male follower of the Sikh religion wearing a turban.

SHERWANI — a long coat-like garment worn in South Asia, very similar to a doublet.

SHLOKA — a Hindu prayer or hymn that is chanted or sung.

SINDOOR — a red powder used by married Hindu women and some Sikh women. During the marriage ceremony, the groom applies some to the parting of the bride's hair to show that she is now a married woman. Subsequently, sindoor is applied by the wife as part of her dressing routine.

TANDOOR — a cylindrical clay oven used to bake breads and meats.

TARRA	a cheap country-made booze.
TAVA	a large, flat or slightly concave disk-shaped griddle made from cast iron, steel or aluminum used to prepare several kinds of flat breads.
TEEN PATTI/ TEEN PATTA	an Indian card game also known as Flush. Usually played during holidays, it is a betting game in which the player with the best hand (three aces or three consecutive cards of the same suit) wins the pot.
THALI	a round steel or brass platter with small bowls traditionally used to serve a large meal.
TILAK	a red mark on the forehead usually applied after aarti.
TOPI	a hat.
TULLI	Punjabi slang for drunk.
UBTAN	a powerful exfoliating and clarifying all-body scrub used by brides-to-be. Generally contains gram flour, turmeric, sandalwood powder and rose water. It is spread on the body and then scrubbed off with jasmine oil.
UPMA	a South Indian breakfast dish made with cream of wheat (semolina), peanuts, spices, curry leaves and mustard seeds.

VIBHUTI sacred ash.

WALLAH a generic term in Hindi meaning "the one" or "he who does." Hence auto-wallah, pankah (fan)-wallah, chai-wallah, etc.

YAAR equivalent to pal, mate or dude.

Note: On page 130 I have quoted from *The God Market: How Globalization Is Making India More Hindu* (New York: Random House, 2009).